Under Lock & Skeleton Key

Also by Gigi Pandian

THE ACCIDENTAL ALCHEMIST MYSTERIES

The Alchemist of Fire and Fortune
The Alchemist's Illusion
The Elusive Elixir
The Masquerading Magician
The Accidental Alchemist

THE JAYA JONES TREASURE HUNT MYSTERIES

The Glass Thief
The Ninja's Illusion
Michelangelo's Ghost
Quicksand
Pirate Vishnu
Artifact

Under Lock & Skeleton Key

A Secret Staircase Mystery

Gigi Pandian

MINOTAUR BOOKS
NEW YORK

First published in the United States by Minotaur Books, an imprint of St. Martin's Publishing Group

UNDER LOCK & SKELETON KEY. Copyright © 2022 by Gigi Pandian. All rights reserved. Printed in the United States of America. For information, address St. Martin's Publishing Group, 120 Broadway, New York, NY 10271.

www.minotaurbooks.com

Designed by Gabriel Guma

Library of Congress Cataloging-in-Publication Data

Names: Pandian, Gigi, 1975– author.
Title: Under lock & skeleton key / Gigi Pandian.
Other titles: Under lock and skeleton key
Description: First edition. | New York : Minotaur Books, 2022.
Identifiers: LCCN 2021046502 | ISBN 9781250804983 (hardcover) | ISBN 9781250804990 (ebook)
Subjects: LCGFT: Novels.
Classification: LCC PS3616.A367 U53 2022 | DDC 813/.6—dc23
LC record available at https://lccn.loc.gov/2021046502

Our books may be purchased in bulk for promotional, educational, or business use. Please contact your local bookseller or the Macmillan Corporate and Premium Sales Department at 1-800-221-7945, extension 5442, or by email at MacmillanSpecialMarkets@macmillan.com.

First Edition: 2022

10 9 8 7 6 5 4 3 2 1

To the phenomenal women in my writers group.
Tempest's story would not have been written without you.

Under Lock & Skeleton Key

PART I

The Lock

Chapter 1

Tempest Raj tested the smooth, hardwood floor once more. Following the floorboards from the beaten-up steamer trunk with three false bottoms to the window letting in moonlight, she didn't hear a squeak anywhere. Good.

In the dim light, she walked the length of the room once more in her crimson ballet flats that were wearing thin over her left pinkie toe. She glanced at the antique clock on the wall. Seven minutes past midnight. There was no way she'd get to sleep for hours.

Satisfied that the floor wouldn't make a sound, she stretched her shoulders, then arched into a backbend kick-over. As soon as her feet touched down, she pushed off into a pirouette. Then another. Spinning, she felt almost free.

Almost.

When she came to an abrupt halt a full minute later, she was breathing harder than she should have been, and she hadn't vanished. Of course she hadn't. This wasn't a stage. There was no trap door underneath her. No audience. She was no longer The Tempest. She was simply Tempest Raj, back at home in her childhood bedroom. And apparently, she was already getting out of shape.

She took a bow for an audience of no one, then kicked off her shoes and flopped onto the bed. Unlike the solid floorboards, the box springs protested with a dreadful screech. The twin-size mattress poking her hip was oh-so-different from the luxurious California king she'd had in Las Vegas up until two weeks ago—when she'd had to sell nearly everything she owned and get out of Dodge.

She was trying to adjust. Really, she was. The schedule of a stage magician meant she never made it to bed until the "wee hours of the morning," as Grannie Mor would say. But she needed sleep. Tomorrow was a big day. No, that wasn't quite true. It *might* be a big day. She knew she shouldn't get her hopes up. The proposal he mentioned might mean a number of things. She'd narrowed it down to the two most likely possibilities, one of which she was desperately hoping for. It was her way out of this mess. As for the other possibility? She'd decide what she thought after she saw him.

She shifted and tried to get away from the most offensive mattress spring. Looking up at the glow-in-the-dark stars from her childhood that still dotted the ceiling, Tempest wondered yet again how she'd gotten here. Everyone believed the stage accident that had wrecked her career and nearly killed her was due to her own negligence. The public, her manager, the venue, and even her supposed friends were quick to accept the worst about her, assuming it was true that she'd replaced the vetted illusions for something far more dangerous. *Tempestuous Tempest, who knew she couldn't top her previous show, but went too far trying to, putting her own life and those of many others in danger . . .* Her actions preparing for the new, unsafe stunt had supposedly been witnessed. But there was someone who could easily impersonate Tempest. Her former stage double, Cassidy Sparrow.

When Cassidy dyed her naturally mahogany hair black,

she looked eerily similar to Tempest. Cassidy wasn't quite Tempest's doppelgänger, but with her strong and curvy five-foot-ten frame, large brown eyes, and wild black hair that reached halfway down her back, she came close.

Cassidy had purposefully wrecked Tempest's career. *Sabotage*. The threat of lawsuits still hung over Tempest's head like a guillotine.

There was no other explanation for what had happened that terrible night. No, that wasn't quite true. There was one other possible explanation, but Tempest couldn't let herself believe it. There was no way it could be true. The first glimmer of such a terrible possibility appeared five years ago, when she first began to wonder if—no. She pushed all thought of it from her mind.

At least one person besides her family believed in her innocence. That's why she was hopeful about seeing him tomorrow. This could be the first step in getting her life back on track.

She closed her eyes, but they popped back open. The constellations on the ceiling didn't mirror reality, but if you looked carefully, you could see that the pinpricks of light formed a constellation in the shape of a skeleton key. A symbol that connected her and her mom, guiding the way home.

Tracing the familiar path of the stars must have been like counting sheep, because the next thing she knew, far too much light was streaming in through the window. She squeezed a pillow over her eyes—then flung it away as she realized it wasn't the light that had awakened her. She'd distinctly heard a jarring sound. Strange noises were to be expected in Vegas. Not in Hidden Creek.

Was someone shouting?

Definitely shouting. The raised voices came from the

direction of the tree house in the backyard where her grand-parents lived.

It wasn't exactly fair to call the structure a tree house. Not for the past fifteen years, at least. What had started as a small child's playroom for a ten-year-old Tempest had, like the rest of the house, grown into something much bigger than its original intention. The original tree house deck still wrapped around the massive trunk of the oak tree that had lent its support for years, and a second deck now surrounded its twin, but in between the trees, the rest of the structure was a proper two-story house that served as an in-law unit for Ashok Raj and Morag Ferguson-Raj.

Tempest leapt out of bed, still disoriented. It wasn't even seven o'clock in the morning. She hadn't been awake at this time of day for years. Crossing the section of floorboards as-sembled in the shape of a skeleton key and opening the an-tique steamer trunk serving as her dresser, she slipped on a pair of jeans and was pulling a T-shirt over her head when she heard her grandfather's distinctive voice give another shout. She shoved her phone in her back pocket and hurried down the secret staircase that separated her room from the rest of the house.

This was the same house Tempest's parents had moved into shortly before Tempest was born. At the time it was a modest 960-square-foot bungalow. The most unique feature of the original house was the land that went with it. Nes-tled into the hillside next to the hidden creek that gave the town its name, the half-acre of land had never been used for a larger dwelling because it was situated on such a steep slope—until Emma and Darius moved in. They had experi-mented over the years on their own house until it was over 4,500 square feet of magical, hidden hideaways across four separate structures.

As her dad loved to say: *What happens when a carpenter and a stage magician fall in love? They form a Secret Staircase Construction business to bring magic to people through their homes.*

The idea was quite romantic. Tempest's parents specialized in building ingeniously hidden rooms for people who fancied a bookshelf that slid open when you reached for *The Adventures of Sherlock Holmes* or *Nancy Drew and the Hidden Staircase*; or a secret reading nook that only appeared when you said the words "open sesame"; or perhaps a door in a grandfather clock that led to a secret garden. Tempest's house—named Fiddler's Folly for her mom's favorite instrument, and a tongue-in-cheek reference to the architectural term for decorative buildings different inside than their outward appearance—had all three features. And many more, including the tree house in back. Tempest loved every inch of it. What she didn't love was the fact that at twenty-six, she'd been forced to move back.

Worse yet, if she didn't receive the job offer she hoped for today, she'd be forced to accept her dad's idea that she come work for Secret Staircase Construction. She'd been named one of the "Top 25 Under 25" young entertainers in a prominent entertainment magazine three years ago, and that success meant she could not only live lavishly but also send money home. It was humiliating enough to be back in her childhood bedroom, but to work as her dad's assistant when she knew he didn't need one? She hoped it didn't come to that.

Tempest rounded the gnarled trunk of the first oak tree and spotted her grandparents. Grandpa Ash and Grannie Mor were the only two people in sight, and they were scowling. Tempest grimaced as she stepped on a sharp root. She hadn't taken time to put on shoes.

"You two finally decided to murder each other after fifty-five years?" Tempest asked, rubbing the ball of her foot.

"Fifty-six years, dear," her grandmother corrected. Grannie Mor's glamorous white hair was perfectly coiffed as usual, an argyle scarf of bright azure and white curled effortlessly around her neck. She always looked as if she'd stepped out of a 1940s Hollywood movie. Except as soon as she opened her mouth to speak, you knew she'd been born and raised in Scotland.

"Where did he go?" Grandpa Ash asked. A plaid newsboy cap covered his bald brown head. Tempest hadn't seen that particular hat before. Her grandfather's hat collection was as extensive as her grandmother's stockpile of scarves.

"Someone else is here?" Tempest whipped her head around.

Grannie Mor hooked her arm through Tempest's elbow. "That rabbit of yours is the devil himself."

Tempest sighed. Now she really wished she'd taken time to put her shoes on. "What did Abra do now?"

Abracadabra was Tempest's five-year-old, fifteen-pound, lop-eared rabbit. He'd already been a big bunny before Grandpa Ash began feeding him under the table. Tempest could have sworn Abra had gained at least a pound since they'd been back. The mischievous, tubby bunny should have been in his hutch in Secret Fort, the unfinished stone tower that made up the most recent Fiddler's Folly structure on the hillside.

"He ran that way." Grannie Mor pointed up the hill. "Whiskers must have attempted to invade his territory."

Abracadabra's favorite pastime, besides eating, was chasing cats. He was used to having free rein during the day, because he always came home. But that was back in Vegas. In his new surroundings, Tempest was keeping him in his hutch unless he was supervised, but clearly Abra was having none of that. The massive gray lop was smarter than your average rabbit.

Or at least Tempest thought so. Maybe all rabbits were this intelligent, but she'd never had the opportunity to find out. In a lifelong attempt to eschew magician stereotypes, she'd never owned a rabbit before receiving Abra as a gift. She hadn't planned on keeping him, but it was love at first bite. The curmudgeonly bunny was a superb judge of character and had bitten the awful woman who was dating Tempest's friend Sanjay. Who could give up such an intelligent creature after that?

"Abracadabra!" Tempest called. "Come on, Abra."

"He'll show up in his own good time." Morag led the way back to the tree house. "Your grandfather was fixing breakfast when he spotted Abra on the loose. He insisted we check on the rascal. I hope his affection for that rabbit hasn't burnt our kitchen down."

"That rabbit is going to get into trouble one of these days," Ash called after them before shaking his head and following them back to the house.

Tempest agreed. She reluctantly went with her grandmother, telling herself that Abra had as many lives as a cat.

They followed the downward slope of the hill to the bright red front door of the tree house. No ordinary key unlocked this door. The door handle was smooth, with no opening for a key. It was the grinning gargoyle door knocker that held the secret to letting you into the house. The person standing on the threshold needed to place a three-inch brass skeleton key sideways in the gargoyle's mouth, as if he was clenching it in his pointy teeth, then twist. As the gargoyle's teeth bit down on the key, the door unlocked.

The door wasn't locked just now. Even if it had been, it wasn't especially secure. This was never meant to be a permanent house. Much like the rest of the dwelling, the front door lock was one of Tempest's parents' many experiments to create whimsical keys for indoor secret rooms. When her grandparents moved in five years ago, they never got around to installing a proper lock. It wasn't like much crime ever happened in Hidden Creek. The only crime of interest that had happened in the town's long history was the one that involved Tempest's own family.

Tempest glanced at the eight silver charms dangling from the bracelet she wore all the time. The thick bracelet, made up of chunky charms related to her mom Emma's love of magic, was the last thing her mom had given her before she vanished live onstage five years ago. The vanishing act wasn't part of the show, and Emma Raj hadn't been seen since. That was the first time Tempest began to wonder if the legendary Raj family curse was real.

Chapter 2

The charms brushed against each other as Tempest climbed the stairs to her grandparents' kitchen. At the top, she closed her eyes and breathed in the fragrant aroma of ginger and cardamom filling the air. When she opened her eyes two seconds later, her grandfather was stirring a simmering pot of jaggery coffee with a wooden spoon, as if he'd been there the whole time.

"Don't do that," Tempest grumbled. "Um . . . How did you do that?"

Ash laughed. At eighty, her grandfather could do a better vanishing and reappearing act than she could. And she knew she was good.

She couldn't take all the credit. Magic was a part of Tempest long before she was born. Ashok Raj was born in the Indian state of Kerala eighty years ago into a family of famous traveling magicians. But Grandpa Ash was no longer a professional magician, and hadn't been for more than sixty years.

"A magician never reveals his secrets." Ash smiled to himself as he turned off the burner and dipped a ladle into the pot of sweet and spicy coffee. He handed Tempest a steaming mug. "It's good to have you home."

She wasn't sure what counted as home these days. She'd returned briefly five years ago, taking a leave of absence from college to join the search for her missing mom. She hadn't returned to school, even after all the evidence pointed to one thing: Emma Raj had died by suicide, drowning herself in the bay.

The sea was at the heart of the Raj magic dynasty—and its curse. From the founding of the magic troupe on the rainbow-colored beaches of Kanyakumari to the Scottish selkie folklore that Tempest's mom and aunt used in their show, water illusions were the soul of all Raj family magic. It was a self-fulfilling mythology. One that had now ensnared Tempest. When her mom vanished and was presumed dead, the idea that had previously seemed ridiculous—really, *a curse?*— finally lodged in Tempest's brain as something that might have been more than superstition born of bad luck. And now, after what happened this summer, she wondered . . . could it really be true?

Tempest gripped the warm mug of coffee, savoring the safe normality. Her mom's presumed death in the water five years ago was too close to her own near-death experience this summer. Pushing thoughts of the family curse aside, she blew on the steaming coffee and ran a hand through her hair. Her fingers caught in a tangle almost immediately. She hadn't glanced in a mirror since waking up, but she knew what her voluminous black hair looked like in the morning.

"Would you like the name of my hair stylist?" Morag asked. "Let me write down her number."

Tempest didn't think she'd ever seen Grannie Mor with a hair out of place, even when she'd been painting in her art studio for hours, oblivious to time and the elements, with her skin and clothing covered in paint.

"I promise I'll look less like Medusa before going out in public, Gran." Tempest laughed and took a sip of the coffee. More than her grandfather's words or sleeping in her childhood bedroom, breathing in the unique scent of the South Indian-style coffee made her feel like she was truly at home. Her mom used to make it for her and her best friend, Ivy. At thirteen, being initiated into the ritual of coffee made them feel like mature adults. Ivy had been Tempest's closest friend when they were kids—until everything fell apart when they were sixteen. Tempest hadn't spoken to Ivy in years. She wished she could erase everything that had happened, but she knew it was far too late for that. It was yet another reason she dreaded going to work for her dad's company. Yet another reason she needed today's meeting to go well.

Tempest savored another sip, then set down the mug. "I should get ready for my ten o'clock breakfast meeting." She didn't say so out loud, but she wanted time to go over some of the better ideas she'd sketched in a notebook. The mechanics of the illusions she envisioned weren't yet fully formed, but the stories behind them were. That had always been one of her greatest strengths. The story came first, and then you figured out how to perform it. Many magicians had tried to mansplain to her why that wasn't how it worked. But not the guy she was on her way to see. She wasn't sure if he'd ask for her ideas today, but Tempest needed to be as prepared as possible. This could be her way back to the stage. Back to having a contribution to make in the world. And most importantly, back to recapturing the sense of wonder she'd once found in magic—that she'd once found in life. That sense of awe and wonder had vanished along with her mom, and she'd been chasing it ever since.

Ashok frowned. "Who eats breakfast so late?"

Tempest stole one last sip of caffeine. "Entertainers who haven't seen seven a.m. in years."

Her grandfather clucked his disapproval before his head disappeared behind the door of the fridge. He emerged a moment later holding a bowl of thick batter.

"For *vada* donuts?" Tempest's mouth watered. *Vada* was a savory South Indian dish that resembled a donut but didn't taste like one. Grandpa Ash had combined the classic dish with the sweetness of Western donuts to create one of Tempest's favorite breakfasts. He'd made it for her the morning after she'd arrived and was thrilled by how many she'd eaten. Grandpa Ash enjoyed food, but his true love was feeding other people.

Ash chuckled. "I knew you were hungry."

"Maybe just one . . ."

Within minutes, the scent of chili pepper and honey filled the air. Ash stacked three sizzling vada donuts into a stainless-steel tiffin and filled an insulated travel mug with coffee. He placed the hearty breakfast into a woven basket and scooted Tempest out the door.

It relieved her to find a fluffy gray mass waiting dutifully on the front porch of the tree house. That was one less thing to worry about. Tempest slid the basket to the crook of her elbow so she could scoop the hefty bunny into her arms and get him back inside his hutch.

"What have you got there, Abra? What's Grandpa Ash been feeding you?" This wasn't a chunk of carrot stuck in Abra's teeth. Or food of any kind. He held a piece of black fabric in his mouth. The edges were frayed, as if it had been ripped. Or bitten.

"Where did this come from?" Tempest looked around the yard and didn't see any obvious signs of destruction. Abra's nose twitched and he nuzzled her hand. As curious as she was, she didn't have time to explore where Abra had been digging. After a moment's hesitation, she tucked the ripped piece of cloth into her pocket. There was more important work to be done. She was on her way to get her life back.

Chapter 3

When the wind cooperated, you could stand in front of Fiddler's Folly, nestled into the hillside, and hear the faint whispers of lapping water from the hidden creek that gave Tempest's hometown its name. The creek hadn't always been hidden. The massive earthquake of 1906 that had destroyed much of San Francisco had also caused a fissure in this hillside across the bay. The water followed a new path, much of which was now beneath the earth. Tempest listened to the hypnotic melody for thirty seconds before stepping into her jeep and setting off to the meeting that could put her life back on track. The bright red jeep was the first big purchase she'd made in her adult life. Thankfully, she'd bought it outright, so it couldn't be repossessed.

Bright morning sunlight shone through the jeep's windows and landed on Tempest's silver charm bracelet as she turned onto the winding road. The jester charm's enigmatic smile appeared even more mysterious as it sparkled in the light. The bracelet lifted her spirits, as it always did. It made her feel like her mom was there with her.

The handcuff charm caught her eye before she turned her attention back to the road. The handcuffs represented

Houdini. Tempest's favorite magician from bygone days was Adelaide Herrmann, who took the world by storm as the Queen of Magic after her husband Alexander died in 1896, but Tempest's mom had loved Houdini above all. Not for his skill, but for his approach to magic. "He wasn't just a master with lock picks," Emma had pointed out. "Houdini's mind and perseverance formed the key. *He was a key that could escape from any lock. If you apply that philosophy to yourself, you can become a key that can enter any world you wish.*" Tempest had rolled her eyes whenever her mother said that, because she knew what was coming next. A pep talk about how once Tempest grew up, worked hard, and forged her way in the world, she'd realize that even though she was different, she belonged. Why hadn't she appreciated those times more when she'd had them? Both her mom and Houdini had been taken from the world far too young—and under mysterious circumstances.

This morning, Tempest was on her way to meet a different Houdini.

When she arrived at Creekside Park fifteen minutes early, he was already there, setting up a picnic at a wooden table. Dressed in black slacks and a slate gray dress shirt, with a bowler hat shielding his eyes from the sun, he must have considered this outfit casual wear. Tempest was used to seeing him in a tailored tuxedo, his costume for the stage. Tempest didn't look much like her stage persona today, either. In jeans and a fitted white T-shirt, with her abundant black hair pulled into a low ponytail, the only touch of theatrics was her favorite fire-engine red lipstick that she couldn't resist.

Sanjay Rai, aka The Hindi Houdini, was Tempest's only magician friend who hadn't turned his back on her after the accident. He believed in her innocence without question, like her family did. Sanjay was a moderately famous stage performer, known for his spectacular illusions that blended Eastern and Western magic. She hadn't imagined he could top the time he escaped from a coffin at the bottom of the Ganges in India, but since then he'd performed the fabled Indian Rope Trick on an outdoor stage in Japan. She still didn't know how he'd pulled it off.

She also didn't know how even a glimpse of him and his gorgeous black hair could always make her stomach flip-flop. At least that answered one question. If he wanted to rekindle the two-second romance they'd had in the past, she would seriously consider it.

Still, she hoped that wasn't the reason he'd asked her here.

"Nice spread," she said, nodding toward the plaid blanket with an oversize wicker picnic basket in the center.

"This?" He shrugged, then yanked on the edge of the blanket. The green blanket was now blue, and the wicker basket was nowhere in sight, replaced by a carafe of coffee, ceramic mugs, and a platter of pastries.

"Show off." She stuck out her tongue and wriggled it at him.

"Who, me?" He grinned and enveloped her in a warm hug. Sanjay had only recently returned to Northern California after a tour, and they hadn't seen each other since they'd both been back. "It's good to see you, Tempest. I hope this spot is okay. I knew you wouldn't want to do a picnic near the water."

Tempest tensed. Sanjay had reached out to her after the illusion-gone-wrong that had nearly killed her. She hadn't wanted to talk about it then, and she didn't now. Not only because lawyers had advised her not to talk to anyone about what had happened that night. She hadn't admitted to Sanjay—or anyone—that had it not been for the actions of one person on that stage, she might not have made it. She still didn't know who it was who'd helped her. Did they not want to admit it because they no longer wanted to be associated with her?

She realized Sanjay was still talking. "It's messed up what everyone is saying happened. Do you want to talk about what happ—"

Tempest cut him off. "Today is about the future, right?"

He tipped his bowler hat and grinned. "It is."

"Then no talk of the past." She breathed in the fresh scents of pine cones and eucalyptus trees. "I could have met you at a café. You didn't have to go to this effort."

"Of course I did. We're celebrating."

"We are?"

"I hope we are." He bit his lip and gave her an innocent smile she knew was far from virtuous. "I had to make a good impression so you'd say yes. I'm working on a new show."

She tried not to let the giddy smile she felt on the inside surface. This was good. Very good. She was hardly disappointed that he hadn't invited her to the picnic to revive a romantic relationship. She was right that he wanted her to work with him on a new show.

Sanjay lifted the carafe. "Coffee?"

"Plenty of cream." She sat across from him at the picnic table in a spot that let sunlight fall on her face.

"I remember."

She accepted the cup of strong, creamy coffee, and imagined how perfect the show would be. "What's the theme of the new show?"

Neither of them was afraid to go big. She expected they'd continue themes similar to those they'd each used in their individual illusions. They both used symbolism from the elements in the stories they told their audiences. Sanjay was so skilled at manipulating air that sometimes Tempest briefly wondered if he possessed a dash of real magic. For Tempest, her magic always came back to water. It had from the start. She'd been born during a tempest so fierce it caused a flood that rerouted her parents' path to the hospital. At least, that was the story her parents told her to explain why she almost entered this world on the bucket seat of an old pickup truck with a broken gearshift, and why they knew they'd call her Tempest. The name had always suited her, especially when she became a magician. The signature line she used without fail before exiting any stage was part of the package that made her famous: *I'm The Tempest. Destruction follows in my wake.* When her mentor Nicodemus had first proposed it, she thought it was a bit over the top, but he'd been right.

Tempest had followed in the footsteps of her mom and aunt, who were themselves following the traditions of their father and the generations before him. The first lesson the Raj magic dynasty stressed was the importance of telling a story during a magic show, not simply performing tricks. A trick was easily forgotten. But a story? If you got it right, that was magic. Tempest wished she had a time machine and could have traveled back in time to see the show that Emma and her sister, Elspeth, had performed in their hometown of Edinburgh, back when they were known as the Selkie Sisters, long before either of them died. But today wasn't a day to think about the past. Today was the beginning of her future.

"Come on, Sanjay," Tempest prodded. "What are your new ideas?"

He shook his head. "Even for you, Tempest, I can't tell you the details until you agree to join me."

She understood. She would have done the same thing in his position.

"I've been looking for the perfect assistant ever since Grace didn't work out," Sanjay continued. "I know you haven't been an assistant in a while, and you're not nearly as tiny as Grace, so we'll have to adjust some things, but I'm willing to put in the effort to make it work."

She blinked at him. "You want me to be your assistant?" His *assistant*?

Rage bubbled up inside her. She'd commanded a far fatter paycheck than he ever had. Performed before larger crowds. Garnered more critical praise.

"Don't worry," Sanjay said. "I can tell from your face you're nervous. But I know you need a job. And I don't care what other people think. You won't tarnish my reputation."

"I won't tarnish *your* reputation?" She wondered if the red-hot rage in her eyes was palpable.

"Bagel?" He tore off a piece and popped it into his mouth. He calmly brushed poppy seeds from his fingers, a contented smile forming on his lips.

"I. Don't. Want. A. Bagel."

"Chocolate chip scone?"

Her mouth felt dry. She took a sip of the coffee, but it scorched her tongue. "I need more cream." Her voice shook as she spoke.

Oblivious, Sanjay obliged with a grin and a tip of his precious bowler hat.

The topped-up coffee was now cool enough to drink, but after one sip to alleviate her parched throat, she had a better idea.

Before she could talk herself out of it, she thrust her arm forward. Her cooled coffee hurtled through the air and hit

Sanjay's chin and splashed onto his dress shirt. It was a strong, chiseled chin and a defined, firm chest. She didn't care that she was hurting her chances of touching either again.

"What just happened?" he sputtered.

She stood and turned on the heel of her red sneaker, then paused to look back. "You should know by now. I'm The Tempest. Destruction follows in my wake."

Chapter 4

Back at her jeep, Tempest gripped the steering wheel and forced herself to breathe. She didn't need Sanjay. She reached into her pocket for a tissue. She wasn't crying. Dirt from the park must have made its way into her eye.

Instead of a tissue, her hand emerged from her pocket with the piece of ripped black fabric Abra had found. She groaned and tossed it aside. As she twisted her key in the ignition harder than was necessary, the engine roared to life. She backed up a few feet before jamming her foot on the brake. Where was she even going? She had officially hit rock bottom. There was no more putting it off. She'd have to accept her fate.

She tapped on the screen of her phone and navigated to her dad's number. His photo was the goofy one she'd taken of him when he was pretending to scale a skyscraper, like The Rock had done in that movie. People were always commenting that Darius resembled the actor. To Tempest, he only looked like her papa.

She hesitated before hitting the call button, thinking back to what her dad had said. He told her his crew could use her help, and maybe it was even true, but during this recession potential clients for Secret Staircase Construction had less money to hire contractors and were taking on more home renovation projects themselves. The company used to have a long wait list. But that was before Tempest's mom disappeared. When she'd gone, the magic had vanished with her. Now they were lucky if they were working at half capacity. It was all her dad could do to keep his three core team members on payroll, let alone hire the subcontractors he used to work with on a regular basis. Tempest had been sending money home more and more frequently. After initially refusing, her dad accepted if she called it a loan. It kept things going—until she lost everything.

No, she wasn't ready to accept either of their fates. She threw her phone onto the passenger seat. She wasn't defeated yet.

💀💀💀

Arriving home at Fiddler's Folly, she walked through the living room and past the fireplace with more secrets than she could remember. Before reaching the kitchen, she paused at the start of the hallway that led to the bedrooms. She lifted the wing of a stone dragon on the wall. Its head tilted to the side, as if the creature was curiously examining the strange young woman who'd returned after so many years. As the dragon's head turned, a panel in the wall slid open, revealing a staircase that had previously been hidden.

Regardless of what was going on in her life, including near-death experiences and friends betraying her, the sight of her own secret staircase that had been hers since she was a kid never failed to elicit at least the hint of a smile on her lips. She climbed the narrow wooden stairs to her bedroom. Her hidden sanctuary.

Her feet didn't make a sound on the sturdy staircase. Every few steps, another subtle light clicked on above her head. Once she reached the top, she turned the key-shaped lever on the wall. The lights in the stairway dimmed into darkness as the sliding wall at the base of the stairs slid silently shut.

Her phone rang as she was kicking off her sneakers at the top of the stairs.

"How did your meeting go?" Her grandfather's voice was unmistakable.

Grandpa Ash's singular accent was approximately 90 percent South Indian, 9 percent Scottish, and 1 percent Californian. He'd left India for Scotland as a teenager, shortly after the accident that killed his brother. He was accepted into medical school at the University of Edinburgh, where he met Morag Ferguson. She captured his heart and sealed his fate that he'd remain in Scotland. They'd given up their Edinburgh flat to come live in the backyard tree house after their daughter disappeared. They hadn't planned on making the move permanent, but life has a way of turning out differently than planned, as Tempest knew all too well. This lack of privacy was something Tempest would have to get used to for the duration of her time at home.

She sighed. "Not good."

"Hmm. Did you eat?"

That brought a smile to Tempest's lips. "A little."

"Ready for lunch?"

"It's ten thirty."

"You can help me cook." He was always cooking.

"Rain check."

When her phone rang twenty minutes later, she was sure it was Grandpa Ash calling again to entice her to help him cook lunch, but it wasn't. She didn't recognize the number, so she thought about declining the call. As soon as she answered, she wished she had.

"I'm at your front door." The voice was that of her former best friend. Ivy Youngblood.

Ivy was once the sole friend Tempest felt completely comfortable with, and the one who always had her back. She knew her family loved her, but she didn't have anyone like Ivy in her life these days, and she missed that more than she thought she would. For as long as she could remember, Tempest had fit in both everywhere and nowhere. Superficially, she blended in with ease, but it was also as if there was a sheet of glass keeping her apart from others. She still heard the "What are you?" question both from people scrutinizing her ethnically ambiguous looks and from those who couldn't fathom that she was the headliner. She was a proud mash-up American and female magician in a profession dominated by men. With a successful stage show, she'd thought she was finally going to find her place in the world. What was she now?

She opened the front door and found her petite, redheaded, former BFF holding two takeout cups. Ivy's formerly long, strawberry blond hair was now cut above her shoulders in a cute asymmetrical style that suited her, but some things remained the same. Ivy wore the same puffy pink vest she'd had since high school and her short fingernails were painted a matching shade of pink, which, as always, had mostly chipped off. She wasn't smiling, but at least she wasn't glowering. Back in high school, Ivy's glower had rivaled Tempest's, even though Ivy was barely five feet tall and therefore often underestimated. Only Tempest's mastery of a solitary raised eyebrow elevated her beyond Ivy as the undisputed champion of scowling.

"Peace offering." Ivy held one of the cups in an outstretched arm.

After misjudging Sanjay's intentions earlier that morning, Tempest was wary of reading too much into Ivy's gesture. She hoped her own peace offering hadn't been in vain. While hastily packing her belongings in Vegas earlier that summer, she'd come across the set of Nancy Drew first editions she'd bought on impulse years ago because she knew Ivy would love them. She hadn't ever sent them. Only when she knew her life couldn't get any worse did she ask her dad for Ivy's address so she could mail her the books. She couldn't remember what she'd scrawled on her note, but it must not have been too horrible.

Tempest accepted the cup. The warming mix of sweet spices told her what was inside. "Spiced chai from Veggie Magic?"

The pair had spent countless hours talking about everything and nothing at a wobbly corner table of the café that had been a mainstay of the town since before they'd been born.

"I was going to ask for extra cardamom," Ivy said, "since I know it's your favorite. But . . ."

"But?"

Ivy shrugged. "I decided against it. I figure we're at the tepid tea peace offering stage of possibly renewed friendship."

"Fair enough." Probably fairer than she deserved, Tempest decided, but she'd take it. "Do you want to come in?"

Ivy shook her head. "I can't stay long."

"How did you know I'd be at home?"

"Ash called your dad. Darius said you didn't get the job you were hoping for. I took advantage of them being worried about you to take an extra break."

Tempest groaned. "This is pity chai?" Her mortification was complete.

"I'd rather think of it as opportunistic chai. I needed a break. We started a new job today. The house is . . . creepy." Ivy zipped up the collar of the puffy vest until it covered half her face, like a turtle retreating into its shell for protection. "I know that sounds ridiculous."

"Speaking of creepy houses, maybe I could contribute a late-night viewing of *Clue?*"

Ivy's eyes lit up and she retreated halfway out of her puffy pink shell. Her frustration with Tempest must have been pretty strong for her not to say yes immediately. "Do you know how hard it is to find someone who'll watch classic mystery movies with me until two o'clock in the morning?"

"Is that a yes?"

"No." Ivy shook her head firmly enough that her hair slapped her face.

"I'm also available to listen to you talk about the well-hidden clues of classic mystery novels." Tempest and Ivy had initially bonded over their love of Scooby-Doo, which led them to classic kids' books: Encyclopedia Brown, Nancy Drew (Ivy's idol), Trixie Belden (Tempest's fave), the Three Investigators. As soon as their ages hit the double digits, they moved on to classic mysteries. Mystery forerunners Sir Arthur Conan Doyle and Edgar Allan Poe led to the Golden Age of detective fiction, including Dorothy Sayers, Agatha Christie, Edmund Crispin, Anthony Berkeley, Ellery Queen, Clayton Rawson (who created Tempest's beloved magician sleuth The Great Merlini), and John Dickson Carr (who wrote Ivy's hero Dr. Fell).

Ivy's eyes grew wide again. "Even my sister cut me off! Can you believe it? Unless a mystery is true crime, Dahlia won't listen to me ramble for more than five minutes at a time. Seriously. She sets a timer on her phone."

"That's harsh. I promise, no cell phone timers on my end." Tempest missed that feeling of getting lost in a deliciously devious book. When she'd made the decision to become a performing stage magician, making it a reality took so much hard work that her free time was consumed with watching playbacks of her own rehearsals or the performances of other magicians, not reading classic mysteries. Whereas Ivy had made her way through the entire John Dickson Carr canon, as well as a lot of others.

"You don't need a timer since you can count perfect time in your head. It's spooky. But I know what you meant," Ivy said, giving Tempest a half-smile. "Just like I know you're the least patient person I've ever met."

"Tenacity is one of my charms."

"Maybe." Ivy held her gaze, her expression inscrutable. "I should get back to the job site. Your dad asked if you could come, too. It's here in Hidden Creek, so not far."

"You don't actually need me, do you? It's not like I'm licensed to do anything."

"Your dad found some discrepancies in the blueprints for the house at the building department. Since you make similar plans when you build sets for your shows and are good at hiding things in plain sight, we could use your help sorting the papers and comparing the drawings."

Huh. That meant they really could use her help.

"I'll text you the address," Ivy added.

"The address to the creepy house where you'd like to avoid spending more time than necessary."

Ivy held up her free hand. "You can't claim I oversold you on the job. Paperwork and a creepy old house. Calvin Knight bought the 110-year-old mansion earlier this summer. He lives there with his six-year-old son. Cute kid. But sad. I bet he misses his old friends."

There was a lot of that going around.

"Let me grab my keys," Tempest said. "I'll meet you there."

☠☠☠

Tempest shook her head as she stepped out of her jeep in front of the Knights' house ten minutes later. Leave it to Ivy and her proclivity to see mysteries everywhere to think such a gorgeous old building was creepy instead of magical.

The façade was straight out of a fairy tale, with two mismatched towers resembling the turrets of a castle. As was common in the American version of the Queen Anne school of architecture, the towers were asymmetrical. It was a style Tempest had always thought of as a Scooby-Doo haunted house.

A handsome man in his forties with dark brown skin, stylish black glasses, and a broad smile answered the door. Behind him, a high-ceilinged foyer led to a curved staircase and kitchen, with two octagonal rooms to their right and left.

"Calvin Knight." He shook her hand and introduced his son, Justin, who was playing with a bright blue robot in a cardboard fort next to the staircase. Calvin was dressed in an impeccably ironed light-blue dress shirt and Blancpain watch—with wrinkled cargo shorts and sandals. He caught Tempest looking at the tan flip-flops on his feet. "Video conference calls only capture the chest up," he said with a wry smile. "I'm working from home until Justin starts school."

Calvin led Tempest through the foyer and kitchen of the sprawling house to the spot where the crew was working. Walking past the weighty classical columns of the grand staircase and ornamental cornices above, Tempest appreciated how a skylight above and sweeping bay windows brought plenty of natural light into the house. The interior architecture of the Knights' new home was as charming as the outside—until they reached the section of the house Secret Staircase Construction would be renovating.

The space was currently a walk-in pantry next to the kitchen. Antique mahogany shelves, now barren, had been built into one wood-paneled wall. The other two walls lacked built-in details except for ornate wooden trim.

Although the Knights appeared to be settled in the rest of the house, with lived-in furniture on the floors and artwork from Southeast Asia and Africa on the walls, this room was bare. It wasn't simply the absence of furniture or housewares. The room felt . . . stagnant. Not exactly a bad odor, though a faint mustiness permeated the air. Ivy hadn't been exaggerating. There was something about the room that felt wrong. The shape. The light. Even the temperature. It was cold in here. Tempest shivered. She wasn't superstitious. Curses and other supernatural manifestations didn't exist. It was Cassidy Sparrow who had wrecked her career and nearly killed her. Not the Raj family curse. Which most certainly did not exist.

Chapter 5

Tempest shook off her worries as she spotted her dad, but they crept back as soon as she noticed his body language. He stood with his tree trunk–size arms crossed and his jaw clamped shut. Tempest got her height and muscular shape from her dad, but even as she'd grown a head taller than her petite mom, people always said she looked more like Emma, with their olive complexions, thick black hair, and eyes the color of night. Darius's light brown eyes matched his light brown skin, and he'd shaved his head for so long that she barely remembered it any other way.

His rigid, protective posture told Tempest as clearly as words that he was worried. About what? If a job was going badly this early, surely that couldn't be a good sign. He looked on as Ivy and the other two members of the crew, Robbie and the new guy, were deep in discussion in one corner of the creepy walk-in pantry.

Tempest caught her dad's eye from the doorway. Darius slipped away from the heated discussion that looked like it was about to become an argument, and led Tempest back through the kitchen, past the half-bath and grand stairway into the foyer. Instead of heading out the front door, they took a right turn into the living room and passed through another arched doorway into a study. She recognized Secret Staircase Construction's handiwork in the bookshelf that lined the back wall of the deceptively small room.

"Which book opens the sliding shelf?" she asked.

He smiled. Regardless of what was wrong with this current job, the delight in his eyes when he thought about a job he was proud of made his whole face light up. "Guess."

She ran her hand across the spines of the books. These weren't for show. The spines showed signs of cracking, and hardcovers and paperbacks of all sizes and shapes were mixed together. The Knights were readers. She stopped on a low shelf crammed full of history books, all of which looked like they pertained to California history, specifically the Gold Rush, with some architectural history in the mix.

"This one." She pulled on a hefty book about restoring a historic home. The book pulled out in her hand. It wasn't attached to any mechanism. She was wrong.

"Too low." Darius grinned and wriggled his eyebrows at her.

"Right. There's a kid in the household." Bringing her gaze higher, she settled on Ralph Ellison's *Invisible Man*. She reached up and gave it a tug. The bookcase swung open. "Nice work. It barely makes a sound."

Darius laughed. "Only you would skip over the details of the exquisite wood carving in favor of how well it can fool people." He pushed the book back in place, and the shelf began to swing shut. Before it closed, she caught sight of a cozy armchair resting beneath a high window in the shape of an oversize wine bottle resting on its side. A metal bar twisted in the shape of a corkscrew cut through the center of the small window. She knew the room would also include a lever on the inside so that nobody could find themselves trapped in the secret room. Her dad insisted on safety features, even when clients wanted to cut corners elsewhere.

This was the first job her dad had done for Calvin Knight, earlier that summer before Tempest had arrived home. She'd heard the job was a success, and she could see why. That was why the crew had been hired for this larger job.

When she turned back to face her dad, he was pointing at two sets of papers spread out on the old desk. "I need you to look at the plans for the house."

Before moving to the antique desk, Tempest glanced up at the intricate cornices and delicate molding in the room. The previous owners had treated its history well. She could imagine it as it was a century ago. "This house is hiding something."

"Ivy told you?"

She met her dad's gaze and grinned. "Architectural misdirection."

A thud sounded from the other room. Darius winced. "I need to get back to them."

"But what am I—"

"I'll leave you to it."

"—looking for?" she finished, speaking to an empty room.

These weren't modern blueprints made with a computer, but old drafting sketches that showed work that had taken place over time.

Within minutes, she could tell that something was off about the different sketches. The measurements in the kitchen and pantry rooms from the 1925 drawing didn't match up with earlier ones. It wasn't simply that they were drawings of the house at different stages of its life over 110 years. It was like a magic cabinet with false panels, meant to look empty when it was really hiding a magician.

Focusing on the jigsaw puzzle pieces that fit together to construct both a house and a stage set, Tempest was certain there was some architectural sleight of hand here. She'd have to measure the space itself to be sure she was on to something, but she already knew she was right. Someone had fudged the measurements nearly a century ago. But why?

Before she could look more closely, her attention was pulled elsewhere. She wasn't alone in Calvin's study.

Tempest was used to people watching her. She knew the feeling well. There was a particular buzz of the direct attention she experienced when she used misdirection to control the audience's attention. And then there was a more gradual awareness that crept up on her when someone was watching her but trying to be stealthy about it. Most people who recognized her in public didn't approach her immediately, instead surreptitiously glancing her way several times while they debated whether it was really The Tempest and if they should ask to take a photo with her.

She knew with certainty that someone was watching her here in this century-old Queen Anne house. Yet nobody was there in the room with her. Nobody visible.

She knew who it had to be. The little boy, Justin, who she'd been introduced to when she arrived. There was a perfect kid-size hiding spot behind the armchair next to the door. Tempest was hundreds of miles from Vegas and a world away from the life in which she'd wowed thousands of people each night, but now that she had an audience, her natural instinct was to put on a show. She smiled to herself as she stepped out from behind the desk and flipped into a headstand.

It took a few seconds to steady herself. She was out of practice . . . good grief, her abs hurt! For a moment she thought she might have to rely on the wall for support, which wouldn't do. But . . . there. She was stable.

Sure enough, a giggle and the applause of two small hands clapping followed six seconds later. Not that she was counting on purpose. But in a career where tracking precise moments in time means the difference between a spectacular vanishing act and being exposed sticking halfway out of a trapdoor in front of thousands of people, you learn how to count with precision in the background of any other task.

Former career, she reminded herself. She flipped down from the headstand.

"Hey, Justin," Tempest called out.

The six-year-old stepped out from behind the armchair where he'd been spying on her.

He gave her a shy grin. "Are you in the circus?"

"Not exactly. Aren't you supposed to be upstairs in your room while my dad and his team have their power tools out?"

"I was, but I don't want to be alone with the monster."

Tempest's breath caught. Was there another part of the house that felt as ominous as the room near the kitchen?

"The monster?" she repeated.

"We never had monsters at our old house." He frowned. "You don't believe me, either. I can show you."

Tempest followed Justin up the grand staircase, holding the smooth balustrade as she went. The light from the many windows didn't quite reach the nooks and crannies, of which there were many. It was no wonder a little boy who was new in town might imagine monsters were lurking.

Justin pointed to the open door of his bedroom. She looked from Justin's sad face to his room crammed full of every toy a child could ask for, from the classic castle blocks she'd played with twenty years before to modern robots that Nicodemus would rant about. Yet she didn't think she'd ever seen a kid so sad. Or so tired.

"Nightmares about the monsters?" she asked.

"Just one. Always the same one, ever since we moved in."

"You know how to beat a monster, right? Did your dad teach you?"

"He tells me it's in my head. Duh. Of course the monster is in my head. I want to get it out of my head."

She tried not to smile at his astute assessment. He was serious, and she'd respond accordingly. "Is it a closet monster, or some other kind?"

He gave her a look that made it perfectly clear it was the world's most ridiculous question. "Closet."

"Good thing you've got everything you need to fight closet monsters right in this room." She scanned the room again and weighed her options. Stepping across the plush rug, she picked up a stack of playing cards from a child-size oak bookshelf crammed with books ranging from *Bunnicula* to the Magic Tree House series.

"This isn't just a deck of cards," she said. "There are many stories inside here, and I'm going to tell you the most important one today." With the flick of her wrist, she fanned the cards into a perfect arc. Well, not quite perfect. Close-up magic used to be one of her biggest strengths, but in the past few years she'd spent more time practicing big illusions than creating these small moments of wonder. She plucked out the joker before waving her hand across the spread, making all the cards except for the joker disappear.

Justin's eyes grew wide. "How'd you do that?"

Her heart swelled at the sight of his excited little face. Even though she hadn't done the trick perfectly, his face held such a sense of wonder.

"Magic." She handed him the colorful joker. She was glad he didn't know who she was. It was easier for people to be impressed when they didn't know how far you'd fallen. "This is the card you need. The jack, the king, and the queen all have their own stories, but this guy? He's the most powerful character in the whole deck of cards. Because he can be anyone he wants to be. The joker can easily fight off monsters."

The kid scrutinized the joker's grinning face. "I don't like him. Aren't jokers like clowns? I don't like clowns."

"Nope. See, he hasn't got a creepy fake smile painted on his face like a clown. His smile is real."

His scrunched-up face told her he remained skeptical.

"The joker is like a court jester," she added. "You know about jesters? They were the guys who entertained kings and queens a long time ago. Jesters have no fear. They speak the truth—even to monsters."

She blew on the card and it disappeared. Justin gasped and giggled. She spread her empty hands wide, and with a flick of her fingers the card reappeared between her index and middle fingers. Sloppier than she would have liked, but from Justin's wide-eyed expression she didn't think he'd caught the maneuver. "Keep this card at your bedside, and he'll make sure no monsters appear."

"Really?"

"Yup. I promise not a single monster will come out of the closet."

She didn't know yet that she'd lied to him.

Chapter 6

empest?" Ivy's face, creased with worry, appeared in the doorway. Her pale skin and light auburn hair, framed by sunlight from the skylight behind her, resembled one of Tempest's grandmother's portraits. "Can you come downstairs?"

"You'll be okay?" Tempest asked Justin.

"Will you teach me to do a headstand later?"

"I already taught you one amazing feat! The *best* one, since you know how to defeat a closet monster."

"Tempest," Ivy cut in. "It's urgent."

"Gotta go, Justin. I'll ask your dad about the headstand." She followed Ivy out the door.

Ivy doubled back and made sure the bedroom door was firmly closed, then clasped Tempest's hand in hers.

Tempest squeezed back. "What's going on?"

"We found something in the crawlspace."

Why did she look so distressed? Crawlspaces in old houses were like time capsules. From crumpled newspapers of long-ago decades to ceramic figurines, a dazzling assortment of random items were used as cheap insulation. Tempest remembered the fun she'd had as a kid as she searched for treasure in the random piles of junk her mom and dad pulled from the walls of old houses. The owners got first dibs on whatever she found, her parents always told her, but the homeowners never seemed to want the treasures.

Then she remembered the time she found something far less pleasant.

"Please don't tell me it's rats," said Tempest. "I hate rats."

"It's not a rat. It's far too big to be a rat."

"Ivy, seriously, what's going on?"

"We couldn't tell what was going on with one of the walls. It should have been lath and plaster, like the rest, but it didn't feel like it was, so we poked a test hole. I was the first one to look inside. It's—" Ivy broke off and pulled Tempest further from Justin's room.

"It's what?"

"I hope I'm wrong," she whispered. "You know how much I hate being wrong. But I really hope I am."

"What do you want to be wrong about, Ivy?"

Ivy's face was ashen when she met Tempest's gaze. "Darius told Calvin we saw something strange inside the wall, and Calvin was insistent we go ahead and open it up. He wants to find out what's going on with that odd space. I don't know if he would have made that choice if your dad had told him what I'd seen through the test hole . . ."

"What did you see?"

"It looks like a body."

Tempest stared at her old friend for seven seconds. Not speaking. Not blinking. Not even breathing. Ivy could read frightening novels by the light of a single candle during a thunderstorm, had entered a profession where women weren't the norm, and drove her moped scooter on Bay Area roads. Intrepid Ivy was frightened. Tempest gave a single nod, and they ran down the stairs together. They passed Calvin on the stairs as the buzz of a power tool sounded.

"We're cutting open the wall," Ivy explained as they reached the base of the stairs and turned toward the kitchen. "Robbie went out to his truck to get respirator masks and a reciprocating saw. We weren't planning on doing more than a test hole, but now . . ."

Thump.

The sound came right as they reached the pantry.

A heavy, six-foot-long bag crashed to the floor.

Ivy jumped. Tempest's heart thudded at the sound and image, but she was used to stifling her reactions while onstage. Her reflexes, however, were quick. While the four members of the crew stood still, Tempest was the first person to reach the dusty sack that had fallen out of the wall.

Robbie stood motionless above Tempest and the heavy sack, a safety mask on his face and the unmoving saw still in his hand. "I didn't think it would be so heavy." His voice was a whisper and his eyes widened as his gaze fell onto the tangled dark mass poking out of the sack. "Is that—"

"Maybe that only *looks* like black hair sticking out." Tempest felt the quiver in her voice as she spoke. Used to breathing through stage smoke and dust, she didn't cough even as she felt her throat constrict. "We can't be seeing what we think we're seeing. There has to be another explanation."

She reached her hand forward, but as she did so she felt a strong yet shaking hand on hers. Robbie gently pulled her back. "We shouldn't touch it."

"He's right," Darius said. Tempest was vaguely aware that her dad, Ivy, and the new guy were in the room with her and Robbie, but she barely registered their presence. It was funny how the mind focused on the strangest things in times of great stress. As the realization hit her of what they were looking at, Tempest wondered if one of the myriad of objects Robbie was no doubt carrying in his explorer's vest could fix the situation, like it did everything else. Tempest had known Robbie since she was eleven years old. She always joked that she wouldn't recognize him if she spotted him without that ridiculous vest, and she wasn't entirely sure she was joking. The beige, water-resistant piece of outerwear wasn't an affectation. If you ever needed anything smaller than a bread box, there was a good chance it could be found in one of the numerous pockets. Tempest remembered him once extracting three kinds of tape (duct, painters, and flex, each wrapped around a different colored pencil), a flashlight, pipe cleaners, compact mirror, and, of course, a Swiss Army knife (Darius favored a Leatherman). Robbie always said he wouldn't always have a toolbox in his hand, but he could always wear the vest.

Tempest willed herself to look up from the comforting familiar image of Robbie's vest into his worried gray eyes. There was nothing in his magical vest that could help this time, and he knew it.

"You think it looks like human hair, too," she whispered.

His eyes watering from the dust, Robbie pulled off his mask, revealing the familiar cleft in his chin that had always made him look young and carefree to Tempest. He looked neither young nor carefree now. When he answered, it was with a shaking voice. "Ivy was right. A dead body was hidden inside the wall."

Chapter 7

"Everyone out," Darius's deep voice boomed. "Gather in the living room, and I'll meet you there in a minute. I'm calling 9-1-1." He already had his cell phone in his hand.

Tempest thought it was a little late for that. This wall hadn't been opened in decades. There was no way the unfortunate soul who'd been inside the wall was in need of medical attention.

Always steady on her feet, Tempest was frustrated to find her legs shaking. Robbie helped her up in time for her to see her dad run a hand across his face and clench his jaw. She knew he wasn't worried about himself, but others. What would this old body mean for Calvin Knight's new home? As for Secret Staircase Construction, the business had been struggling since her mom had vanished, and things had only gotten worse with the recession, which was why she'd been sending money home. Back when she could afford it. Cassidy might have wrecked far more than Tempest's career. If it ruined her dad's business, too, Tempest would never forgive her.

The lines of her dad's face deepened as he spoke to the operator in a hushed tone. A cold draft made Tempest shiver.

It was warm outside, so her arms were bare in a T-shirt. Why was it so cold in here?

"Tempest?" Darius looked surprised to see her still standing there. Everyone else had listened to him. He had that kind of voice. That kind of presence. "You don't want to be here."

She did, though. She wanted to be there with her dad to help, and she also couldn't ignore the macabre curiosity tugging at her. Something else tugged at her more forcefully. Her dad took her hand in his and led her out of the cold pantry.

"Come on," he said. "What? No, I was speaking to my daughter. My daughter who's *leaving*." He pulled her out of the pantry and through the kitchen, not stopping when he bumped into one of the two barstools at the granite kitchen island, then around the corner into the foyer.

Entering the living room, she spotted the new guy first. What was his name? Gideon. That was it. Her dad had told her about the new guy, but she hadn't met him yet. Gideon stood alone, not scrolling on a cell phone but simply looking out the window. Ivy and Robbie sat together on the couch, huddled in a quiet conversation. A thin layer of dust was still visible in Robbie's light brown hair, but he didn't seem to notice. Ivy's pink vest was zipped high enough to cover her mouth and nose, but her wide eyes peeked over the collar.

"What's happening?" Robbie stood as Tempest and her dad came in.

Darius shook his head and pointed at the phone at his ear. They all waited in silence as Darius spoke a few more hushed words to the person on the other end of the line before sliding the phone into his pocket.

"Why'd you hang up?" Tempest asked. "I thought 9-1-1 operators stayed on the phone with you until help arrived?"

"I guess not if the body is a century old. But they're sending someone." Darius ran a hand over his face. "Where's Calvin?"

"Upstairs with his son," Ivy answered.

"I guess it's time for me to go upstairs and tell him he bought a house with a dead body inside it."

Tempest stepped in front of her dad. "Let me send him downstairs so you can talk to him alone. I'll stay with Justin." She bounded up the steps of the grand staircase.

Justin must have heard her coming, because he ran to his doorway and greeted her with a wide smile on his face. "Time for a headstand?"

"We were going to ask your dad, remember?"

He ran back into the room, with Tempest following. "Miss Raj was going to teach me a headstand. She's in the Not-Exactly-Circus."

"The Not-Exactly-Circus, huh?" Calvin caught Tempest's eye. His amused expression shifted when he saw the worry on her face. "I'm guessing you didn't find buried treasure in my crawl space. Everything okay downstairs?"

"My dad needs to see you."

"Old houses," he muttered. "I did research and thought I knew what I was getting into . . . Back in a flash, J. You can tell me more about this headstand then."

Justin scrunched up his face, but smiled as his dad left. "Want to play robots?" He held up the bright blue and silver robot she'd seen earlier. She hadn't noticed its creepy crimson eyes before.

"First, I need to tell you more about what the joker protects you from."

The smile faded. "Why?"

Smart kid. When he learned about the old bones in the house, what could possibly make him feel better? She thought back on the days when she was around his age. "Do you like pirates?"

"Nah. Robots."

She looked around the room and counted eight robots. "No pirate treasures for you?"

He shrugged. "I don't care about treasure. I'd rather have my mom back."

"Me too."

"You don't have a mom?"

"I did. Until five years ago."

Tossing the robot aside, Justin threw his little arms around her. The force took her by surprise. It shouldn't have. She knew how raw those emotions could be. As quickly as the strong and forceful hug was around her, it was gone. He let go and pulled his knees up to his chest.

"Why'd you ask about pirates?" he asked. "Is there a pirate monster in the house now? I thought you vanquished them?"

"Big word, little man."

He grinned. "Daddy reads to me. A lot. And he lets me read anything I can reach on the bookshelves myself—climbing on chairs doesn't count." His expression turned serious. "Are you hiding something about the monster?"

"You know that room off the kitchen where your dad hired my dad and his crew to build a magical playroom for you?"

"The creepy room."

Tempest froze. "Why do you say that?"

"It always feels so cold in there."

"It's normal for old houses to have drafts." Tempest spoke the words to convince herself as much as Justin.

"Not like that," he said. "That room is where the closet monster comes from."

Chapter 8

While waiting for the authorities to arrive, Calvin stayed upstairs with Justin, and Tempest joined the crew where they'd gathered in the living room. Light flooded in through the bay windows and the skylight of the foyer adjoining the spacious room. An unlit fireplace dominated the wall opposite the windows, stretching from floor to ceiling. Nobody spoke.

Before retreating to the living room, Robbie had made sure there were no dangerous power tools left out and Darius and the whole crew had taken a closer look at the wall. Everyone avoided the bag with the body and nobody touched anything more than necessary. Though Darius didn't say so out loud, Tempest knew why he wanted to do so: to assure themselves that Secret Staircase Construction wasn't working for a murderer. The verdict? The wall wasn't as old as the house—the lath and plaster had been replaced by sheetrock in the mid-1900s—but it was definitely an old one that hadn't been worked on in a long time. Whoever had been stuffed into the crawl space of the pantry had been there for a lot longer than Calvin Knight and his son had been there.

Still, even though the crime wasn't personally connected

to any of them, it was an eerie feeling to be inside a house with a murder victim. And surely that's what this was. Why else stuff a body inside a wall?

Tempest watched her father pace back and forth in front of the hearth, dividing his gaze between the windows and the people in the room he cared about—which meant all of them. Darius Mendez was a father figure not just to Tempest, but to just about everyone in his life. A combination of fatherly caregiver and someone willing to do whatever it took to protect the people important to him. He adopted people in the same informal way he'd been adopted himself. He'd grown up with the surname Smith, but learned later it was the name of the first couple who'd taken him in before giving him up when he proved too difficult. After bouncing around from one foster home to the next as a kid, as an angry teenager he landed with a loving woman who didn't give up on him. Mona Mendez formally adopted Darius not long before she died, and he changed his name to hers.

Darius would never give up on his misfit crew, even though they didn't follow instructions any better than his daughter did. Even if they lost this job and he had to give up his own salary to pay theirs.

Ivy sat with her knees tucked up in the bay window, her face half hidden in the puffy collar of her vest. An unopened book lay in her lap. She'd escaped into books as a kid to escape a bad family situation. Tempest's parents let Ivy stay with them during a rough patch, and Darius had let her try out the tools in his workshop until she found which ones she liked, and he helped her find classes to become a welder. Never mind the fact that Secret Staircase Construction projects didn't frequently require those skills. But Ivy was willing to help out with the less desirable tasks, which were more enticing than sitting in front of a computer or finishing college.

Robbie fidgeted in the armchair next to the fireplace. He was their creative thinker who didn't follow directions well enough to survive in a traditional crew, and who Tempest didn't think she'd ever seen sit still. Darius put up with him at first because he was too brilliant not to take a chance on, and in time he became Secret Staircase family. He was the guy who could use only a paperclip and wedge of wood to coax open a sliding bookcase that refused to budge after an earthquake. Their very own MacGyver.

When Tempest was little, her mom and aunt had always called friends of their parents "Uncle" or "Aunty," so Tempest assumed that's how the world worked. When she was eleven years old and called twenty-something Robbie "Uncle," he'd laughed his head off but told her he loved it and wouldn't have it any other way, and that he had a nickname for her as well—"Twirls," since that was her preferred method of not standing still. She'd thought of him as Uncle Robbie ever since. With sandy blonde hair and a wiry frame, he looked nothing like Tempest's mom or dad. But he was family. He'd been the core member of the Secret Staircase Construction crew for the last fifteen years.

Tempest didn't know the full story of the new guy, Gideon, who was standing next to the window looking out, but she knew enough to see her papa was following a similar pattern. A stonemason by training, Gideon was afraid of heights, so he couldn't get on a ladder or scaffolding, but that hadn't deterred Darius from hiring him.

Darius himself was a carpenter who got his general contractor license when he and Emma decided to form their own business. Emma brought the creative vision for the stories they could tell through architecture, and was also the project manager and bookkeeper. Darius had managed to learn the last two jobs since Emma vanished, but never the first.

It was a haphazard team of misfit craftspeople, not a carefully planned and efficient crew, but it worked. A welder for a business that rarely needed welding. A jack-of-all-trades who couldn't follow directions. A stonemason who couldn't climb to the top of a wall. And a carpenter dad who held them all together after they lost the heart of the business. This was never a normal construction business. This was a family business that brought magic into homes. But today they'd brought something else into this home.

Tempest couldn't stand the waiting any longer.

"I need to go to the bathroom," she said. "I'll be right back."

She stepped into the foyer and turned toward the small bathroom tucked underneath the stairs, before the entryway gave way to the kitchen. She didn't, of course, need the bathroom. She needed the room beyond the stairs. She held her breath and crept through the kitchen into the pantry.

The room was the way they'd left it, with the wrinkled, dusty sack lying on the floor, black hair spilling over the cinched top. That's why she'd been drawn back. It wasn't merely curiosity. There was something familiar about the curl of that hair. Or perhaps it was the faint scent . . .

Tempest pulled open the top of the musty old sack, just a few inches. It was enough to reveal what was inside. Enough to make her wish she hadn't come back.

This was no skeleton or decaying body. Instead, looking up at Tempest was the bloodied face of someone she had seen alive and well a month ago. The woman who'd wrecked her career. Tempest's stage double. Her doppelgänger.

"Cassidy Sparrow," she whispered into the cold air.

Which was impossible.

Not only had one of those impossible crimes she and Ivy used to read about come to life, but the victim was a woman who could easily be mistaken for Tempest herself.

Tempest gripped the selkie charm on her charm bracelet. *The Raj family curse isn't real*, she told herself. *The curse isn't real.*

Chapter 9

When Tempest was little, as a bedtime ritual her mom would regale her with magical stories from far-off lands beyond their own enchanted little hillside folly. Emma Raj, after all, had grown up in a magical land of faeries and other mythical creatures, and Emma's father was heir to a magical dynasty.

Tempest and her parents would climb the ladder to the tree house strung with lights that looked like fireflies, and Emma would ask Tempest to pick any subject under the stars. Once she did, Emma spun an enchanting story out of thin air, filling Tempest with wonder. A sense that anything in the world was possible. One of Tempest's favorite subjects was the selkie, the mythical creature from Scottish, Irish, and Scandinavian lore: a woman who's only human on land. As she emerges from the sea, the selkie sheds her seal skin to take human form, but only for a brief time. She's always called back to the sea.

Her mom's stories would often end with a small magic trick, before Tempest climbed her own secret staircase to be tucked into bed by her dad.

An only child with plenty of time to observe adults, Tempest realized that many grownups were sad, and a lot of kids, too. But not Tempest and her parents, who had magic all around them. They had very little money, but a home filled with love and magic. By the time she was five years old, Tempest knew she was going to be a magician. What better purpose in the world could there be than to give people a sense of wonder?

As with all things that seem too good to be true, there was a catch. Tempest learned about hers the first time she visited her aunt and grandparents in Edinburgh.

It was the summer she turned seven years old, when her parents' business was growing and they had a commission to renovate a mansion in southern California. Emma and Darius thought it would be best for Tempest to spend the summer with her grandparents instead of living in the motel where her parents would be staying for six weeks. Her grandparents had visited Hidden Creek before, but she'd never met Aunt Elspeth. Grandpa Ash was a medical doctor, Grannie Mor a musician and artist, and their daughter Elspeth? She made a living as a stage magician. Tempest's mom never said much about Elspeth, and her papa told her not to ask, so Tempest never knew the sisters had once performed on the stage together as the Selkie Sisters before Emma moved to California.

The Selkie Sisters performed to crowds of adoring fans before Emma left Scotland, spinning a story that they were daughters of a selkie from the Scottish waters and a sailor from India. Born on a boat—a realm between land and sea—and always pulled back to the sea. Elspeth told young Tempest about their biggest illusion, called the Tempest. Images from a magic lantern cast shadows across every surface of the theater, creating the illusion of waves from a fierce storm. The sisters stepped into a steamer trunk for shelter, but fell overboard and tumbled to the bottom of the sea. They appeared moments later on top of a seaside cliff on the opposite side of the stage, having defeated the storm. Safe. Reunited.

Why don't you perform as the Selkie Sisters anymore? seven-year-old Tempest asked Aunt Elspeth.

Do you have a favorite fairy tale? Elspeth answered. With her long black hair, large brown eyes, and a smattering of freckles on her cheeks and nose, she looked so much like her younger sister.

The ones where the princesses save themselves, Tempest answered. With her mom's imagination, Tempest never knew which stories were known to anyone beyond the wooden walls of her magical tree house.

Why do they need saving in the first place?

Tempest scrunched up her face. *Because someone is trying to do something bad to them.*

Sometimes, said Elspeth, *there are bad people we need to fight against in the real word as well. The magic we give people comes at a price.*

I don't understand.

My appa—

Grandpa Ash?

He doesn't like that I perform magic. He worries that it can be dangerous. He's not wrong, but some things in life are worth doing even if it means you need to step outside of your safe and cozy home.

That was all Elspeth would tell Tempest that summer. It wasn't until years later that she heard the word "curse."

The Raj Magic Dynasty had existed for five generations—as had its curse. At least, that's the way the family legend went. As with all legends, the story varied, depending on who you asked. Depending on what day you caught them, they might or might not admit to believing in it.

Regardless of which version of the story was told, one key element remained the same: *The eldest child dies by magic.*

That was also the one piece of information that could be confirmed as true. The cursed magic began on the rainbow-colored beaches of Kanyakumari with Devaj Raj. It remained in India for three generations before crossing the ocean to Scotland, where it found Ashok Raj's eldest daughter Elspeth in Old Town Edinburgh, where she died in a stage illusion gone wrong when a guillotine sliced off her head. The curse led to the deaths of the eldest child in each generation. At least that's what it did until it went a step further and came for Tempest's mom, following Elspeth's little sister Emma Raj to California. Emma was only the eldest after her sister died in that stage accident. Which seemed to Tempest like cheating.

Tempest knew it wasn't rational, but now, after everything that had happened, how could she *not* wonder if the curse was coming for her? Especially when the staging of her doppelgänger's body looked like a magic trick.

The eldest child dies by magic.

It was meant to be Tempest herself in that wall, not Cassidy.

Chapter 10

This isn't the family curse, Tempest told herself as she backed away from Cassidy's body. It doesn't really exist. Magic could be a dangerous profession if you weren't careful. Before her grandfather's eldest brother had died while performing an underwater escape, Ash hadn't believed in the Raj family curse. But with the tragic death of his brother Arjun Raj, the whispers of a curse that had begun two generations before turned into a full-fledged legend.

The eldest child dies by magic.

Tempest couldn't know what exactly had occurred over the past 150 years. What she did know was that a month after she nearly died on stage, her stage double was dead—and presented to Tempest like one of her own seemingly impossible illusions.

During the frantic aftermath of that summer's spectacular stage accident (or "Tempest's negligence" as the lawyers had called it), Tempest's resolve wavered. It was ten years after her aunt had died in a stage accident and five years after her mom had vanished and was presumed to have taken her own life. It had to be bad luck, not a curse. Right?

She couldn't take her eyes off of Cassidy's face. Not unlike Tempest's own, but not her twin. Cassidy's hair was shorter now, her olive skin had a touch of sun, and her thick eyebrows were plucked to look less like Tempest's. Otherwise she looked as she had earlier that summer on opening night.

Tempest closed her eyes and took two deep breaths. When she opened her eyes again, nothing had changed. Cassidy lay here in front of her. Dead.

Tempest hadn't imagined she'd ever feel pity for her double-crossing stage double. Cassidy had done a terrible thing, but she didn't deserve to be killed and stuck inside a musty old sack in a crawl space.

The reality hit her that it didn't make sense on so many levels. Her dad and the rest of the crew insisted that the wall was old and hadn't been tampered with. Yet Tempest had seen her fall out of the wall with her own eyes. There had to be a trick with the wall.

Tempest knew she should really get out of there. Instead, she shone her light into the hole in the wall. Nothing indicated that anything had been disturbed for decades. Maybe above or below? No. There was too much dust.

Tempest could imagine people wanting to kill the cunning Cassidy. But how had her body gotten into that wall? Why was Cassidy even in Hidden Creek? She had wanted to stay in Vegas to step into the void left by Tempest's ouster. Cassidy hadn't been able to step into the role immediately, but Tempest suspected that had been her plan. Why head to Hidden Creek? *Unless she'd been there to see Tempest.*

Footsteps on creaking floorboards.

There was no time to check the walls more thoroughly. Tempest ran through the kitchen, her heart thudding in her chest far more furiously than it did when she was on stage—and crashed into someone next to the stairs. New Guy. He smelled like coconut and a forest in a monsoon.

She extricated herself from thin, muscular arms and leaned

back on her heels. "Normally people step back when they see a tall woman running."

"I thought you might crash into the built-in cabinet. It's original."

"Thanks, New Guy. Um, I think."

"We haven't officially met. I'm Gideon. Gideon Torres."

"Tempest. And I need some fresh air." She pushed past Gideon and opened the front door.

Gideon followed. He closed the door behind them and sat down on the top step of the porch. "I'm shaken by what we saw in there, too. That old sack with the skeleton inside."

The adrenaline from falling onto a virtual stranger had momentarily pushed the image of Cassidy from the forefront of her mind. It flooded back.

"I feel like I'm covered in the dust of old bones," Gideon continued, "even though I know I'm not. I was heading to wash my face. But fresh air is better. Thanks."

Tempest willed herself to focus. Gideon was around her age, she guessed, and an ethnically ambiguous mash-up, like her. His dark brown eyes held an intensity that both startled and assured her. How he watched not just her, but the world. The whole time she'd been at the house, she hadn't once noticed him distracted by anything. She imagined him sitting in a cabin in the woods reading a Dostoyevsky novel without once scrolling on a cell phone.

Tempest, however, was aching for distraction. For answers. She sat down next to Gideon and tucked her knees under her chin. "I don't understand what's taking the authorities so long."

Gideon shrugged. "I guess they think Darius mistook the bones of an animal for a human skeleton."

"Why would they—"

"It happens a lot on construction sites. I like your charm bracelet. May I take a closer look?"

She extended her wrist. Who said, "May I"? She understood why he wasn't freaked out, though. Only distressed. She was the only one who knew it was Cassidy inside the wall, not something much closer to an old skeleton.

He leaned closer and she again smelled the sweet and nutty scent of coconut. "It's intriguing, like they each tell a story. They're bigger than average charms, too."

"Only big enough for the details that tell the story." Tempest touched the fiddle charm, its left side more of a square shape like an Indian sarangi, the right more like a rounded western fiddle.

She rubbed the familiar shapes between her fingers. The silver felt cool on the skin of her wrist. She could identify each one of the charms with her eyes closed. Tempest didn't meditate—at least, not the traditional way by sitting still— but each charm brought her calming memories. The bracelet was her inheritance—the last gift her mom had given her before vanishing.

The bracelet remained on Tempest's wrist even when she performed onstage. She wasn't a close-up sleight-of-hand artist these days, or the bulky object on her wrist would have been seen as a cheat she was using to hide props. Onstage, however, there was another solution. Cassidy had worn a duplicate bracelet when they were performing an illusion that required Cassidy to pass as Tempest for the blink of an eye. Details were important for the illusion to work.

She and Cassidy had spent so much time going over the details, down to the second. The millisecond. She closed her eyes and saw Cassidy's lifeless body in the pantry. Who had done that to her? And why would they have put her inside of that wall?

"What's the deal with the mermaid with the curling tail?"

"She's a selkie, not a mermaid. There's a difference." She opened her eyes to see him looking intently at the bulky silver charm. "See how she's peeling out of her seal skin to become fully human? And . . . you're trying to distract me from the fact that a body just tumbled out of the wall."

"Is it working?"

A police cruiser pulled up in front of the house.

"Time to go." Tempest stood and pulled Gideon up along with her. She really didn't want to go back inside. She shivered at the thought of the cold spot.

"Where are we—?"

"This way."

They followed the porch where it wrapped around the side of the house. Tempest's view was mostly obscured, but she caught snatches of movement through the bushy lemon tree. A tall, young officer stepped out, pressing his lips together as he shielded his eyes from the sun and looked up at the asymmetrical features of the house. Calvin Knight opened the front door and jogged down the steps to greet the newcomer. Tempest's dad was a few steps behind. The three men spoke a few hushed words and disappeared into the house together.

"We should get back inside," said Gideon.

"Or not. I like it better out here."

"I thought you'd want to hear what's going on."

"I do." Tempest rubbed her arms. "I just don't want to go back inside."

"I bet we can hear them better if we go to the back." He pointed. "It's a full veranda that circles around most of the house."

Tempest was already walking before he finished the sentence. "I like the way you think, New Guy."

"Gid—" He broke off as a shout came from within the house. His eyes squinted at Tempest in an unspoken question.

She knew the answer, but she couldn't tell him. The officer had seen Cassidy's body. The authorities would take the discovery seriously now. Sure enough, the exclamation faded into anxious, muffled speech calling for backup.

Tempest refused Gideon's suggestion to go back inside with him. She was completing her seventh pirouette to clear her mind when a black sedan screeched to a halt in the driveway. Her ruby red sneakers came to a full stop with a squeak. Seeing the man who emerged from the car, she nearly tipped over.

Unlike the first officer to arrive, this one Tempest knew well. He hurried toward the house so quickly he barely closed the car's door behind him. He surely would have noticed Tempest, even in her obscured spot, if the younger officer hadn't ushered him inside.

Detective Blackburn. The detective who'd worked on her mother's disappearance. *The vanishing.* That's what he'd called it. Tempest reached for the silver charm of a Scottish selkie riding the waves of the ocean. The detective's gray hair she remembered was now completely white. How much had her mom's disappearance contributed to that?

She followed the veranda to the back of the house and heard what was being said inside.

It wasn't difficult. Detective Blackburn was practically shouting. Four words rang out: "Tempest Raj is dead."

Chapter 11

Detective Blackburn thought that poor girl was you?"
Ash pulled Tempest close. *"Ada kadavulae."*

Tempest's Tamil was nearly nonexistent, but the strength of her grandfather's embrace conveyed the seriousness of the exclamation. She rested her head on his shoulder and squeezed back. With her eyes closed, the scents swirling through her grandparents' warm, cozy tree house kitchen worked magic to counteract the horrible discovery of earlier that day.

But the culinary magic of her grandfather's kitchen was no match for their family's tragic stage magic history. Their curse. The very real possibility that Cassidy Sparrow was killed in Tempest's stead.

Two hours ago, Tempest was the first witness to be questioned—after nearly giving the detective a heart attack when she appeared in the doorway of the small room where her doppelgänger's body lay. She'd identified Cassidy's lifeless form, and after additional crime scene technicians arrived and she answered more of Detective Blackburn's questions, she was free to go. She'd wanted to wait for her dad, but Darius asked her to go home and let her grandfather know what was happening. Her dad had reached Ash in time to let his father-in-law know not to bring them lunch as he usually did, but hadn't gone into details.

"You must tell me everything," Ash said, releasing Tempest. "But first, have you eaten?"

"I couldn't possibly—"

"Tempest. It's midafternoon. Starving yourself won't do anyone any good."

Tempest breathed in the scents of cumin, onions, vinegar, and chili peppers. Grandpa Ash had been making his famous Rajaloo, a roasted potato curry that was a mash-up of flavors from South India, Portugal, and Scotland that made up his signature dish he'd based on the Euro-Indian dish vindaloo that was popular in Britain.

The kitchen was the largest room of the tree house. Like a traditional South Indian kitchen, the space between indoors and outdoors blended together, with the doors to the dining room deck open from dawn until well past dusk. Grandpa Ash was cooking a feast, as he did most weekdays. After his forty-year career as a medical doctor, Ash had reinvented himself as a chef and self-described *dabbawalla*: a purveyor of the complex lunchbox delivery system that kept Mumbai running. Cooking a delicious lunch for the Secret Staircase Construction crew, then delivering the home-cooked feast to their job site, was his contribution to his son-in-law's business. It was widely known to be one of the perks of working for Tempest's dad, and however many additional contractors were working on a job on a given day, Ash always made sure to include them.

It was also Ash's way of staying in shape. True to tradition, he carried stacked tiffin lunch boxes on his bicycle and rode to any Bay Area location where the team was working. The circular, stainless-steel, stackable lunch boxes were widely used in India, as they were the easiest way to transport home-cooked meals via bicycle to workers at lunchtime. As would have been the case in Mumbai, Ash's *dabbawalla* bicyclist's journey would often include a train ride. In Ash's case, this resulted in him collecting a stack of business cards from people interested in home-cooked vegetarian lunches if he ever expanded his service.

Ash accepted the cards with a warm smile and gave out free samples (he always brought extra, because the scents never failed to entice onlookers), but politely declined offers to expand his business. As long as he was feeding people and surrounded by his loved ones, he was a happy man.

Tempest looked through the open door that led to the porch dining room. It was empty except for a hummingbird hovering above a pot of lavender. "Where's Grannie Mor?"

"She walked to the park to paint. Her mobile phone is always turned off when she's painting. I asked your father to pick her up on his way back from the murder house."

The murder house. He wasn't wrong.

"What I don't understand," Ash said as he handed her a glass of water and joined her in the cozy breakfast nook, "is how your assistant is connected to Calvin Knight."

Cassidy hated it when people referred to her as Tempest's assistant. *Had* hated it, Tempest reminded herself. She shook her head. "She isn't—wasn't. This isn't about the Knights' house. She was brought to me." Tempest told him about the discovery.

"As if it was staged for you," Ash murmured when she was done. "Who would do that?"

A magician, she thought to herself. The fear in her grandfather's dark brown eyes told her he suspected the same thing. "There's no reason that makes any sense."

"You need sustenance." Ash jumped up and returned to the stove. "Ah! That must be Morag and Darius."

Two sets of footsteps sounded on the stairs. When the first newcomer appeared, Tempest was startled to see that Grannie Mor's hair was actually out of place. Not compared to that of a mere mortal, but Morag probably considered her hair a rat's nest. She darted straight to Tempest and pulled her up from her seat. Tempest didn't exactly tower over her grandmother's five-foot-five frame, but Tempest's muscular legs and strong arms made her appear taller than her actual height, whereas Morag had a petite body that made her appear smaller—until she opened her mouth or picked up a paintbrush or a fiddle. Or, apparently, when she squeezed her granddaughter's broad shoulders.

"You're nae hurt?" Morag must have been shaken for her Scots to surface so prominently. One of Ash's old dress shirts was Morag's favorite painting smock. The light blue shirt was dotted with bright specks of color—mostly purples and blues today. A swath of indigo that looked like a raven dominated the breast pocket.

"Only shaken," Tempest assured her.

"Your father refused to tell me much of anything before we were all at home together. We're here now. *Och!* Now tell us what's happened."

"First"—Tempest turned to her dad—"how's everyone doing?"

"I stayed long enough to make sure they weren't hassling Calvin Knight. The crime scene crew was still collecting evidence, but the detective seemed most interested in Cassidy's boyfriend as a suspect, not the Knights. A bunch of movers and tradespeople they didn't know well were in and out of the house this summer after their move—like us. Good call to tell them about the boyfriend."

Tempest frowned. She knew it was right to mention Isaac to Detective Blackburn. But a crime like this? He was a stage-hand, not a magician, and not an especially good one at that. He was clever only in the sense that he relied on his good looks and charming smile to get others to do things for him. "Isaac was abusive. But I don't really think he could have—"

"Didn't the two of them live in Las Vegas?" Ash asked.

"Why bring her to you?" her grandmother added.

Ash took his wife's hands in his. "She wasn't only brought to Hidden Creek. The poor girl was stuffed inside a wall, before falling into our Tempest's lap. It's like a magician's trick."

Grannie Mor swore a string of Scots Gaelic. "Pack a bag, Tempest. You can stay with Nicky in Leith. I'm sure he'll—"

"You want to put me on a flight to Scotland?" Tempest gaped at her grandmother.

"*Dunnae* you see? It was meant to be you."

Ash frowned. "Your grandmother is right that we need to keep you safe."

"I'm not sure," Darius said slowly, "if she's free to travel."

Ash's wooden spoon clattered to the tile floor. "When were you planning on telling us you're suspects?"

"We're not suspects," Tempest said more forcefully than she felt. "But we're involved in the investigation."

Ash turned off the stove. "You can't think straight on an empty stomach. Sit down at the table. I'll bring food. And my magic Rolodex."

Five minutes later, the foursome was seated around one end of the outdoor dining table. The trees swayed in the wind. Even when it rained, the outdoor dining room worked. The awning was a proper roof above the table, and the shelter of the tree provided added protection. Only the fiercest tempest would force them inside.

It was a comforting meal, and somewhat simple by Ash's standards, with only three dishes. Fresh chapatis to scoop the Rajaloo, and yogurt raita to cool the intense spice. Grannie Mor peppered her and her papa with questions, most of which they couldn't answer, while Ash scrolled through his magic Rolodex of business cards he'd picked up from people he'd met on his *dabbawalla* outings.

Abra was napping, curled up in Darius's left arm. The rabbit slumbered between his hand and the crook of his elbow, forcing him to eat gingerly so as not to disturb the bunny. Abracadabra never fell asleep in Tempest's arms, but her papa's massive size belied a gentle nature that anyone who spent more than a few minutes with him picked up on.

"Ah!" Grandpa Ash cried when he reached the card of an IT expert. "Marcus, if I recall, is a genius who has hacked government computers before. We could ask him to hack into Detective Blackburn's investigation—"

"I don't think that's called for, Grandpa. How do you even know that about this guy?"

Ash chuckled. "It's amazing what a good meal will do for a single man who's skin and bones because he often forgets to eat while in front of his computer. Besides, he said the hacking was at the behest of the government, to test their security. Ah! No, no, you're right. Ayumi would be better." He pulled another contact from the mountain of cards. "She has the ear of multiple governments."

Tempest would have thought he was joking except for the fact that the crown prince from a small European country had once attended Tempest's stage show. When he complimented her at a backstage meet-and-greet, he told her he was in attendance at her grandfather's suggestion.

"What's taking the rest of the crew so long?" Ash asked Darius as Morag gently moved the Rolodex beyond his reach.

Darius shook his head. "Nobody comes over until we know what's up."

Ash gasped. "You don't think they—"

"No." Darius set down squirming Abra, who no doubt sensed the anxiety of the person holding him. "But until an arrest is made and I *know*, our priority is keeping Tempest safe."

"That's why you didn't want to invite the Knights, either?" said Tempest. "Justin was already worried about his new house."

"The kid will be fine, Tempest." Her dad tried to smile. He half succeeded. "Before I left, Calvin told me they were heading to stay with family in Sacramento while their house is a crime scene. They were there for a couple of days last week as well. That was another time when anybody could have broken into the house. There's no sign of it yet, and I still don't get how they got through the wall . . . I'd swear nobody had touched that wall in decades."

Morag stood and thumped her fists on the table. "Because nobody did."

Nobody moved. Except for Abra, who scampered from the deck into the kitchen.

"I don't think there's a secret passageway," Darius said finally. "Structurally—"

"*Och!*" Morag shook her head. "How can you not see this settles the matter for good?"

Tempest didn't like the fierce look on her grandmother's face. "Which matter?"

Morag's blue-gray eyes narrowed. "Magic. The magic stops now. As an only child, Tempest is technically the eldest—"

"Don't start with the curse, Mom," Darius cut in.

"There is no curse!" Tempest shouted. Maybe if she was loud enough, it would be true.

"The dead woman," Morag said crisply, "is your doppel-gänger, who you worked closely with for years, who ruined your career—and who was dropped into your lap with no earthly explanation." The fact that she didn't raise her voice made her cold words all the more forceful.

"You've all stopped eating again." Ash placed an additional chapati on each of their plates, even though none of them had finished their first ones. "Fresher. Eat."

"There has to be a rational explanation," Tempest protested. She said the words aloud to convince herself, not just her family.

"Maybe." Ash stood and pointed at their plates. "Keep eating. I need to get dessert."

For dessert, Ash served *cranachan*. Tempest adored the rich Scottish pudding with summer berries on top, but she hardly had an appetite. Apparently neither did her dad.

"Where are you going?" Grannie Mor asked Darius as he stood up without touching his dessert.

"Hardware store. This house isn't secure enough. Tempest, you don't go anywhere on your own until we solve this. Are we all agreed?"

"I'm glad you're taking this seriously," Ash said, "but I don't know what you can do to stop the curse."

Tempest picked up Abra. "I'll take Abra back to his hutch. Don't worry, I won't leave Fiddler's Folly."

Along the highest slope of the hillside, a partially constructed stone turret sat abandoned. Christened Secret Fort by Tempest's mom, the structure was one of Secret Staircase Construction's "lesson-learned experiments"—a term Emma and Darius preferred over "failed experiment." The idea was to build a freestanding stone structure in the style of a medieval castle. Emma had spent quite a bit of time on it the year before she vanished, especially after she sprained her ankle and threw herself into a project that didn't require her to travel off-site. It wasn't a practical project, and Darius hadn't had time to help her with it while he was managing the crew on several large jobs, but Emma had a story in mind to tell about a magical castle turret, so she spent her extra time giving it a go.

The only part of the Secret Fort that had been completed was a stained-glass window in the shape of a skeleton key that cast golden light onto the unfinished floor. The key-shaped window was made of thick glass, not the thin modern glass made possible by the industrial revolution. Chunks of orange, yellow, and a reddish-gold tint (which Tempest was sure her grandmother would know the proper name for) were fitted together inside metal framing. It didn't look airtight, but that wasn't much of an issue, because the circular stone structure had no roof, and a hole where a door should have been. It stretched fifteen feet in diameter, and was barely one story high, so it hadn't served a practical purpose until Tempest returned home and put it to good use as a cozy home for Abra's hutch.

Tempest climbed the steep incline and returned the escape artist to his home. She hadn't noticed earlier that the door handle was damaged. The key-shaped handle must have broken off in transit from Vegas to Hidden Creek. That was how Abra had gotten out last night. Since Tempest's carpenter dad had built the hutch, he'd given it beautiful elements like a handle in the shape of a key and castle ramparts on top. Abra gladly accepted the leftover greens she left for him. The only one who wasn't worried for her, he chomped happily and ignored her.

She heard the sound a fraction of a second before a voice spoke.

"Is that really you?"

Tempest whipped around, startling Abra, who thumped his leg against the matting in his cage.

Sanjay stood in the stone archway where a door should have been. Dressed in a full tuxedo and with his bowler hat on his head, he looked as if he'd come from a performance. Yet there was something disheveled about his attire. His bow tie was askew, his cummerbund was nowhere to be seen, and his normally pressed vibrant white shirt was creased with wrinkles.

Was it her imagination, or had his voice cracked just a little there?

"Of course it's me, silly."

Strong arms pulled her into a crushing hug. She let him hold her, feeling the thudding of his heart and the warmth of his breath, until he showed no sign of letting go. She pushed him away. "What's the matter with you? Do I need to sic Abra on you?"

The bunny wrinkled his nose. The expression was wasted on Sanjay, who didn't take his eyes off of Tempest.

"According to social media," he said, "you're dead."

Chapter 12

'm pleased to see rumors of your death have been greatly exaggerated." Sanjay slid a handkerchief across his eyes so quickly Tempest couldn't be sure she didn't imagine it.

She groaned. "What are people saying?"

"Do you want to know?"

"Probably not."

"Here's one that sums it up. *The Tempest is dead at 26. The Raj family curse has struck again, this time claiming the life of Emma Raj's disgraced daughter* . . . I think I'll stop there. You get the picture."

"Does it say how I died?"

"No details on that yet. Which really, you'd think click-bait would lead with. A teaser about the horrifying details to follow and all that. Wait. Has something actually happened?"

"Not to me."

"What do you mean," he said slowly, "*not to you?*"

"Remember Cassidy?"

"That dreadful social climber? One of the good things about your show being canceled is that you don't have to work with her. What's she done now?"

"She's the one who's dead."

Sanjay swore in Punjabi. Tempest couldn't help smiling just a little at that. One of the challenges for performers of wholesome live shows, like hers and Sanjay's, was that under stressful circumstances one might accidentally be tempted to swear. Not a good look for a family-friendly performer. If you let yourself swear in real life, it was bound to pop up on stage at some point. If most of the audience didn't know you'd sworn, though, it wasn't nearly as bad.

Sanjay didn't speak much Punjabi, but he'd learned strategic pieces of the language: basic conversational phrases to make visiting family in India easier, magic-related terminology to use in certain acts of his stage performances, and he'd deliberately learned a handful of words that would come in handy to express frustration. She didn't know what this one meant, but she remembered it from when he'd been caught with a dirty hand—the magician's term for a sloppy move— during a small performance.

Tempest scooped Abra into her arms. He objected until she took his food as well. "Let's go inside."

"You worried about your grandparents hearing something, since this tower doesn't have a door?"

"Or a roof." Tempest pointed up to the sky.

"Ash speaks Tamil, not Punjabi. He won't know what I just said."

"He wouldn't care about your foul mouth even if he did hear you. I'm worried about what I'm about to say to you."

Inside the main house, Tempest lifted the dragon's wing, revealing her secret staircase. Sanjay had been here before, so he didn't comment on the hidden space as they climbed the stairs. He hadn't, however, ever seen the room where she was taking him.

"No way." Sanjay watched incredulously as Tempest stepped

onto her steamer trunk and activated a hidden panel. "There's a *secret*-secret room up here?"

He followed her up a narrow staircase, barely wide enough for adults, to the tiny turret above her bedroom. Tempest's magic nook. Only eight feet in diameter, the turret was circular on the outside, but on the inside had seven walls plus a doorway.

One of the walls was taken up mostly with a window, and the other six each held a framed magic poster. Houdini, Adelaide Herrmann, Nicodemus the Necromancer, The Hindi Houdini, the Selkie Sisters, and The Tempest. Each of the posters featured an illustration showing the headliner not simply performing a skillful trick, but telling a story. Houdini's illustration showed the handcuff king shackled and handcuffed, surrounded by any lock a man could devise, with the words *Nothing on Earth Can Hold Houdini*. Adelaide Herrmann's poster followed the style of her male counterparts, with ghostly figures floating above her, and a skull at her feet. Decades later, Nicodemus kept the same classic style with devils whispering in his ears, as had Sanjay. Both Tempest's and the Selkie Sisters' showed the women not on a stage, but in the sea, their voluminous black hair swirling in the water and melding into the waves. If you looked more closely at the water, you could find hidden words and objects.

Besides all being hand-drawn illustrations that told a story, there was something else all of the posters had in common, which Tempest hadn't realized until today. There was a hint of the supernatural in each of them. All except for Houdini's—he had crusaded against spiritualism.

Sanjay tipped his bowler hat at his own poster. "I'm honored I made the cut."

"Don't flatter yourself. There was an extra spot on the wall."

"What didn't you want the grandparents to hear?"

Tempest touched the poster of Adelaide Herrmann, who'd survived a theater fire not unlike the one Tempest had barely escaped. "I tried to play down the idea that I was the intended victim instead of Cassidy, but . . . I had to be."

Tempest spun around from the poster of her idol and told him how her stage double had fallen out of a sealed wall in front of her eyes. "They were clever," she concluded.

"Rather like a magician," Sanjay mused. "Preston the Prestidigitator is one of the few people online saying you're not dead."

"Preston?" She hadn't seriously considered that her self-declared superfan and aspiring magician could be involved. "How does he know I'm not dead?"

"He says you two are connected, so he'd feel it if you were dead."

Tempest shuddered.

Sanjay frowned at his phone. "At least that's what he says on his feed. Assuming he's lying, if he killed Cassidy thinking she was you, he could have belatedly realized his mistake." Sanjay's phone disappeared from his hand. Tempest knew he must have maneuvered it into a pocket, but she didn't catch how he did it.

"Preston doesn't want to hurt me." Tempest didn't know much about Preston beyond the fact that he'd only ever been considerate. Hapless, but sweet. She suspected he'd been the person to start many of her standing ovations, and whenever he asked her to pose for a picture, he'd waited respectfully until it was a good moment, not forcefully intruding like so many people did.

"What if he believed Cassidy wrecked your career and was the one who took you away from him?"

"With her as the intended victim?" Tempest shook her head. "Doesn't matter who was the intended target. How could he have pulled off the trick of getting her into that wall?"

"There's probably a secret passageway."

"Even if there is, this is the guy who spectacularly failed his performance test at the Castle and was denied membership. The secret passageway—if there is one—is hidden better than I or my dad could find."

"The killer had more time."

"But they *didn't*." Did they? Calvin and Justin had only moved to Hidden Creek that summer. Secret Staircase Construction had built him a bookcase that hid a library, but until that day the pantry area was untouched.

"Why hide Cassidy in the wall at all?" Tempest took a step toward her own magic show poster. "It's a trick without a story."

She stretched out her hand toward the barely visible image of a second selkie in the dark ocean waters. The illustration teased the audience with the question of what would happen to the two selkies at opposite ends of a tempestuous sea. In the show, Tempest got to write herself a happy ending. The only story that made sense in real life was one she didn't want to think about. Cassidy's body appeared, impossibly, in front of Tempest, almost as if it was a warning. As if the curse was coming for her.

Chapter 13

"Y ou don't believe in curses, do you?" Tempest asked her captive audience.

It was nearly midnight. With the darkness of the night sky outside the windows, and illustrations of performers with devils whispering in their ears surrounding her, she didn't know what she believed herself.

Sanjay had gone home, and her dad and grandparents had gone to sleep hours ago, but Tempest knew she wouldn't sleep. She'd climbed the narrow secret stairs to the topmost room of the house again to process her theories.

She waited for a reaction from her companion. "Don't you have anything to say to that?"

Abra looked up from the hay he was munching. His nose twitched as he observed her for a few seconds, then returned to his meal. She wanted company, so was giving them both a midnight snack. She'd raided her dad's fridge and found a few leftovers cooked by Grandpa Ash. Biryani and baked beans. Not a natural combination, but she'd scooped the beans onto the baked rice and vegetables. Not a bad mash-up.

"With no objections from the honorable Abracadabra Rabbit, I'm going to take that as an agreement. There's no such thing as curses."

The clock struck midnight. Figuratively, of course. It was only her silent cell phone that lit up as one day turned into the next.

"If it was a real curse," she told the rabbit, "something would happen at midnight, right?"

The sound of hail on the window startled her. *Hail?*

She clicked off the overhead light—a medieval candelabra hanging from the pointed spire high above—and opened the curtain. A dark figure tossed pebbles at the window. He had good aim. And a bowler hat. Sanjay.

She pushed open the window. "Sanjay?" she hissed.

"Who else?"

"Five seconds." She turned the dial of the oversize clock face on the wall above the door. She hadn't tried this since she'd arrived, so she had no idea if it still worked. The hands of the clock groaned in protest, but when they aligned to midnight, a click sounded. Then . . . nothing. Fine. Her secret escape hatch wasn't working. She left her room the old-fashioned way. Through the secret staircase and out the front door.

"That was longer than five seconds," he said when she reached him. "You're losing your touch."

"Technical difficulties. Why are you here?"

"You weren't answering your phone."

"I turned it off."

"You *turned off* your phone?" The shock in his voice made it clear the words didn't compute. "Who *does* that?"

She raised an eyebrow at him. "Me."

"Don't turn off your phone. I was worried."

"So you throw rocks at my window at midnight?"

"Your light was still on up there, but downstairs was dark. I didn't want to wake your dad. He scares me."

"We're talking about the same guy, right? The one who takes in aimless young people."

"Who's over six feet tall, has arm muscles bigger than the tires on my truck, and whose daughter I once dated."

"Fair point." She lowered her voice. "Let's go inside."

He dropped the remaining pebbles in his hand and followed her inside.

"What's up that was urgent?" she asked once they were through both secret passageways in the high turret, the furthest spot from her dad's bedroom.

"Two things. First, Carisa called me and told me Isaac has been arrested."

"That was fast."

"Apparently they found her blood in his car." Sanjay glanced out the window and tugged the curtain shut.

Tempest grasped her charm bracelet. "Is someone there?"

"No. But I've been monitoring things online. Preston has his location posted. That's the second thing you needed to know. Your superfan is in town."

"That doesn't surprise me."

"Internet rumors are blowing up in general, so I wanted to make sure you called—"

"Nicky." Tempest groaned. How could she have been so selfish not to think about letting Nicodemus know what was going on?

"So you called him already?"

"Not yet. But news of my death broke during the middle of the night in Scotland. I doubt he's up yet."

"Yeah, it's only eight o'clock in the morning there. Is he still on a performer's schedule?"

"Probably." She hated to think of him waking up to the news of her supposed death. "But it's not a completely unreasonable hour now."

"I bet he'd rather lose a bit of sleep and hear from you."

Tempest turned her phone back on.

"Why on earth are you calling me at this ungodly hour?" As was the case with Tempest's grandmother's, Nicodemus's Scottish accent grew thicker when he was upset.

"It's good to hear your voice too, Nicky."

"It's barely eight o'clock in the morning." He yawned, but the words that followed had a renewed sense of urgency. "You wouldn't be calling if it weren't an emergency. Now tell me, what's wrong? Is it Morag? Ash?"

"It's me. And the opposite problem. I needed to be sure to tell you I'm not really dead."

"Not dead?" He fell silent. When he spoke a few moments later, the tired urgency of his voice was gone, replaced by alert confusion. "Hmm, yes, I see your point. Rumors of your demise have crossed the pond, as they say. Now tell me, was it a publicity stunt gone wrong?"

Tempest groaned. If that was Nicodemus's first thought, the press would undoubtedly vilify her like they had before.

"No," she growled into the phone. "It's my stage double, Cassidy Sparrow, who's dead."

"Your doppelgänger," Nicky murmured. "I'm relieved you called. Waking up to news of a loved one's death is not good at my age. I miss you, my dear girl. Let me call you back on video."

"You think the sound of my voice is a trick?"

"I've no doubt the artificial intelligence is out there to fake your voice. But no, I simply want to see your face."

When he called back less than a minute later, he was dressed in a white dress shirt and had styled his wild gray-blond hair. Like some people who wouldn't be seen without their makeup, Nicodemus insisted upon being properly dressed and with his hair styled in a wave-like splash atop his head, rather like David Lynch.

In the background behind him, Tempest spotted the brick wall of the studio below his bedroom. The classic automata still worked, at least the last time she'd been there. You could wind them up and the figures would do things like sign their names or do backflips. The earliest form of mechanical robots. She was both drawn to and creeped-out by the two fortune-teller automata, and she adored the centuries-old miniature woman who played a toy piano, even though the doll's frame was reduced mostly to wire. Or perhaps *because of* it. The woman played a mesmerizing tune in spite of her body being nearly entirely stripped away.

Tempest held up her phone so her Nicodemus the Necromancer magic poster was in the shot. It was a small gesture, but one she thought he'd appreciate as his career wound down.

"Sanjay is there with you?" Nicky said, spotting him over Tempest's shoulder. "Are you two—"

"No," they said in unison.

"A stage accident? I didn't realize you were performing so soon again. You could be better at keeping me apprised of your life."

"It wasn't an accident, stage or otherwise."

"What do you mean," he said slowly, "that it wasn't an accident?"

"She was murdered." Tempest wished she hadn't agreed to the video call. The look of horror and concern spreading across his face broke her heart.

"Your doppelgänger was murdered . . . Where are you now?" Nicodemus's voice picked up in speed and urgency. "Do you have police protection?"

"There's no reason to suspect I'm in danger. They already arrested her boyfriend." But something didn't feel right. The more she thought about it, the more she knew Isaac couldn't have pulled it off any more than Preston could have.

Tempest hated to admit her fear. But she couldn't stop thinking about the phrase that had dominated so many years of her life.

The eldest child dies by magic.

Chapter 14

"D idn't sleep well?" Tempest asked her grandfather, surprised at the small size of the breakfast on the tree house deck. "After learning Isaac's been arrested, I thought you'd be relieved." She'd briefly woken her dad and grandparents after Sanjay's intel, to tell them the news of the arrest.

Grandpa Ash was sporting a brown felt fedora and a serious expression. Breakfast was a simple affair today. Scottish porridge and Indian coffee.

"We ate a proper breakfast hours ago," Ash said. "I saved this for you. Porridge and coffee last well warming on the stove. Soufflés don't."

"I missed a soufflé?"

Ash's expression lifted as he chuckled. "We'll make you a morning person yet."

Grannie Mor gave her a sly grin. "I wasn't a morning person until I met your grandfather, either. My schedule as a musician was much the same as yours. But a medical doctor—and now a cook—wakes up early. So, so early."

"Where's my dad? I thought the job site would be closed for at least a few days."

"I'm surprised the noise didn't wake you."

"What noise?"

"He and Robbie spent the last few hours building a tempo-rary fence around the property."

"A fence?" She groaned. "The press?"

"Only a few of them." Grannie Mor turned her sly smile to Tempest. "You're not *that* famous, dear."

"Do I even want to look?"

"Probably not, dear."

Tempest's phone buzzed.

I'm sorry, Sanjay's text said. *It was a mistake for me to post online trying to clear things up. Said I'd seen you. Now I'm part of the cover-up.*

Tempest groaned. Attached to Sanjay's text message was a screenshot of online rumors spreading faster than a California wildfire.

How bad is the rest? Tempest texted back.

Bad. But I couldn't have known!

Never follow an apology with the word "but," she replied, then turned off her phone.

Two minutes later, her grandfather's phone rang from where he'd left it inside. Ash grabbed it from the breakfast nook and came back outside. "So good to hear from you! I must apologize for my granddaughter not inviting you to stay for dinner last night. Ah, that's kind of you to say. Yes, she's right here." He offered her the phone.

Tempest grudgingly accepted. "I know it's not your fault, Sanjay. I'm not mad at you."

"Then why did you stop replying to my texts?"

"I'm having breakfast with my family. What did you want to say?"

"That I'm sorry. With no 'buts' attached. I'm sorry, Tem-pest."

"You're forgiven. I'm handing the phone back to Ash."

"Have you eaten?" Ash asked once the phone was next to his ear. He clicked his tongue. "A cappuccino from your fancy coffee contraption isn't breakfast."

After finishing her porridge and coffee, and helping Ash clean up, Tempest was ready to see how bad it was. Sanjay had either exaggerated, or things had gotten better in the last hour. The mainstream press now had it right, at least. There were still rumors about her being dead on social media, but the reputable sources were now reporting that Cassidy Sparrow was the dead woman and her abusive boyfriend had been arrested.

After Tempest had returned home to Hidden Creek, the media coverage of her career's disastrous ending had started to die down. Now it was back full force. She'd changed her phone number when she deleted her social media accounts, so very few people had the new number. Trolls were no longer calling her. The drastic measure also prevented anyone she used to know who might have good intentions calling her. Still, the break was worth it. There were far more people who wished her ill than well. She'd grudgingly given her business manager, Winston Kapoor, her new number, though she dreaded him using it. She was certain Winnie believed she was guilty. He made the proper sympathetic noises, but was more concerned with making sure she had the contact information for the list of law firms he gave her in case one of the threatened lawsuits came to pass.

Tempest spotted the chain-link fence jutting jaggedly across the front of the property line. The fencing was an affront to the craftsman aesthetic of everything Secret Staircase Construction did, but it was staunchly in line with an even more important goal—keeping everyone safe.

As she made her way down the hillside, Tempest didn't get

too close, in case anyone was still waiting outside to talk to her. But through the trees, she thought she recognized a familiar face in the crowd of six. Technically, it wasn't his bland face she recognized. It was his ill-fitting clothing she spotted first. He'd told her once that the oversize tuxedo jacket was his good luck charm, since he'd been wearing it the first time he met Tempest. Her superfan Preston wasn't just in town. He was here at Fiddler's Folly. She backed away, hoping he hadn't seen her.

She found her dad in the cedar-clad barn that served as the Secret Staircase Construction workshop. "Thanks for the fence. You didn't have to—"

"Of course I did. It's not a real installation, but it ought to do the job for as long as it needs to."

"You look beat. We finished the rest of the food, but I'm sure Ash would be thrilled to make more."

"Had a hearty breakfast hours ago. Now that we know you're safe, I've gotta grab a few things and get going."

"Isn't the job at the Knights' house suspended?"

"When have you ever known me to take a day off?"

It was true.

"Since we ended up with a free day," he continued, "the crew have a job to check up on, and I've got a favor to repay."

"Always looking after everyone else, Papa." She'd always called him Papa, never Dad. The Tamil word for father was "*Appa*," so her mom and aunt had called Grandpa Ash *Appa*. Tempest didn't speak Tamil, so to little kid Tempest it always sounded like her mom was saying "Papa." While other little kids were calling their fathers "Daddy," and then "Dad" as they grew older, she stuck with "Papa."

"I'm expecting Gideon in a few—" The faint ding of a buzzer sounded. "Good to see the new doorbell at the fence is working. I need to see about making it louder, though . . .

Hey, I didn't tell you yesterday, but after you left, Gideon said he wanted to talk to you about something."

"What?"

"Dunno. I'll be right back after I get him. We didn't have time to put in an automatic opener, so it's old school."

But when Darius got back two minutes later, it wasn't Gideon with him, but Detective Blackburn.

"This place is a fortress," the detective said, noticing that the newly erected fencing circled the entire property. "Did you know there's a guy performing magic tricks for people out front? He's not very good, though. At least he's not getting inside."

"There's nothing I won't do to protect my baby girl."

Tempest held her breath as the detective gave Darius a measured look. He couldn't possibly think her father had anything to do with Cassidy's death, could he? All the same, she wished her dad hadn't said that.

"Our people looked over that wall." Detective Blackburn looked from Darius to Tempest as he spoke. "And the ceiling. And floor. There's no way for Cassidy to have gotten into the wall at the Knights' house."

"But clearly she did." Tempest was sure his words were chosen carefully.

"She certainly did. Landing in your lap, as you all confirmed. You, who comes from a family that creates the impossible."

"Hang on." Darius stepped protectively in front of Tempest. "Are you saying we're suspects? You arrested someone already."

The detective glanced in the direction of the front gate. Nobody had followed him up the path. "Not me. Las Vegas Metro. Their evidence against Isaac Sharp is solid."

Tempest gaped at him. "They know how he got her into the wall?"

"We don't yet know why he brought her to you—"

"But *how*? I know the guy. I'm not saying he's not capable of killing someone. I'm saying he's not capable of pulling *this* off—"

"There's evidence."

"What evidence?"

"You know I can't tell you that."

"I'm trying to help."

"And I'm trying to tell you to let it go. You know as well as anyone that we don't always get the answers we want. Life doesn't give us the neat packages we hope for."

No, but the more she thought about it, the more she knew something was wrong. "It can't be right."

Tempest knew Cassidy's boyfriend well enough to know. Before he was Cassidy's boyfriend, he'd been hers.

Chapter 15

I t might have been a slight exaggeration to say that Isaac had been Tempest's boyfriend. They'd dated shortly after her arrival in Las Vegas.

Like so many talented performers struggling to stand out in the city, he could charm just about anyone he met. Tempest, craving connection in a big new place that could feel so anonymous, had fallen for his charming act. And that's exactly what it was. An act. To be fair, it wasn't for a malicious reason. Isaac's goal wasn't to con people. His goal was to be loved. An insecure soul, he lashed out when he felt he was under attack. She could see that after a few dates, and had ended things shortly before he met Cassidy. Tempest was relieved to have him out of her life and didn't see any reason to set the record straight, even after Cassidy told everyone that Isaac had dumped Tempest for her.

Tempest knew that he'd physically abused Cassidy on at least two occasions. Cassidy had come to rehearsal with makeup covering a bruise supposedly caused when she "accidentally" tripped. The woman never tripped onstage, even during quick set changes. Cassidy was frustrating in numerous ways, but her balance was impeccable.

Isaac was capable of violence. That could explain the blood they found in his car. What Isaac wasn't capable of was setting up the way they found Cassidy's body. Of that she was certain. She needed to tell the one person who would believe her when she said the police had it wrong. The person who'd look at a seemingly impossible crime in the same way she did.

"You okay?" Her dad startled her from her thoughts.

"You said you're sending the crew to a site. Is Ivy already there?"

Darius looked at the calendar on his phone and shook his head. "They're not due there for another hour."

She pivoted on her heel. "Do you need anything else from me, Detective?"

"Where are you going?" Darius asked as Blackburn shook his head.

"To see an old friend."

☠☠☠

Ivy lived in a duplex near Hidden Creek's Main Street. She occupied the one-bedroom upper unit above her older sister, Dahlia; Dahlia's wife, Vanessa; and their young daughter, Natalie. It had originally been a single-family home, one of Hidden Creek's many century-old houses, but had been converted into a duplex in the 1960s when nearby universities were expanding. Professors and students liked the idea of living in a historic building but didn't need a full 3,500-square-foot house to themselves.

Tempest hadn't been to this house before, but it was easy to tell she was at the right place. A carving of Janus, god of passageways, rested atop the ivy-draped archway. But unlike the traditional Roman image with profiles of two men facing opposite directions, this depiction of Janus was of two red-headed sisters. Their stone faces remained unpainted, but the stone tendrils of hair had been painted a shiny copper that gleamed in the summer sun.

On the path beyond the arch entryway was another grouping of painted ceramics, only these were a bit different. Three whimsical garden gnomes—a red-headed gnome holding a magnifying glass (Dahlia, a true-crime writer), a dark-haired gnome holding a gavel (Van, an attorney), and a baby gnome (Natalie).

Ivy's portion of the dwelling was accessible via a circular staircase along the left side of the house. The hand of Secret Staircase Construction was evident in the method to gain entry to the staircase. To pass through the gate, it was necessary to stick your hand inside a comically oversize lock that had room for a hand to slip through the keyhole. Inside was a wooden carving of a key. Tempest grasped the stem of the faux key and gave it a gentle tug. It didn't budge. But when she twisted it to the right, the result was a faint click, and the gate swung open. This was why the mailbox was on the outside of the gate.

"I have another peace offering," Tempest said when she opened the door. "A big one this time."

"Bigger than those Nancy Drew first editions?"

"Much bigger. I come bearing a real-life mystery to solve."

Ivy's pink lips parted, and she looked from Tempest's hands on her hips to her arched eyebrow. "You don't think Cassidy's boyfriend killed her."

Tempest felt a surge of hope as she looked at the woman who used to be her best friend. Who felt like she still was. Even after all this time, Ivy knew her better than anyone. "He didn't."

"Which means the police have the wrong man."

"This isn't about Cassidy at all." Tempest took a deep breath. "I think it was supposed to be me."

Ivy bit her lip. "You don't really think the family curse has come for you."

"Why was her body brought here? I don't mean a supernatural curse that magically transported Cassidy inside that wall for my dad's crew to find. But *someone* is doing this to me and my family."

Ivy raised an eyebrow. "For five generations?"

"I know, I know. Meaning, it's got to be a trick. You in to help me figure it out or not?"

"Oh, I'm in." Ivy gave a single, resolute nod. "Where do we start?"

"I thought by now you'd already have a dozen classic mystery movies lined up in your mind that could offer a possible explanation. All those mysteries we read and watched when we were kids."

"Harrumph."

"Um, did you just say, '*harrumph*'?"

Ivy pressed her pink fingertips to her temples. "I'm channeling Dr. Fell, John Dickson Carr's famous sleuth. If you hadn't been gone so long, you'd remember—"

"I remember. It's just, now that you've grown up, I didn't know you still wanted to be Dr. Fell."

"What bigger aspirations could a woman have? He's the master at solving seemingly impossible crimes. We need his methods here. Because I agree with you. Something doesn't feel right about what we saw yesterday."

"You game for a classic mystery movie night to kick-start our creative thinking?"

"How about Agatha Christie's *And Then There Were None*

for a mystery movie with a completely unexpected twist, and Hitchcock's *North by Northwest* for the mistaken identity?" Ivy glanced at her phone and swore. "I've gotta meet Robbie at a house in Marin, and it might take most of the day. Meet me at my place tonight at eight."

Chapter 16

Tempest stood at the edge of the sand at Ocean Beach, watching and listening to the rhythmic waves of the Pacific Ocean as the seawater lapped over her bare feet. The frigid water made her toes clench, but she stood firm and savored the feeling. Neither water nor flames had killed her earlier that summer. Yet . . . even though her jeans were rolled to her knees, her feet stayed frozen in place, refusing to take her even a single step further into the sea.

She wasn't here to fight with herself. She needed to get some physical activity to think straight. Usually she practiced hours on end each day, but being home had thrown her. She was planning on going on a hike, but first, the sea called to her. Letting her feet sink into the sand, she grounded herself and stretched, then flipped into a backbend kick-over. Then another. She stopped when she realized a small crowd was clapping. She'd gone so far she'd lost sight of her shoes. She took a bow and ran back toward the dots of red that proved to be her sneakers.

After a long hike at Lands End, it was nearly sunset when Tempest reached Fiddler's Folly. The light was beginning to change color as it pushed its way through the hillside trees.

Tempest fed Abra. She needed to remember to ask her dad to build a ramp to the hutch and construct a safe pen, so Abra could let himself into and out of his little house. He knew how to use a litter box, so he'd been a house bunny for a short time, but Abra was always happiest outdoors.

Tempest's own outdoor excursion had been a bust. What she'd seen at Calvin Knight's house reminded her, more than anything, of an illusion. She knew an illusion when she saw one. She created them for the stage. But *off* the stage, she had more questions than answers, and was eager to see Ivy that evening to talk things through. She'd forgotten to ask her dad or Ivy for Gideon's number, since her dad had mentioned that he wanted to talk to her as well. If it was important, surely he would have called or texted her himself.

As she changed out of her sweaty, sandy clothes in her room, a nostalgic sound filled the air. She hadn't thought about the jingle of the secret doorbell outside her window in years. Maybe a whole decade. The buzzer that had been installed when she was a kid didn't buzz like a traditional doorbell, but instead sounded like wind chimes.

Ivy was the only person who used that secret doorbell, back when they would sneak out for grand adventures—or rather, to build a fort in the tiny "woods" behind the house, watch an old movie, then sneak back inside. Had Ivy decided to come over to Tempest's house instead? Someone must have opened the gate for her. Tempest looked out her bedroom window, expecting to see her old friend.

But Ivy wasn't there. Nobody was.

The sound of wind chimes must have drifted from elsewhere. Tempest was about to turn back—until another familiar sound reached her ears. A melody from a fiddle. A wave of intermingled sorrow and delight washed over her as she recognized the song. This was a ballad her mother used to play. Her grandmother was a fiddler as well, but Tempest had never heard her play this tune.

"Grannie Mor?"

Tempest held her breath. As someone who kept time perfectly, she had always hated the expression that time froze. Yet that's exactly what happened when she caught a glimpse of the figure. This wasn't her grandmother.

A woman holding a fiddle in her arms stood at the base of the gnarled oak tree Tempest had climbed as a child.

A *transparent* woman.

Not just any woman, but the most important woman in Tempest's life. The one she hadn't seen in five years, since she'd vanished.

"Mom?"

Chapter 17

The ghostly figure levitated, floating higher with the oak tree still visible behind it—then vanished.

Ten years after Elspeth's accidental death onstage and five years after her mother's disappearance, Tempest Raj stood frozen in place, staring at the ghostly presence that so resembled her mom.

It took Tempest too long to regain her senses. Cursing herself for letting her imagination get carried away and frighten her, she ran downstairs and looked at the base of the tree where she'd seen the apparition.

Nothing.

She stood still and listened. Had there been a noise? Yes. Abra was thumping his foot. Tempest felt herself stiffen. Why was the bunny making a fuss?

On the steep hillside shrouded with trees, she stood in shadow as the sunlight faded into the western horizon. She crept toward the Secret Fort. She was running on adrenaline. Only as she rounded the front of the unfinished tower did it occur to her that she didn't have a plan if she found someone hiding inside. It had to be a person. A flesh and blood person. Right?

Tempest knew her legs were powerful, and had learned a few kicks that could knock out—or at least knock over—an opponent. And there had to be a person behind the trick. *This isn't a ghost.* She repeated the words to herself as she crept forward.

She jumped into the doorless entryway. The only living being in the tower was the surly bunny. He sniffed at her, then turned his back.

She hadn't imagined the ghostly fiddler, had she?

She spent the next five minutes looking around for evidence that a person had been there, but of course there were footprints of all kinds around the yard. After all, four people lived there, one of whom loved entertaining and one of whom ran a business out of the workshop on the property. She was beginning to think it was impossible to know what was relevant—until she saw a footprint she recognized all too well.

There on the windowsill underneath her own bedroom window was a footprint that left behind the impression of a rose. A rose that matched the sole of the shoes Cassidy Sparrow had always worn.

💀💀💀

Seven minutes later, Tempest banged on Ivy's door. Her hand shook. She was half surprised she hadn't crashed the jeep on the short drive over here.

No answer. She was half an hour early.

Ivy popped her head around the corner of the house. "Tempest, I have a life. I'm finishing dinner with my sister and her family. You can't just roll back into town and expect me to—"

"I just saw—" Tempest stopped herself. What else was

she going to say? That she'd just seen the ghost of her dead mother?

"You saw *what*, Tempest?" Ivy trudged up the circular staircase until she stood in front of Tempest. "Are you going to tell me or not? If I'm gone too long, Natalie is definitely going to eat the last piece of baklava before I get back."

"I saw something . . . *a ghost*, outside my window."

Ivy gripped the handrail. "Don't go anywhere. Back in two seconds."

It took Ivy two minutes to extricate herself from her sister's family dinner. At the top of the stairs, Ivy handed Tempest a plate with two pieces of baklava and unlocked her door.

"Could it have been one of your fans who got past the fence?" Ivy peeked out the window overlooking the front of her house before drawing the white curtains shut.

"I thought about that at first. There's a guy who came to nearly all of my shows, and couldn't deal with it when my show was shut down and I cut off all social media. Preston. He's an amateur magician, so he could make a figure vanish." Tempest shook her head. "But he's not someone who'd do that to me. And he couldn't have made it look like my—never mind."

"What did the ghost look like?"

Why couldn't she admit to Ivy she was convinced she'd seen her mom? "Translucent. And I know there are a dozen ways to make a see-through image appear, some through traditional magical setups like Pepper's Ghost, some using modern technology. But still . . . It seemed so *real*."

"Someone has to be messing with you."

"There was a strange footprint."

"There you go."

"Cassidy's footprint."

Ivy's eyes bulged. "You think it was *Cassidy's* ghost?"

Tempest hadn't considered that. As much as she wanted to laugh at the idea and roll her eyes, instead, she wondered: Was that why it had looked so much like her mom? "That's not exactly what I was thinking. Cassidy had these designer shoes she loved, with the print of a rose on the bottom. I found that footprint on a windowsill underneath my bedroom. Someone is going to a lot of effort to mess with me, if they're even stealing her shoes . . ." The more she explained, the less a rational explanation seemed, well, rational.

"Eat a piece of this baklava." Ivy held the plate under Tempest's nose. "The sugar rush will do you good. Because honestly, you do look like you've seen a ghost."

Tempest pushed away the sweet.

"What are you thinking? It's gotta be bad for you to refuse dessert."

"This is how magicians fool people. Not the technical sleight of hand. But the psychology of it. Distracting the audience with misdirection. Relying on their imagination to fill in the blanks." The rational part of her brain knew it had to be a trick. But her heart wouldn't let her believe it. She knew what she'd seen. What she'd felt.

"Maybe it's simpler than you think. Could Cassidy have faked her death?"

"Impossible." Tempest pressed her eyes shut and saw Cassidy's lifeless face.

"Yeah, but none of us actually saw the body. It could be mistaken identity."

"Detective Blackburn asked me to identify her. It was Cassidy."

Ivy's cheeks turned pink. "I didn't know."

Tempest brushed away the concern. "It doesn't matter." But

it did. She couldn't stop thinking about Cassidy's face. "Her hair."

"What?"

"Cassidy had cut off her hair recently. Why would she have done that? She didn't just keep it long so it would match mine. She loved her long hair. None of this makes any sense. Not unless there really is a curse."

"You get a free pass for saying that tonight. You nearly died onstage, and now your doppelgänger has been killed and left somewhere it was impossible for her to be."

"I was so sure it was Cassidy who wrecked my show. But what if—"

"Back up," Ivy said. "I don't know what happened at your last performance. Only what the media reported. You haven't talked to me in years."

"You work with my dad. I know he tells you—"

"You think I ask him for details about everything you do? God, your ego, Tempest! You haven't even asked me what's been going on in my life."

Tempest blinked at Ivy. "An hour after we first saw each other, my stage double's dead body fell out of a wall. It wasn't exactly the right time to ask what you've been doing lately."

Ivy stood up and glared at Tempest. "Some of us have to get up early."

"I thought the job was stopped?"

"I've got something else I'm working on. Which you'd know if you bothered to ask."

"*Something else?* Could you be any more vague?"

"You ran away before I could tell you what was going on with me when we were sixteen—and before you object, I know that's terrible to say, because you were dealing with the death of your aunt. I'm not mad that you left without a word, or even that you stayed in Edinburgh. I'm upset because when you stayed to finish high school there, you didn't get in touch. Ever."

"You didn't, either."

"I'm the one who was left behind."

"With *my* parents! I know you moved into the tree house. You had them—"

"Only because life at my own house was unbearable. Which you knew, but you still didn't call."

"My parents were there for you—"

"They weren't the same thing at *all*. I needed my best friend, even on the phone, and I think you needed me, but you chose to run away instead. You were running away from both of our lives—from me, and also from yourself. You did it again when your mom vanished. You ran away from everything except for writing a script you could perform to pretend to get her back. You stopped living your own life. And you stopped caring about those of us who were still here." Ivy paused and lowered her voice. "I can't trust you, Tempest. If I let you in, you're just going to run away again. I'm beating you to it this time. Goodbye, Tempest."

Chapter 18

Tempest drove home feeling more alone than she thought possible. After her mom had vanished, her heart was broken and her spirit crushed. But there was also something inevitable about what had transpired. At some level, even as she'd denied it to her conscious self, Tempest had been resigned that the curse would come for them. But now, to have Ivy's friendship dangled in front of her only to be ripped away so soon was unbearable.

She shouldn't have pushed Ivy away ten years ago, even as she grieved for Aunt Elspeth. She shouldn't have ignored the signs that Ivy's family life had gotten so bad that she'd rather sneak into the unfinished Fiddler's Folly tree house to sleep instead of listening to her parents scream and throw bottles at each other. When Darius had discovered Ivy sneaking out at sunrise, he and Emma let her stay in the guest bedroom, and Darius taught her how to finish building the tree house. It was Ivy who'd done most of the work finishing the small house her grandparents now lived in, even though Tempest hadn't known it at the time. When she found out, she should have felt relief that her friend was safe. Instead, she'd been consumed by jealousy. Tempest wasn't proud of the reaction, which she knew wasn't fair. But she had been figuring out her place in the world—she still was.

Tempest had always found herself in the awkward position of being comfortable both everywhere and nowhere. Comfortable in her own skin, until questioned as if she was occupying someone else's. She was a mash-up American and a female magician in a profession still dominated by men. Not Scottish or Indian or the mash-up of her dad's unknown ancestry, even though she was all of those things. Not a magician's assistant but the headliner. She was simply Tempest, who knew she was a kick-ass performer and a force to be reckoned with, even though she was lost.

It was that feeling of being lost that shook her. She was treading water in the middle of a dark and stormy ocean. She'd briefly hoped Ivy would be that beacon, but she'd screwed it up already. She'd alienated too many magician friends who either saw her as jumping the line or diminishing the sleight-of-hand aspect of magic. She'd lost touch with her casual friends after deleting her social media accounts. And even before that, when she met new people, they usually started off on the wrong foot either because they'd formed impressions of her from the headlines or because they expected her to be someone completely different—someone they'd imagined in their mind because of how she looked. Her reaction was to say she didn't need anyone. She was fine on her own.

Was Ivy right that she always ran away? She wasn't going to run away from this. She needed to prove the curse didn't exist by solving Cassidy's murder, either with or without Ivy's help, and then worry about getting back to Vegas.

Her tires screeched as she stopped abruptly in front of the new gate. She'd forgotten it was there. Nobody was lurking, so she climbed out and unlocked the gate. She knew it was just a temporary measure, but her dad had gone all out, more than he'd admitted. She doubted he could afford it.

Fiddler's Folly hadn't always been theirs, even after they turned the tiny bungalow into the assortment of whimsical structures. It was originally owned by Zola George, an eccentric, wealthy woman who took a shine to Darius when he was a young man in Southern California. She was nearly three times his age, and her interest was more motherly than romantic, in spite of Emma's teasing insinuations. Back when Darius was employed as a carpenter in Los Angeles, he was fired fairly regularly, because he always wanted to do things differently from his bosses. He was willing to spend more time on projects to make them better, but that impacted everyone, so it wasn't practical. One of his boss's clients, Zola, saw him get fired from her job. She held a different opinion of the young man, and hired him to do some specialized carpentry, to build a desk for her writing.

Darius and Emma were living in a tiny studio apartment with a view of the Coldwater Canyon exit of the highway, and Zola's job was perfect. After they made her a grand writing desk filled with secret drawers, Zola asked them to build whatever they wanted in her huge backyard. She didn't even care about permits, but Darius did. He'd just gotten his general contractor's license. Emma interviewed Zola to find out what would be a meaningful story for her, making up a magical tale based on one of Zola's books, a fairy tale about an orphan who finds a genie. They built her a floating carpet as the centerpiece. She loved it.

After they'd done a lot of work for her and a few others in L.A., Emma became pregnant with Tempest. Zola had the perfect idea for the couple. She had a small bungalow on a good size plot of land in Hidden Creek, which she'd always meant to fix up for her no-good son, Arlo. It was a precarious plot of land in many ways, perched on a steep hillside covered with rocks and trees—the kicker was that the trees were protected, so you couldn't cut them down. Even so, it was an expensive property, because it was the Bay Area.

Zola rented it to Darius and Emma for a fraction of what she should have. She said they could experiment to their hearts' desire there, and have a good spot to raise their child, but there was one condition—that they invite her to Thanksgiving dinner each year, so she wouldn't have to spend it with Arlo and his wife, whom she detested. She spent Christmas with her girlfriends, who dwindled in number as the years went on, and finally she herself dwindled. Tempest had enjoyed seeing Aunt Zola once a year. Zola always brought her a treasure trove of books for one of Tempest's secret bookshelves. And when she passed away, she left Fiddler's Folly to Darius and Emma.

Tempest locked the gate behind her, climbed the familiar steps of her secret staircase, and curled up in her bed, still in her clothes.

That's when she heard it.

A fiddle.

Not only the sound of a fiddle, but the ballad her mom used to play. It was unmistakably her mom's tune.

And it was everywhere.

"You're in my head," Tempest whispered as she clutched her charm bracelet. Her fingers wrapped around the silver fiddle and she squeezed her eyes shut. The music didn't stop. The melody surrounded her. The fiddler was no longer on the hillside—but inside the house.

Chapter 19

The air in the music-filled room felt as if it was being sucked out, leaving only a heavy brick in Tempest's chest as she gasped for air. Was this what a panic attack felt like? She'd experienced her share of grief, but she'd never had anything resembling a panic attack until the night she nearly died on stage.

Tempest ran downstairs to get her dad out of bed.

"Nightmare?" He felt her forehead.

"You didn't hear anything?" She was clammy and out of breath from fright, not exertion.

Darius's muscles flexed as he yanked a baseball bat from under the bed. Tempest recognized it as one she'd used as a kid. With her naturally muscular arms, she'd been good at Little League but found it boring.

"What did you hear?"

"I thought—" She broke off and listened. As soon as she'd descended her secret staircase, the fiddler's ballad stopped. "I thought I heard someone in the house."

"They must have jumped the fence," Darius said. "I should have built a better one. Lock this door behind me. I'll check it out."

"I'm coming with you."

He opened his mouth to protest, but he knew her better than that. He nodded and gripped the bat more tightly. Room by room, they searched the house together.

They found nothing.

With her dad at her side, the fiddle felt oceans away. "I must have imagined it," she said as they made a second loop. By the time she'd convinced her dad, she'd nearly convinced herself. Nearly.

☠·☠·☠

After lying awake for most of the night, Tempest got up and flung open the window curtain. She squinted at the ridiculously bright light.

Her cell phone rang ten seconds later.

"Want breakfast?" her grandfather's voice asked.

She *really* needed to get her own place. "I just woke up. No need to save anything for me."

"You need breakfast."

She ran her fingertips over the fiddle charm on her bracelet. As sure as she was that she was talking to her grandfather right now, she knew it was her mom who'd been there with her. Had her mom come for her?

She shivered. She couldn't face anyone in the state she was in. "I'll have some coffee and cereal in Papa's kitchen."

She heard a disapproving click of his tongue, and she thought he was going to give up without more of a fight, until he went on. "Don't you want today's gossip?"

Her fingers froze on the neck of the fiddle charm. "What gossip?"

"I'll put another batch of pancakes on the *tava*."

She took a quick shower and climbed the stairs of the tree house fifteen minutes later, after checking on Abra and letting him out of his tower hutch. "Don't make me regret my decision to give you some freedom," she said to the bunny. He twitched his nose at her, then hopped away.

Her dad had left her a note on their own kitchen counter that he'd be at another job as a trade for the fencing he'd borrowed. She knew he hadn't been able to afford it. He was paying off the loan in labor.

"What's the gossip?" she asked her grandfather.

"Eat."

She broke off a corner of the cornmeal pancake. Grandpa Ash was right. The pancake instantly made the morning better. With maple syrup, it tasted sort of like the pancakes her friends ate—er, her *former* friends—except Ash was incapable of making pancakes that weren't at least a foot in diameter, like a *dosa*. Also like a *dosa*, his version of pancake was thin, crispy, and delicious.

Ash tossed a few sheets of paper in front of her. He'd printed an article from a Las Vegas newspaper, writing about Cassidy's death and her boyfriend Isaac's arrest.

"It's not the curse." He smiled and joined her at the table.

"You didn't believe it?"

"Confirmation is reassuring. Do the pancakes need more syrup?"

"They're perfect. Hey, did you hear anything strange last night, Grandpa?"

"Strange like what?"

"Never mind."

"The burglar scare?" Ash frowned. "Darius told me it was nothing. The house was secure. He thought you were dreaming."

"Yeah, I probably was."

"Maybe he should add security cameras. Why are you looking over at the workshop? Are you still worried? Or is there something wrong with the food?"

"I thought I heard something."

"Gideon arrived a while ago. But you've reminded me I need to make a lesson plan for Robbie's younger brother, Liam."

"A lesson plan? You're learning the construction business as a fourth career?"

Ash chuckled. "Liam wants to become a chef."

"I saw him at Veggie Magic right after I got back to Hidden Creek. He wasn't a chef. He was my waiter." She didn't mention that she'd been disappointed by how much he'd changed since Robbie had brought him to one of her shows, or what he'd said to her. *Last meal before they haul you off to jail for that stunt?* he'd asked as he took her order. Even though a lot of people were surely thinking it, only the truly uncivilized would have said it to her face.

"He's working as a waiter for now," Ash said, "since he just graduated a couple of months ago and moved in with Robbie. Robbie asked me earlier this week if I could take Liam under my wing. What do you think I should begin with? I know. *Dosa* preparations, since it will need time to ferment. We'll get three types started soaking—black gram and rice, chickpeas, and oats—before turning to spice mixtures." He nodded to himself and checked the cupboards for supplies.

When Liam turned twenty-one two years ago, Robbie took him to Las Vegas to celebrate the occasion. Robbie was already in high school when Liam became an unexpected addition to the family, and he figured it would be a good way to bond with the little brother he'd barely known when he was growing up. Plus, by taking him to Vegas himself, Robbie felt he could make sure his little brother didn't go *too* wild. They fit in one bit of family-friendly entertainment: Tempest's show, *The Tempest and the Sea*. Robbie had told her they were coming, so Tempest invited them backstage to visit with her and the cast and crew. She'd really liked him then, so she'd been disappointed by their exchange when they met up again this summer. Maybe he'd just been having a bad day. Tempest certainly knew what that was like.

After finishing her breakfast, Tempest took two cups of coffee to the workshop.

Gideon didn't stir from his task when she came in. He wasn't wearing headphones, at least not that she could see from the door. Crouched in front of a stump of wood with a foot-high stone lion resting on top, his lips parted as he inspected the similarly open mouth of the creature.

The stone animal had so much personality, she could almost imagine him coming to life. She rubbed her eyes. That's what she got for not getting any sleep.

Tempest stepped closer and watched as Gideon tugged at the lion's sharp, massive stone teeth. He paid more attention than anyone she'd ever seen. He was also thinner than she'd realized. His cheeks were almost gaunt. He gave a final tug on a spot at the far side of the animal's mouth, then smiled to himself and stood.

He pointed at the mug she'd placed on the table. "This one for me?"

She shook her head. "Nope. This one is for the lion. Anyone ever tell you it's not nice to say you want to talk to someone about something mysterious, then fail to follow up?"

"Your dad told you?"

"Of course. You were going to tell me something, but you didn't text me—"

"I knew I'd see you soon. Besides, I only have a land line."

"You don't own a cell phone?"

"I don't need one. Most people don't. Not really. In this case . . ." He shook his head. "After I left the Knights' house, I realized what I was going to say sounded . . . Never mind. I don't even know what I was going to say. I was weirded out by what was going on. My imagination was playing tricks on me."

"There's a lot of that going around," Tempest murmured as she looked at the lion.

"I didn't catch—"

"Tell me what you *think* you saw. I don't care that it was only your imagination."

"That's just it. I don't know what I saw. It was more of a feeling."

"Fine. If you're not going to tell me, then tell me about this lion." The details in the carving were exquisite.

He picked up the coffee and took a sip. "I'm sure lots of people will bring him coffee after he opens their secret espresso bar, so I'll take this one."

"A secret coffee bar?"

"That's what the client said. My guess is that it's a *bar* bar, but he's free to put whatever he wants in the little nook with a sink, mini fridge, cabinet, and marble countertop."

"It's not like Prohibition is going on."

"You'd be surprised what people don't want to tell us. We're in the strange position of being in between craftspeople and the help. Some people totally open up, and those are the ones who get the best work that reflects what they're really hoping for. I heard that your mom was the best at that." He paused, as if waiting to see if it was okay to have brought up Emma.

"She was. How does the lion work?"

"Come look." He was so enthusiastic that coffee splashed across his hand as he set down the mug. "At first glance, he's only a decorative grotesque. I wish I could have made him bigger."

"You carved this?"

He nodded. "He'll sit perched on a built-in mantel, with his head a little higher than the line of sight, to hide his secret. Feel his tooth on the left side of his mouth—our right."

"He's not going to bite my hand, is he?"

"I promise he won't bite."

She knelt, as Gideon had, and touched the cool, stone teeth. The texture was a strange combination of smooth and rough. She wouldn't have liked it for a magic trick, because the sensation was confusing. With only the sense of touch, it was a baffling texture. As her fingers slid across the teeth, they came to rest on something different.

She looked at Gideon. "He's missing a tooth."

"That's the spot where the trigger goes. Push the button and a panel slides open, revealing the bar beyond."

"I don't see any holes in the stone. It's wireless? Like a garage door opener?"

"If your dad ever hears you call one of our secret passageway levers a garage door opener, he'll put an end to Robbie building them like this. It's a lot easier than the mechanical setups Darius likes. I get the feeling that's because it's what your mom liked to do. Your dad is still true to being old-school. I think that's why he hired me. In spite of hearing that I wasn't a team player because I couldn't climb a ladder or scaffolding." He hesitated.

"You're still dying to tell me whatever it was you wanted to say to me."

"I'm torn. I rather like the fact you don't currently think I've lost my mind."

Tempest's breath caught. "You saw something?"

"Maybe." He set down the mug and ran both hands through his hair. "There's no way for her to have gotten inside that wall."

"It's an impossible *illusion*. I create them. You're not crazy."

"Did you tell the detective your thoughts?"

"He's no longer investigating. His counterpart in Las Vegas took over and made the arrest. I get the feeling it's not like on TV where law enforcement fights over jurisdiction."

"Not much is. But you should still tell him. You know what you're talking about when it comes to illusions. You're The Tempest."

"Was. I *was* The Tempest. Now I'm just plain old Tempest." Tempest patted the lion's stone head and stood up. "How did my dad find you?"

"I attended one of your grandmother's art shows and he was there. I asked Morag if she sold reproductions of any of her paintings, because I was unemployed and couldn't afford the original of the one I wanted. The three of us got to talking, and before I left I had a job. I was supposed to follow in my dad's footsteps and become an architect. It was bad enough for my parents that I did an apprenticeship and started working as a stonemason instead of going to architecture school straight away, and now I'm helping with whatever Secret Staircase Construction needs. Not exactly a solid career choice."

"Welcome to the club of disappointing children."

Gideon tilted his head. He studied her face, but took his time before answering. "Your dad is so incredibly proud of you, you know."

"He hated that I went to Las Vegas."

"Only because you called yourself a magician. He was worried."

"I know that look. You think he's crazy to wonder if the curse is real. But it's not as crazy as it sounds. It's been going on for five generations. It's natural that an otherwise rational person would wonder." She thought of the music from her mom's fiddle, and the translucent figure that looked so much like her mother. There were at least five ways a magician could have pulled it off. Everything except for the fact that it looked exactly like her mom.

"You wonder," Gideon said softly. He glanced at his watch. Not a phone with a clock, or an electronic watch connected to a cell phone, but a watch with a dial that needed to be wound, that looked like it could have been a hundred years old. "There's somewhere I need to be now, but there was also something else I was thinking about. Are you free in an hour?"

"Maybe. Why?"

"Meet me here." In precise, small letters, he wrote an address on a sheet of graph paper. As he handed it to her, he took her hand, and for a strange two seconds she thought he might have been about to kiss it. Instead, he lifted it closer to his face and looked at the charm of the Janus-faced jester. "I've decided that one's my favorite."

"Why?"

"He's not trying to pretend to be something he's not. There are two sides of him, and he's not hiding it. If only the rest of us could be so lucky."

Chapter 20

The jeep bumped over the uneven road as Tempest followed Gideon's directions. She reached the address he'd given her. The street was filled with potholes and a row of run-down houses that sat next to a cracked sidewalk and in the shadow of a renovated live-work building of overpriced lofts. Gideon's address led her to the house at the end of the street, a yellow stucco cottage with a sandstone carving of a Great Dane to the right of the natural wood front door. The dog's body was posed as if he was standing guard, but the expressive face of the carving held too much laughter and joy to even pretend he was meant to frighten.

Gideon's note said to use the side gate, not the front door. A note with the word "Enjoy" written in a granite pencil was tacked to the wooden gate. The stone path was nicely tended but narrow.

"It's a secret garden," she murmured when the path opened up to the backyard. "Garden" wasn't the right word for it. This was a menagerie. Stone carvings of animals surrounded her. It felt almost as if they were magically alive, each imbued with a unique personality.

Tempest passed an owl with eyes that watched you wherever

you went and feathers that Tempest could only tell were stone once she reached out and touched them. A dragon with mischievous eyes and wings that rose majestically into the air as if hovering on the edge of the breeze that was picking up. A gargoyle with an inquisitive expression that made him look as if he was about to speak. When a voice did speak, Tempest imagined it had come from the gargoyle.

"There's some cake," the voice said. "It's purple, and incredibly tasty." Past a fig tree, Ivy was seated at an iron table. Across the table was an empty chair. "Gideon isn't here. I think this is his idea of a meet-cute for us to make up."

Tempest barely noticed the sound of honking cars on the nearby freeway as she looked from Ivy back to Gideon's artwork. She immediately knew this was why Gideon considered himself a disappointment to his parents. These creations weren't a hobby he dabbled in. This was commitment. He wanted to be an artist. "This is all his work?"

Ivy nodded. "He left the place to the two of us while he's off to source some stone for a new project."

Tempest walked over to the gargoyle that looked like it was about to speak. The detail in the stone face was astonishing. "This is what he wants to do with his life."

"He's already doing it." Ivy cut Tempest a piece of cake. "I'm the only one who hasn't gotten my act together."

Tempest turned from the gargoyle to her maybe-friend. "You're a kick-ass welder."

"Who stumbled into it, works for a business that doesn't need her skills, and who's had her favorite pink vest from high school mended half a dozen times so she can keep it as a security blanket." Ivy jammed her hands into the pockets. "Come over here. You need to see something else."

Ivy beckoned Tempest toward a window of the cottage.

Whatever reservations Tempest had about spying on Gideon vanished when she looked through the window into the small living room. The mantel surrounding the fireplace had been replaced by the open mouth of a dragon. It looked like stone, but she wasn't close enough to tell. The dragon's long teeth encroached on the opening of the hearth, but the rest of the carving took up the space to the sides and above the fireplace, where you'd normally see brickwork. The dragon's stone eyes followed her as she moved from one side of the window to the other to get a better look. Tempest could see why Darius had adopted Gideon into the Secret Staircase family. These were the details she'd seen in high-end jobs her dad had done in the past year.

"I'm sorry I blew up at you last night." Ivy's voice startled her.

Tempest pulled her eyes from the dragon's. "I'm sorry I abandoned you."

"You didn't. You were grieving and you had a loving family to go to in a place that let you feel close to your aunt. It wasn't about me, and I should have realized that." She paused and gave Tempest a shy smile. "Nissed zoo."

Tempest smiled at the code. One of their basic ones.

"Nissed zoo, uoo. I haven't thought of that code in years."

"Technically it's a cipher," Ivy pointed out. "And way too easy to work for a secret conversation. But I figured I'd go for the simplest one so I didn't need to hand you a key. Why was that so hard for us to say at sixteen? But more importantly right now, *why*—" Ivy lowered her voice, "did you tell Gideon you were looking into Cassidy's death?"

"I didn't."

"When I got here right before he left, he told me—"

"I only told him I agreed he wasn't crazy for thinking it

was an impossible situation. Besides, he had no connection to either me or Cassidy, so it's not like he's involved in what happened to her."

"He could be a serial killer."

"You sound like your sister. And may I remind you we're sitting in his garden."

Ivy shrugged. "I didn't say it was likely. But if this were an Agatha Christie novel, he'd be the bad guy."

"Good thing it isn't, then." Tempest considered what Ivy had just said. What was it that the Queen of Mystery always did? "If this was an Agatha Christie novel, I can think of an even less likely suspect. It would be that young police officer."

They stared at each other.

"No . . ." Ivy said. "You don't really think he—"

"I can't imagine how. But I can't imagine anything that makes sense right now. Add him to our list of suspects."

"We have a list of suspects?"

"It's probably time to start one." Tempest took a bite of the purple cake. "*Ube* cake." She'd eaten far too much of the delicious Filipino cake when she'd done some tour dates in Asia, back when she was doing enough physical exertion to eat as much cake as she wanted.

Tempest took another bite of cake instead of saying the next thing she wanted to say. Why wasn't she telling Ivy that she'd heard the fiddle again? She knew the answer. It was the same reason she hadn't admitted it to her dad. She didn't want their pity. She'd had far too much of that lately. If they thought she was losing her mind, she wouldn't be able to stand it.

"What do you want to do next?" Ivy asked.

"I thought you'd have a plan based on those books you love.

You were *harrumph*ing yesterday. Channeling Dr. Fell not working as well today?"

Ivy looked as if she was going to say one thing, but changed her mind. "You've always been The Tempest, with the rest of us caught in your orbit. Even when we were little. It wasn't being a stage magician that made you The Tempest. You were simply stepping into the spotlight that was always waiting for you. I understand if you need to go back to the literal spotlight once this is over. Just make sure you're running *to* something, not *from* it."

"Don't tell me Ivy Youngblood has grown up while I've been away."

"Never at heart." Ivy paused, and again looked like she was about to say something before a barely perceptible shake of her head. "I never properly thanked you for those first edition Nancy Drews."

"I couldn't *not* buy them for you. It's like I had no free will at all, so there's no need to thank me."

"In that case, I'll thank your subconscious." Ivy burrowed her nose into the collar of her vest for two seconds, and when she emerged her expression had changed from hesitant to decisive. "We've got a ton of crap to work through."

"I know."

"But that dead body could have been you. Or any of us. I don't care about 'working through' things. Life is short. I want my BFF back."

As the sun shifted the shadows of the stone carvings, they talked for the next two hours, picking up the same easy banter they'd had before. Conversation flowed from one random topic to the next, from the secrets of Old Town Edinburgh Tempest had discovered to how welding equipment worked. They hadn't reached the present or the strange death of Cassidy Sparrow when they were interrupted by Ivy's phone buzzing. Her face turned pink as she looked at her message. "I didn't realize how late it was. I promised I'd babysit my niece this afternoon."

"Can you meet up tomorrow?"

"What about later tonight? I should be free after eight."

"I've already got plans tonight."

Ivy grinned. "Gideon?"

"What? No. Why would you think that?"

"No reason. Then what have you got going on tonight?"

"Actually . . . I can't tell you."

"Tempest!"

"Really, it's for your own good."

"I like the sound of that even less."

"I'll tell you when I see you tomorrow."

Chapter 21

Tempest didn't know how to pick a lock.

It's a common misconception that all stage magicians know how to do the range of standard tricks that people think of as magic. Many of the world's most talented magicians know only one style of trick. But they know countless variations on it, and are better at it than anyone else in the world.

Tempest Raj could create an indoor storm and make thousands of pounds of props disappear from a stage, could do backflips and levitations that would land her impossibly far from where you expected her to be, and could conjure beautiful and baffling performance art using only a good story and a great sense of timing to add a twist of misdirection.

But she couldn't pick a lock.

Tempest spread the blueprints across Sanjay's granite worktable. Before meeting up with him, she'd spent the afternoon practicing close-up magic and hoping the methodical practice would jar something loose in her brain. Some secret of illusion that would make her think the answer was staring her in the face. It didn't work.

She secured the rolled edges with four hefty books from

Sanjay's vast magic library. He made sure she didn't select books from his shelf of first editions, so she picked up well-read books by Jim Steinmeyer, Peter Lamont, John Zubrzycki, and a modern reproduction of Jean-Eugène Robert-Houdin's memoirs, and placed them on the four persnickety edges that kept curling.

"There are no secret passageways marked," Tempest explained after Sanjay returned from the kitchen with two lattes from his fancy espresso maker.

He hesitated before handing her the black ceramic mug. "You're not going to throw coffee at me again, are you?"

"You're not going to insult me again, are you?"

His face reddened as he handed her the mug. She had a feeling his friend Jaya had set him straight as to why his offer to be his assistant was insulting.

"It has to be a secret passageway, right?" he said. "Some way in and out that doesn't show up in the plans and that everyone missed."

"That's my thought. The house is definitely hiding something."

Tempest hopped up onto a window seat in front of the ceiling-high wall of windows in this industrial live-work apartment in the South of Market neighborhood of San Francisco known as SOMA. The area had gentrified around Sanjay in the last few years, and the once-vast views of iconic downtown skyscrapers and the Bay were now obscured by expensive high-rise apartment buildings.

It was a good space for Sanjay, who created midsize magic. He wasn't a close-up artist, but he was far better at cards, coins, and cup-and-balls than Tempest. His favorite type of performance was a midsize stage show, working with one or two others and performing in a formal theater setting that wasn't too big. Not like Tempest, who needed a far bigger crew. She still felt like she'd let them all down. Even though it wasn't her fault, and they'd unfairly blamed her, it wasn't their fault, either. She wondered how many of them were still out of work after the show shut down.

Sanjay's tricks were mostly things he could fit into a steamer trunk or slightly larger props that went in the open back of his sleek pick-up truck.

"How," Sanjay asked, "did her boyfriend find out about the Knights' house and its secret passageway?"

"I don't think he did."

"Of course he—" Sanjay broke off and groaned. "You aren't only trying to solve the impossible situation. You're trying to solve the *murder*, aren't you?"

"They're the same thing. That's why I need to get inside."

"I only use my lock-picking skills for good—meaning entertainment. Not actual crime."

"Crime solving and freeing an innocent man definitely counts as good." Isaac was hardly innocent, she knew, but he was innocent of this particular crime.

"If it did," Sanjay said, "you could simply ask the detective to see the crime scene again." The twitch that emerged on his lips as he spoke told her she'd be able to convince him.

Sanjay had never wanted to go to Vegas. He'd had a good thing going at a Napa Valley winery theater until it had burned down in a California wildfire.

Sanjay liked to think of himself as an escape artist, like his idol and namesake Houdini. He usually escaped from a stage out of a locked trunk, cabinet, or sack, but had also staged a few high-profile escapes, like from a coffin in the Ganges River.

Tempest's mom had a different idea about Houdini's motives. Houdini wasn't *escaping*, she'd say. He was *setting himself free*. Semantics, perhaps, but those were two different things. Houdini couldn't be confined. He chose the terms of his confinement so he could set himself free into the world he wanted to see: the adoring public. He was a showman. So was Sanjay. He only needed one more performative nudge . . .

"It's better to seek forgiveness afterward than to be denied permission up front," she said.

"Nice try." Sanjay gave her a smug smile.

Just one more nudge. "You probably couldn't get us inside anyway."

The smile faltered. "Why do you say that?"

She had him. "The house had these really cool old locks. I think they're original. Like more than a hundred years old, made of brass."

"I'm completely aware you're trying to manipulate me, so you should stop before I change my mind about helping you."

"You're in?"

"I was always in. Don't you know me by now?"

"I thought I did. Until the picnic incident two days ago."

"I get it." He flipped his bowler hat onto his head. "Now let us never speak of it again."

Chapter 22

Sanjay parked his truck two blocks away from the house. It was nine p.m. Late enough for the cover of darkness, but not late enough for it to seem suspicious if anyone saw them walking up to the house.

Tempest stopped short when the house came into view. In the darkness, the spires of the Queen Anne house made it look more like a haunted house than ever. She wouldn't have been surprised to see a bat fly above one of the turrets. Sanjay, oblivious, kept walking. She caught his jacket and pulled him back.

"Hey, this is a designer jacket."

Tempest pointed. "There's a light on in the house."

"The killer?"

"Look at the driveway."

"A killer stupid enough to park in the driveway?"

"I'm pretty sure that's Calvin Knight's car. They're back earlier than expected."

"What are you doing?" Sanjay hissed as Tempest strode forward.

"Saying hello to Calvin, and asking for his permission to inspect the room. You're coming with me. You're good at this stuff."

"Which stuff? Impressing tech millionaires or finding secret passageways?"

"Both."

They reached the front door and Tempest knocked. Calvin Knight opened the door holding a mug of steaming coffee. He was dressed in the same mismatch of formal top and casual bottom, but he'd replaced his black-framed glasses with cobalt blue ones.

"I wanted to say how sorry I am about everything that happened," Tempest said. "This is my friend Sanjay. We were out nearby, and when I saw the light, I made him stop."

The two men shook hands. Tempest fought back an eyeroll as Sanjay unnecessarily adjusted his jacket to hide his lock picks.

"You two want to come in for coffee or cocoa?" Calvin asked. "I just got Justin to bed after a single mug of cocoa, so there's a bunch left on the stove. I caught your eyes lighting up, Sanjay. Cocoa it is."

Sanjay's sweet tooth rivaled that of any small child. Ash loved him for it.

"So he's doing okay?" Tempest asked. "I feel so badly that we brought this to your house."

"I don't know what magic you used, but that joker from a deck of cards to fight closet monsters is doing its thing."

"I'm glad. And I'm sorry I missed him before he went to sleep."

"Me too. He needs more smiling faces after the year we've had. He hasn't met any kids his age yet, since school hasn't started. Ivy mentioned she'd bring her niece by sometime. I hope we can figure out how to move forward. We weren't expecting to be back so soon. But they arrested that poor girl's boyfriend." Calvin leaned back against the counter and adjusted his glasses. Tempest knew it must have been

her imagination, but it looked as if he was adjusting the focus of a microscope directed at her and Sanjay. "I know you
weren't just driving by. This residential street is too small
for that."

Sanjay took a gulp of cocoa and coughed. Tempest made a
mental note that as good a performer as Sanjay was, he'd be
terrible at a life of crime.

"I have a confession," Tempest said, as Sanjay tugged nervously at his jacket again. "I asked him to take this street
as a detour, because I was hoping you'd be home. Detective
Blackburn told me about Isaac as well, so I thought you might
be back. I did want to apologize, and also . . . I'm still curious about what actually happened. I was there in the room
when the crew found her."

"The secret of the wall itself, you mean?"

Tempest nodded. "Something doesn't feel right about the
whole situation in this house."

"Tell me about it." Calvin clicked his tongue and shook his
head.

"You agree?" Sanjay asked.

"Let me tell you the story of this house." Calvin set down
his coffee and jogged out of the kitchen. He returned with
two books.

"California Gold Rush history?" Sanjay read.

Tempest smiled. "I noticed you were a history buff when I
looked at the sliding bookcase my dad built."

"My grandma was the one who taught me to be proud of
Black history, long before they taught it at school. Justin will
have a different experience than mine, but this is still living
history. This house—" Calvin paused and looked wistfully
around the high ceiling and off-kilter walls. "This house was
built more than one hundred years ago by the children of a

formerly enslaved couple who discovered gold in the Gold Rush. You can imagine the precarious situation they found themselves in."

"With the Fugitive Slave Act?"

"It didn't technically apply in California, but there were a bunch of laws—or lack thereof—that made it easy to steal from them, since Black and Native folks couldn't testify in court."

"That's why the blueprints are hiding something," Tempest murmured. "An escape hatch?"

Calvin chuckled. "I don't think it's anything as dramatic as that. Not in this particular house. It was their children who built it. This style of architecture wasn't revived in the U.S. until the 1890s, and this house was built shortly after 1900. The original couple who found gold were quite elderly by then, and their wealthy son built it for the whole family to live in together before they passed away. The son and daughter ran a local business making tailored clothing for people who weren't served elsewhere; he was a tailor who made suits, and she was a seamstress, sewing dresses. I was interested in the history of the house. It's a good story to tell Justin about triumphing over adversity, and I like the idea of preserving the history, while also making it our own. I didn't think about the possibility of anything hiding in the walls until we felt the cold spot."

"Cold spot?" Sanjay asked.

Calvin's eyebrow rose above his glasses. "You didn't tell him?"

"He's a little superstitious."

"I am not," Sanjay huffed.

"A crawlspace hiding something other than insulation," Tempest said. "That's why it was so cold. The reason that area felt wrong and creepy wasn't because it's haunted, but because of a draft in a place where we wouldn't expect one."

"You thought it was haunted?" Calvin asked.

Tempest flushed. "Not really. But if you know the story of my family . . ."

"You mean the 'about' page of the Secret Staircase Construction website?" Calvin asked, clearly confused.

"You don't know who she is?" Sanjay asked.

"Tempest Raj," Calvin answered. But there was a slight question in his voice as he spoke. "You're Darius's daughter."

"That's me," Tempest said. "I know it's too late to look tonight . . ."

"It's only nine thirty," Sanjay pointed out.

"I was being polite," Tempest snapped at Sanjay as Calvin laughed. "I don't want to wake Justin."

"Once he's out," said Calvin, "he's out. Let's look for this supposed secret passageway."

They pushed open the door to the pantry. Dust hovered in the air from the work various people had done to inspect the crawlspace that had contained the body, but the difference in temperature was no longer detectible.

"The cold spot must've been your imaginations," Sanjay said. "What were you having the Secret Staircase crew build in here, anyway?"

"A magical playroom for Justin," Calvin said. "One that's visible from the kitchen. I love to cook. I work a lot, so when I've got free time, I want to spend as much of it as possible with J."

Tempest could see what a great space it would make. "How did you find my dad?"

"Indigo Bishop. She's the one who posted about the history of this house."

Tempest smiled at the memory of Indigo. Tempest hadn't seen her in years. For a short time Indigo was the in-house architect for Secret Staircase Construction, right after she'd graduated from Berkeley. Even when Tempest was a kid, she could tell that Indigo wouldn't stay long. Not because Indigo didn't get along with Darius and Emma, but because she had other aspirations for herself. A Black woman who'd grown up in San Francisco, she saw how the architectural history of Black neighborhoods had been erased. She wanted to restore as many old houses as she could, saving them for people who were too often being pushed out of desirable neighborhoods.

Sanjay stepped through the newly opened cutaway in the wall. "There's a whole little room inside here." He stepped past a dusty ream of fabric and picked up an even dustier glass jar of green beans. There was a whole row of home-jarred fruits and vegetables.

"It's a closet that was sealed up," Tempest said.

Sanjay stepped back into the main pantry with a mason jar of peaches. "You look disappointed. Do you think these are still good?"

Tempest snatched the jar before he could open it and poison himself. "Of course I'm disappointed. If it's not a room for people to hide in, it's less likely to have a secret exit."

"The most recent owners didn't know about this extra little room?" Sanjay asked Calvin.

"The police looked into that, too. The last owners were an elderly couple who passed away. I bought the house from their middle-aged son, who hadn't lived here and knew nothing about it. Besides those blueprints that don't tell us much, we're on our own."

Fifty-seven minutes and two cocoas later, the threesome were dusty and tired, but had no solution to the puzzle to show for it. No escape hatch. No secret passageway. No false panels. Not even anything that had been cut through to get in from the floor or ceiling. It was simply a long-forgotten closet.

"I'm glad there wasn't a secret hiding spot for people," Calvin said.

Sanjay brushed plaster from his sleeves. "Why?"

"Because," Tempest said softly, catching Calvin's eye, "it means the occupants weren't worried for their lives."

As glad as Tempest was for the previous owners of the house, she was far more disturbed about the present. There was truly no earthly way Cassidy could have gotten into that wall.

She paused in the foyer to look back at the house as Sanjay picked up his bowler hat from the coatrack. They thanked Calvin and stepped out of the impossible house into the night.

"Penny for your thoughts." Sanjay displayed empty hands in front of him as they walked down the driveway, then snapped the fingers of his left hand. An oversize coin designed like a copper penny appeared between the thumb and index finger of his other hand.

"Is that Houdini's face on that penny?"

"Of course." Sanjay tossed it to her. "If one is going to make a novelty penny, why not make it interesting?"

Tempest caught the heavy disk and twirled it between her fingers. As they passed underneath a street lamp, she vanished the coin.

"Hey," said Sanjay, "you only get to keep that if you tell me what you're thinking."

Reaching the spot where they'd parked his truck, she stopped and faced him. "I really thought I'd be able to figure out the trick of how she got into that wall, and that would lead us to who put her in there. The illusion is where I thought I'd be useful."

"There's more to an illusion," he said, "than where it's staged."

Tempest's senses tingled under the street lamp. "You're brilliant."

"I know." He was entirely serious. The man had a healthy ego. He leaned forward and touched her cheek. "Plaster dust." He brushed it from her face, but his hand lingered a moment longer. For a second she thought he was going to kiss her. Instead, he pulled another Houdini coin from behind her ear and grinned like the mischievous child she had a feeling he'd been.

She sighed. "How many of those things do you have?"

"Don't ask. They offered me a discount on a bulk order. Hey, the night's still young. Do you want me to come over?"

Realizing how much she wouldn't have minded if he'd kissed her, she decided that would be a very bad idea.

He took a step closer.

The shrill sound of a phone ringing caused him to take a step back.

"Nicky?" Tempest put her phone to her ear. "Is everything all right?"

"Ay. Did you forget?" Nicodemus left the question hanging.

Tempest closed her eyes. She'd promised to stay in touch. How many days had gone by? It was a full two days since she'd spoken to him.

"Ye trying to give an old man a fright?" he continued. "When I saw I *hadnae* missed any messages during the night, I was worried."

"I'm sorry."

Tempest hadn't put the phone on speaker, so Sanjay paced on the asphalt. "Everything okay with Nicodemus?"

"Is that Sanjay?" Nicodemus asked as Tempest switched to speakerphone.

"Hi, Nicky." Sanjay tipped his hat to the phone, even though Tempest was the only one who could see it.

"Together at midnight again? Are you sure you two aren't—?"

"No," they said in unison.

Chapter 23

Sanjay dropped Tempest off at Fiddler's Folly after everyone in the household had gone to sleep. Storm clouds were gathering in the west. She wondered if they'd reach Hidden Creek.

From inside the protective fencing, she watched Sanjay drive away as a crash of thunder sounded in the distance. Every structure on the hillside property was dark, aside from the porch light that looked like a lantern containing a flickering flame. The illuminated lantern reminded her that she hadn't yet visited the secret garden at night. She'd spent time in the cozy spot since arriving, but like so much else at Fiddler's Folly, the secret garden was magic: it was one thing in the day, yet transformed into quite another at night. Maybe the different perspective would help jar some ideas loose.

Tempest let herself into the house and walked quietly to the kitchen. The picture window above the sink opened to a forest-like view, with a steep slope of greenery directly in front of the window. To the left, a rustic wooden fence was covered with tendrils of ivy and a hanging vertical garden of herbs Ash used in his cooking. What the decorative fence enclosed remained a mystery—unless you knew the secret

way in. You couldn't reach the secret garden from the outside. It was only accessible through the grandfather clock in
the kitchen.

To the left of the sink and picture window, an eight-foot
cherrywood grandfather clock was nestled into a nook in the
wall that looked as if it had been made for the clock. Which,
in fact, it had. The clock functioned perfectly well to tell
time, but it wasn't a grandfather clock. The clockface on top
was a real antique, one that Zola had left in the house for
Tempest's parents, but it didn't need the pendulum mechanism below to operate. The five-foot-tall case containing the
pendulum was yet another illusion. The copper pendulum
swayed back and forth, yet the gesture was purely ornamental. Through an optical trick, the pendulum seemed like it
filled the eleven-inch depth of the clock's body, but it only
took up the front three inches. Beyond the faux pendulum
lay the secret garden.

Tempest unlocked the secret door by giving a boost to the
wooden griffin climbing the side of the clock. As the griffin
climbed an inch higher, the pendulum door swung open.
Tempest pushed the pendulum aside and ducked her head
to step through the entryway to the secret garden. With the
clouds above, there wasn't much light, so she flicked on the
lanterns. Her breath caught as she did so. All around her,
the night blooming section of the garden was alive. The
beautiful bright white flowers of Queen of the Night, the
orchid cactus, surrounded her. The orange fronds around
the white petals swayed in the wind. Stretching higher than
the Queen of the Night, delicate white moonflowers veined
with purple peeked out from their vines and filled the enclosed garden with a fragrant lemony scent.

Her dad wasn't a night person, so it had been her mom

who'd maintained the night-blooming flowers. Who had kept it up these last few years? The light from one of the flickering lanterns caught her eye and gave her the answer. Two spots of dark red paint dotted the wrought iron chair tucked into a corner of the tiny garden. Her grandmother must come here to paint.

The flickering lanterns told their own story, as just about everything in this house did. Robbie had found them at a salvage yard for a job they were working on, but Emma had fallen in love with them and taken them for her own secret garden. The client said his heart was set on having authentic Victorian street lamps in his back garden, but it turned out he didn't care about actual authenticity, only an aesthetic. Instead of simply flickering lights that resembled real gas lamps, the client wanted to change the gentle white light into violent red flames. When Emma gently prodded him about what he was going for with the red flames, he confessed to her that he loved Bram Stoker's *Dracula*. Not only did he get his faux Victorian gas lamps with strong red flames, but also a trick of the light that cast the shadow of bats. The client was thrilled. From there, Secret Staircase Construction knew exactly what they'd design for the outdoor pizza oven he'd requested in his secret back patio. Instead of installing a standard stone pizza oven, they crafted one to resemble a stone mausoleum.

When there were kids at a house where they'd been hired for a job, Emma would write the children their very own stories that were theirs alone, with a main character with their name. For adults, the magic was often modeled after their favorite book or story, such as the cemetery-themed pizza oven for the *Dracula* fan. For a Poe fan, there was a raven with a beak that opened a secret drawer, and a claw that served as a key to a music box.

That was one of the main reasons the business had struggled after she vanished. Darius was a brilliant craftsman, and he had a great core team, as well as extra contacts he hired for bigger jobs, but once the magic was gone, what was Secret Staircase Construction?

Tempest touched the familiar shape of the selkie charm, with its twisting tail. She'd had the charm bracelet for five years now. She hoped silver didn't wear down over time. She didn't know what she'd do without the comforting touch of the charms that made her feel close to her mom.

Shortly before Emma Raj vanished, Tempest had returned to Fiddler's Folly for a visit. She came home to see the stage show her mom would be presenting at the Whispering Creek Theater to honor her sister Elspeth on the fifth anniversary of her death. It was shortly before Tempest's twenty-first birthday. Her mom handed her a box covered in silver wrapping paper decorated with a pattern of gold keys. Thick red ribbon looped across the mug-sized box, and tied to the bow on top was a Houdini bobblehead toy. Emma had looped the red ribbon through the spot where the plastic toy's wrists were handcuffed. This was Tempest's twenty-first birthday present, Emma said, to be opened on her birthday. Tempest honored her mom's request to wait until the actual day, so she didn't open the present until it was too late to ask her mom more about it. A folded piece of notepaper on top of the charm bracelet inside read, *Happy 21st! A magical inheritance for my magical daughter. Love love love xxx Mom.*

The charm bracelet had kept her grounded in those horrible weeks after her mom vanished, during that time when the investigation unearthed Emma's increasingly erratic behavior leading up to her disappearance. Whatever was going through Emma's mind that caused her to break with reality had also led her to create the most beautiful gift Tempest had ever received. One she would always cherish.

Tempest checked on Abra before heading upstairs. Like the rest of the household, he was fast asleep. The bright moonlight shone through the stained-glass key window of the unfinished tower, bathing the space in a warm glow.

Yet . . . why did it feel as if someone was there?

The feeling of a presence was her imagination, surely. Because of what happened the night before. It *had* happened, hadn't it? She touched the bolt of lightning on her bracelet and pushed the thought from her mind.

Back inside the main house, Tempest lifted the wing of the stone dragon on the wall. In the shadows of night, as its head tilted to the side, more than half of his face was hidden in darkness. The soft whir of gears echoed through the silence. The panel of wall opened with a louder *whoosh* than was audible during the day, but you still had to listen to hear the well-oiled levers.

A nightlight clicked on as the panel stopped moving, illuminating the stairs. Tempest had hated that safety feature as a kid, since she considered forced lighting to detract from the mystery. She ascended the now-visible staircase. The wooden steps held familiar grooves.

Tempest opened the door to her bedroom. With her stockinged toes, she traced the wooden key shape made from the hardwood flooring, then looked up to the pinpricks of stars on the ceiling that formed her key constellation. Her mom had always said that Tempest was a key that could open any lock and be anyone she wanted to be, and maybe that was true. But she was still missing the piece that would show her how to get there.

The curtains of her bedroom hadn't been drawn, and a

flicker of light in the window caught her eye. She ran to the window. The light was gone. But a crash of thunder sounded in the distance. *Lightning.* That's what the flash of light had been. Nothing more.

She unlatched the window and slid it open. The air was cool. She closed her eyes and breathed in the scents of pine and water. The air was so still and silent that she heard the babbling of the hidden creek.

That's when she heard the sound that made her skin prickle. *Please let it be thunder,* she wished, gripping the bolt-of-lightning charm.

This was no thunder. Another sound was out there in the night. There was no mistaking it. What she heard was closer than the sound of the distant storm. This was no trick of the wind or her imagination.

Notes from a sorrowful fiddle cut through the air. Again, it was the melody her mom used to play. One that began as a Scottish ballad, but had a touch of the rhythm of the sarangi.

Was it coming from above? The stars on the ceiling twinkled, but revealed nothing beyond the key their pinpricks formed.

As the music surged, she skidded backward and tumbled onto her steamer trunk. One of its hidden drawers popped open. She scrambled away as if it had burned her skin, but there was nothing inside the secret drawer except for an extra pair of jeans.

She would have laughed at herself if it hadn't been for one thing. The fiddler was coming closer. The ghostly presence was in the room with her.

Chapter 24

When Tempest created her breakout stage show, she was following in her mom Emma and Aunt Elspeth's footsteps, decades after the sisters performed as the Selkie Sisters. She wrote the script in lieu of therapy, after losing both of them. The magical fable that grew out of her raw grief became *The Tempest and the Sea*, the show that got her funding as a headliner.

While onstage, thinking of nothing except keeping precise time as she followed through on the promise she'd made the audience, the rest of the world fell away. She was no longer a grieving daughter. She was a wizard bringing the gift of two hours of wonder to skeptical people who'd suffered their own losses and disappointments.

Her signature illusion of flying in a swirling tempest and disappearing, along with other strong illusions, were key to it being a success, but she knew the heart of the show—and the secret to why it was such a success—was the story.

A story from the sea, told in the universal language of music, illusions, and movement. A story told with no spoken words. The only sound was music.

The fiddle.

Two fiddles, to be precise.

The fiddle idea came from her mom and aunt's original show in Edinburgh, but Tempest developed this initially minor element into the theme of the show. Nicodemus found the composers who created the score, one from Inverness and the other from Edinburgh by way of Bangalore.

The idea of dueling fiddles was nothing new. The fiddles in Tempest's show were a Scottish fiddle and a sarangi, the Indian fiddle. East and West. The Indian fiddler stage right, the Scottish fiddler stage left.

Tempest and Cassidy played the two sisters. Tempest was the little sister whose elder sister is pulled back to the sea in a storm where they lose each other. Cassidy's role was small; she only appeared in the beginning and end as her character, and in the middle as an occasional stage double when one was needed.

The two-hour show told the story of a woman searching for her beloved sister through a series of water and sea-themed illusions. After her sister is pulled away to sea at the end of the opening sequence, Tempest's unnamed character wakes up alone on a Scottish island and has many adventures, illusion after illusion, always trying to find her way back to her sister.

The push and pull of the two fiddles lured her in both directions of the stage. Finally, she sees she doesn't need to pick. Instead, she embraces her true self, spins and spins until a tempest parts around her, then dives into the ocean in the center of the stage, emerging above the waves in an illusion that takes her high above the sea—and the audience. The top half of her body is the one from the beginning, but her legs are the tail of a seal. A selkie. There in the ocean, she finds her selkie sister.

It was a happy ending—the one Tempest, her aunt, and her mom never got in real life. A new beginning, in which they were free.

Chapter 25

Tempest woke up with her face in a pile of clothes.

She'd ransacked her own room after the fiddle player's music had invaded it. There was no sign of trickery. Only the echo of her vanished mom and the curse that had claimed too many members of her family until it accidentally captured Tempest's doppelgänger.

The eldest child dies by magic.

Streaks of sunlight cut through the room like knives. What had she really heard the previous night? Although the storm hadn't crossed the Bay to Hidden Creek, claps of thunder had continued to echo in the distance for much of the night. Had the wind played tricks on her, leaving her imagination to fill in the rest?

Had the other members of her family who had died from the curse seen or heard their dead loved ones before they were claimed? She was reminded of the story of Houdini's death. Even though he was a spiritualist debunker who proved that mediums were nothing but tricksters, before his death he told his beloved wife, Bess, a secret word he would use to contact her from beyond the grave. Nobody else knew the word, so if a medium used it at a séance, Bess would know it was truly

Houdini who'd come through from the other side. Harry Houdini died under mysterious circumstances on Halloween. As for contacting Bess after his death? If he did, she kept it to herself.

That wasn't the first time Houdini had exposed this contradiction in himself. These two sides of his convictions. When his mother died, the man who exposed the trickery of spiritualists was also desperate to find one who was real. One who would let him see his beloved mom.

Tempest needed coffee. After a quick shower, she was dressed and at the bottom of her secret stairs within five minutes. There was no need to fuss. Nobody to be "on" for. She'd forgotten how easy it was to be with family. How right it felt.

On the tree house deck, Grandpa Ash greeted her with a smile so warm it was as if Tempest had just solved world hunger. He was sporting a Panama hat this morning, the cream color of the straw matching Morag's cashmere sweater. Her grandmother gave her a satisfied nod. "Good to see you're learning how to get out of bed before half the day is over."

Tempest was glad to have pushed herself out of her comfort zone in Vegas. But it was hard work on many levels. Being at home felt like . . . well, *home*.

A faint noise from a distant buzzer sounded an hour later, while she and her grandparents were finishing the newspaper crossword puzzle.

"I didn't know you had a doorbell at the tree house," Tempest commented.

"We don't, dear." Morag set her coffee mug on the newspaper and listened. "Is that the front gate buzzer your father installed?"

The buzzer sounded again.

"I'll go check." Tempest left her grandparents as they quibbled about the second-to-last crossword puzzle answer, and found Robbie and Liam standing outside the make-shift gate. Liam looked even more like his brother than Tempest remembered. He wore his unruly light brown hair longer than his older brother's, but their hazel eyes and the cleft in their chins were identical, and they were both a few inches taller than Tempest, putting them over six feet tall like her dad. They would have looked like twins if Robbie hadn't been nearly two decades older than his brother.

She gave them a smile as she unlocked the gate, but it was only returned by Robbie.

"Thanks, Twirls. I must have the new key to this gate some-where here with the dozens of others, but I can't for the life of me remember which it is. You remember Liam?"

So much for giving him the benefit of the doubt that he'd been having a bad day when she saw him at Veggie Magic. The sullen man who stood before her met her gaze, but his hazel eyes were checked out, not really seeing. The sense of wonder she remembered from their first meeting in Vegas had vanished. It had been a rough couple of years for a lot of people, but there was something more here. A bitterness she recoiled from, even before he spoke.

She forced herself to keep smiling. "Good to see you again, Liam."

He gave her a brief upward nod before turning back to his brother. "Can we get this over with?"

Robbie scratched his neck in embarrassment and gave Tempest a half-hearted smile. "We're heading to the workshop so I can show him around. I thought we'd come early before

Liam's cooking lesson with Ash, since he said he might want to check out carpentry, as well."

"I hear you're interested in becoming a chef," Tempest said.

Liam looked at his brother instead of Tempest. "I thought I'd only have to look at the workshop if he wasn't ready for me."

Tempest settled on the word "bratty" to sum up Liam Ronan. Which was unfortunate, since he was twenty-three, not thirteen.

"We've got time." Robbie followed the fork of the entryway path that led to the workshop and slid open its side door. "You can stand outside and sulk, or you can see if you might want to follow in your big brother's footsteps."

Liam looked as if he was going to object, but changed his mind and followed Robbie. "What's in that corner?" He pointed at Ivy's welding equipment.

"Not to be touched by us," Tempest said as she caught up to them.

"Could you do the honors of giving him the workshop tour?" Robbie asked. "I'll go let Ash know we're here, in case he wants any help in the kitchen."

Great. Alone with the brat. That wasn't fair. Maybe he was just having another bad day. She'd certainly had enough of those lately.

"I don't know this studio as well as Robbie and the rest of the crew, but—" She broke off as she turned, finding Liam right in front of her.

Unlike the spark of curiosity always twinkling in Robbie's eyes, anger dulled Liam's. "Let's get this over with."

She forced herself to relax. "Do you want to get a studio tour or not?"

"Not. I thought that was pretty obvious. I thought you'd be smart enough to see that."

"Smart ass."

"I try. Hey, I think you've got a rat over there."

"That's Abra." The rabbit perked up at the sound of his name.

"A magician with a pet rabbit? That's a bit cliché, isn't it?"

"He's a guard rabbit, I'll have you know. And a great judge of character." She crouched next to Abra. "Go on, boy. Say hello to Liam Ronan."

Liam sat on his knees next to Tempest and held out his hand for Abra to sniff. "Hey, little fella." Abra nuzzled his hand and Liam laughed.

"Judas," Tempest mumbled to the bunny.

Liam scratched a contented Abra behind the ears again, then stood and went over to the photo and carved wooden plaque next to the main door. Darius and Emma's wedding photo still hung above the bench where the crew dumped their jackets and bags.

This is what happens when a stage magician and a carpenter fall in love, the chiseled lettering read. Underneath the words, a selkie holding a key. Darius wasn't an artist, so while the letters were made with confident strokes of precision and beauty, the seal woman and key were rudimentary.

"So this is what makes Secret Staircase Construction so special?" Liam ran his fingers over the indented letters.

The words themselves were innocent. Said in a different tone, it would have been a compliment, acknowledging the love, magic, and craftsmanship that went into the business. But not from Liam's mocking mouth.

Tempest raised an eyebrow, activating her scowl.

Liam turned and caught her expression. "Is that the famous scowl? You must use filters online to make it look more fierce."

Robbie stepped back into the workshop. "Hey, you two. Ash would love a taste-tester in the kitchen, so you can go on up, Liam. I left their front door ajar—I've broken their dragon knocker lock one too many times for Morag's patience. I've got a few things to clean up here, so I'll be there in a few."

"He's a good kid," Robbie said after Liam had departed.

"The fact that you had to say that means you're either trying to convince yourself or me."

Robbie scratched the cleft in his chin, but remained silent.

"I remember him being so different when we met a little over two years ago," Tempest said. "I would have agreed with you then. But now? It's like he's two different people."

"Just an adolescent. I know, I know, he's twenty-three. But since I left home when Liam was a toddler, he grew up with only my mom and sister, no father figure. And he had to finish college during a bad economy—"

"Make excuses much?"

Robbie forced a laugh. "I'm hoping your grandfather will knock some sense into him. How are you holding up, Twirls?"

"You mean after we—"

"I can't stop thinking about how that sack felt when it fell out of the wall. When Blackburn told me what was inside, I, uh . . ." He fiddled with one of the numerous pockets of his vest and flushed. "I threw up in one of the Knights' potted plants."

"You feeling any better?"

"That's supposed to be my line. I was asking to make sure you were okay, kiddo. I should have known you would be. You've always been strong. You can handle anything."

Maybe she could. But looking at Robbie, remembering when

she used to call him Uncle Robbie and think he had all the answers, she wondered if that was a good thing. Part of her didn't want to solve the mystery of what had happened to Cassidy, because it might tell her what had happened to her mom. Did she really want to know?

Chapter 26

That afternoon, Tempest had offered to take Justin to a play date with Ivy's niece, Natalie, since the kids were the same age and Justin would be attending Natalie's elementary school that fall.

"Would you like to do the honors, Justin?" Tempest asked as they reached the magical key of Ivy's gate.

"What do I do?"

"It's a puzzle."

He stuck his hand through the keyhole that was large enough to be straight out of Alice in Wonderland, and grabbed hold of the wooden skeleton key. Unlike Tempest's methodical puzzling out what to try, within two seconds Justin had pushed and pulled in every direction, settling on the clockwise twist that opened the gate.

"That was too easy," he said as the gate popped open. "Can I have a harder puzzle?" He giggled and bounded up the circular staircase.

"Hi, Ms. Youngblood," Justin said as he opened the door.

"It's so nice to see you, Justin. You'll be hanging out with my niece downstairs, but I thought you might like to see the key riddle first."

"That doesn't count as a riddle," he said.

"Why not?"

"Too easy. Real riddles are bigger. But they make me happy when I work them out."

"You're a wise man," Tempest said. "My grandma loves riddles. She's from Scotland, so you might not have heard some of hers. I'll see what she's got for you."

"Why isn't your gate puzzle harder, Ms. Youngblood?" he asked.

Ivy laughed. "I don't want to discourage *all* visitors. Just the ones without enough imagination to stick their hand into the lock. Not everyone has enough imagination. We're the lucky ones."

Downstairs, Ivy introduced Tempest and Justin to her sister's family. Tempest hadn't seen Dahlia in a decade. Her auburn hair was brighter and curlier than her sister's, as it had been when they were teenagers, but her contact lenses had been replaced by bright yellow cat-eye glasses. The frumpy T-shirts she'd worn to disguise her ample figure were now swapped for a svelte purple tunic in a cut that flattered her curves, and red knee-high boots that made a statement. Like Ivy, Dahlia was only a little over five feet tall.

"It's been way too long." Dahlia's strong and friendly hug told Tempest both that she was at ease with the body she used to hate and that she was truly happy to see Tempest.

Tempest hadn't met her wife, Vanessa, before, or their six-year-old daughter, Natalie. She would have loved to stay longer to get to know them both, but Natalie, bored with the adults, immediately dragged Justin off to see her toy collection. Vanessa told Tempest she had to come over for dinner one day soon, before chasing after the kids.

"Want a cup of tea before you two head off?" Dahlia asked.

"I almost forgot." Tempest set a metal tiffin filled with Grandpa Ash's cardamom shortbread on the kitchen countertop. "I brought cookies."

"Are you sure I can't help you two?" Dahlia started a kettle onto the stove and hopped up on a barstool.

Ivy zipped her pink vest so it covered her face.

"You told her?" Tempest asked.

"She's my sister," Ivy's muffled voice said.

"It's about time I get to help solve a real mystery." Dahlia cracked her knuckles.

"You gave a tip to that true-crime podcaster one time," Ivy reminded her, poking her head out.

"Not the same."

Dahlia Youngblood was five years older than her sister, and her love of true crime began when she was a sixth-grader. That was when she learned about the Black Dahlia, the famous unsolved murder from 1940s Los Angeles. Dahlia wasn't named after the glamorous victim—she and Ivy had been named for plants by their garden-enthusiast mom—but the fact that she shared a name with the woman who'd been called a "beautiful and mysterious" figure made her read everything she could find about the case. True crime wasn't as popular at the time, so when she checked out history books from the library, her parents were none the wiser about the sordid, salacious details inside the pages. Her passion for the genre was what led Dahlia to become a journalist. After Natalie was born, she'd switched to writing books on true crime, a job with a flexible schedule that worked with her family life.

"We're not approaching things from that angle." Tempest raised an eyebrow at Ivy.

"You sure?" Dahlia unlatched the tiffin. The kitchen was

immediately filled with a sweet and spicy scent. "Ivy said you thought it might be a serial killer."

"Not exactly—" Tempest began.

"Dahl." Ivy scowled at her sister. "You know, pretty soon Natalie is going to be old enough to know a serial killer isn't someone who sneaks into people's homes to destroy their cereal boxes. And you haven't seen Tempest in years. Maybe at least pretend to be a normal human on day one, and not have a big grin on your face when you talk about serial killers."

"Anyone," Dahlia said, "who has a mentor who calls himself Nicodemus the Necromancer isn't a normal person. And you're both terrible detectives if you're ruling out any possibility."

"I'm not a detective!" Tempest insisted.

"Yes, you are. You're trying to prove her boyfriend didn't do it."

"I'm not exactly trying to prove that. I'm trying to make sense of an impossible situation that happened in front of my eyes and break my family's curse."

"Which you don't believe exists."

Tempest hesitated before speaking. She no longer knew what she believed.

Dahlia hopped off of the counter stool and poured three cups of mint tea. "Does anyone have a vendetta against you or your family?"

Tempest accepted a warm mug. "Too many social media haters to count."

"Rival magicians?" Ivy suggested. "OMG is Sanjay from a family of magicians?"

"He's the black sheep in a family of lawyers. And Sanjay is no Romeo." Tempest told them about him wooing her to be his assistant.

"No," Ivy gasped.

"That's the worst," Dahlia agreed. She bit into one of Ash's cardamom shortbread cookies. "And these cookies are the best."

Ash's recipe was a mash-up of traditional Scottish shortbread and a North Indian shortbread called *Nankhatai*. Like the Indian version, he used ghee or coconut oil instead of butter, included chickpea flour, and added cardamom, but the overall effect was quite similar to the Scottish version most people in the US and UK were familiar with.

"These cookies," Dahlia continued, "might be the top reason I'm glad you and Ivy made up. Tell me about Cassidy."

Dahlia spoke so authoritatively that Tempest answered without thinking. "Cassidy was jealous of me. I know that's terrible to say now that she's—"

"Lying about someone to be nice, just because they're dead, won't get her justice."

Tempest watched the swirling steam of her mug of tea as it twirled higher and higher until it disappeared into the air. "She thought because she *looked* like me, she could easily replace me. She kept pressing for a larger role, but she didn't have the skills—because she didn't have the discipline to get there. She couldn't keep time accurately, so we needed a crew member to help her know when to appear. We had a system that worked well, but I wasn't going to give her a bigger role. She wasn't a magician. She had charisma, so she did well in a lot of performance-oriented jobs. One of my magician friends saw her singing and mentioned my job opening to her. He found her charming, so he overrated her skills."

"The magician's name?" Dahlia looked up with a pen poised in her hand.

"Julius couldn't have had anything to do with her death."

Dahlia set down the pen. "You're a terrible detective, Tempest."

"I told you, I'm not a detective."

"Then what's Ivy helping you with?" Dahlia adjusted her glasses and pursed her lips. It was disconcerting how, even though she was a head shorter than Tempest, Ivy's sister appeared to be looking down her nose at her.

"Her library."

"My library?" Ivy repeated.

"I need to reread the book with Dr. Fell's locked room lecture. The secret of the trick will tell us what's going on, and there's no better place to begin. Do you have a copy?"

"Of *The Three Coffins*? I'm offended you'd even need to ask."

"Can I borrow it when we go upstairs?"

Ivy drummed her pink fingertips together. "I can do something even better."

Chapter 27

W hat *is* this place?" Tempest asked.

The first floor of the cozy Victorian house across the bay in San Francisco was bursting with books, but even more intriguing were the details of the converted house. Two gargoyles loomed over guests as they stepped through the front door. Inside, a knight's gleaming suit of armor stood next to the information desk, a full-size train car was visible beyond the desk, and back-to-back reproductions of classic paperback dime novel covers lined the highest reaches of every wall.

The space was divided into three large rooms. The main room, beyond the front desk, was laid out like a library, with bookshelves and desks with reading lights. Beyond the bookshelf-lined room was a doorway with a sign above it that read *Museum*. The windows of the train car revealed that it, too, contained a room. The effect was absolutely magical.

"This," Ivy said, "is the Locked Room Library, a library for readers of classic detective fiction." Instead of grabbing *The Three Coffins,* aka *The Hollow Man,* from her own bookshelf, Ivy insisted this was the place that would help them.

"I never knew this was here."

"It's pretty new," Ivy said. "Isn't it the best?"

"I can't believe you didn't tell me about this until now!"

"I love your charm bracelet," said a librarian hurrying past them with a stack of books. She was dressed straight out of the 1940s, in a plaid A-line skirt, white blouse with puffy shoulders, and an emerald green scarf in her hair.

Ivy led them to the corner of the library in which the classic, black-paneled train car had been parked. Upon closer inspection, it wasn't a true train car, but a curved wall that began two feet off the floor. Huge black wheels and gears rested underneath, and retractable stairs descended in front of its door with a glass-paneled window. A sign dangling from a suction cup on the glass read *Reserved*.

"That's for us." Ivy removed a key card from her pink fanny pack and waved it at the doorknob.

"The modern key card kinda ruins the effect."

Ivy snorted. "Tell me about it. It started as a real key, since this is the private meeting room they like to keep locked, but book clubs who reserved the room kept losing it, so they had to switch to these cards. I don't believe they actually lost the key—and for the record, my own book club wasn't one of the offenders. It was a beautiful iron skeleton key, more ornamental than secure. So beautiful the temptation was too much."

Ducking her head to step through the small doorway, Tempest half expected Poirot himself to appear at the bar located at the end of the room and was slightly disappointed when he didn't. It looked so much like a train car, she felt as if she was standing in a dining car from a BBC period piece drama.

Tempest leaned over and traced the faux windows with her fingertips. "The Secret Staircase Construction crew built this. My dad told me about a train car they made for a historical building in San Francisco. He did the carpentry details and Robbie found the seating and bar area at salvage yards, right?" She took a few seconds to text her dad about what a great job he'd done.

Ivy grinned. She picked up a skeleton key decoration hanging on the wall and placed it in a lock and turned it. The scenery behind the window began to slide by, accompanied by the sound of a steam engine, as if the train had begun chugging along. She gave a contented sigh and turned back to Tempest. "I learned how to heat wood to make rounded pieces for this job, and Gideon built a door of bricks in the main section of the library."

"You mean the brickwork around a doorway?"

"Nope. Literally a bricked-up door to nowhere. It's meant to represent a scene from John Dickson Carr's novel *The Burning Court*. Fix yourself a coffee at the bar if you'd like. I'll be back in a few minutes."

True to her word, Ivy returned four minutes later with an armful of novels. The binding of the books themselves didn't look old, but many of the titles were classic mysteries Tempest had heard of. *The Three Coffins* and *The Crooked Hinge* by John Dickson Carr. *Murder on the Orient Express* by Agatha Christie. *Death from A Top Hat* by Clayton Rawson. And also some she hadn't. *The Poisoned Chocolates Case* by Anthony Berkeley. *The Moving Toyshop* by Edmund Crispin. And more recent novels in the impossible crime genre, including *The Tokyo Zodiac Murders* by Sōji Shimada and *The Fourth Door* by Paul Halter.

The narrow table swayed under the weight of the books Ivy had pulled from the shelves.

"Somewhere in these books is the answer," Tempest said. "Or the key to it."

"You brought up Dr. Gideon Fell's locked room lecture from *The Three Coffins*, where he explained all the ways an impossible crime could have been committed."

"I haven't read the book since I was fifteen," said Tempest, "but I know that if this is a trick, it should give us the answer to how Cassidy's body got into that wall."

"What do you mean, 'if'?" Ivy squinted at Tempest as if she'd grown another head—an illusion Tempest had once tried but didn't like. "Of course it's a trick."

"Slip of the tongue." Tempest felt color rising in her cheeks. Why couldn't she admit to Ivy what she was so sure she'd seen and heard? Why didn't she say aloud that a big part of her wondered if it was truly the curse? "Anyway," she said instead, "if Dr. Fell doesn't give us the answer, I'll declare that his creator John Dickson Carr was wrong—"

"Blasphemy! There are *infinite* variations. This lecture just lays out broad categories, but it doesn't explain everything. What fun would that be? But between it and these books before you are some of the more ingenious ways people have pulled it off—"

"Not people. Fictional characters."

"Fiction gets at the truth of life precisely because it can get at the most meaningful elements of true human experience. You know that. To tell your family's true story, you performed a piece of fiction for thousands of people a night." Ivy paused and bit her lip. "What was it like? When we were talking in Gideon's garden, we went off on so many tangents that we didn't get to the present."

Tempest set down the paperback she was holding and stood to look out of the faux train window. The scene of a blurred field of yellow flowers was painted on the wall behind the glass. She pressed her palm to the plexiglass and looked out over the fake scene.

"Sorta like this faux scenery," she answered. "Exquisite if you use your imagination, but you don't want to look too closely under the surface." She lowered the train window and stuck her head out. Looking down, she saw where the canvas of scenery met the floorboards at the base of the wall. The truth behind the illusion.

"I want to hear more about it, since all I got was snippets from Darius." Ivy shook her head. "But I know now isn't the time. We need to focus on the matter at hand."

"Back to the books." Tempest sat back down, but Ivy was still looking out the false window.

"Let's begin," said Ivy, "with Dr. Fell's Locked Room Lecture."

Tempest shook her head. "The more time I spend with you, the more I know what we need is the Ivy Youngblood Locked Room Lecture."

"Ha."

"I'm serious. After I moved on to magic, you kept reading your way through these books. I know misdirection in *physical* actions, which is how I know something is wrong. But you know what's behind that."

Ivy clasped her hands together. "This is the moment I've been waiting for all my life, you know." With the smile on her face, she looked like she'd won an Oscar.

"You have the stage."

"*Harrumph*," Ivy began. She smoothed her hair. "We'll begin with a refresher. We're talking about an impossible crime here. Otherwise known as a 'locked room mystery.' Not to be confused with a 'closed circle mystery,' in which everyone is trapped on an island or in a manor house during a snowstorm. They often overlap, but they're not quite the same."

"Our situation with Cassidy is most clearly an impossible crime, aka a locked room mystery."

"John Dickson Carr had his corpulent detective spell out

eight methods of setting up an impossible crime. Sort of. Seven categories, plus five methods for the various ways to trick a lock and key, so I really don't understand how he made them five separate points. Thus, for clarity, we're left with eight."

"Do you give lectures here at the library?"

"Oh! Do you think I should?"

"Totally. But we shouldn't get distracted. Go on with the Ivy Youngblood locked room lecture."

"This is where I slightly diverge from Dr. Fell. His categories claim to be open-ended, but are in truth overly specific. The Ivy Youngblood version has five, not eight, methods. First, a time shift. Being wrong about the time the victim was killed. Either they were already dead far earlier than realized, or we think they're dead, but really it's a trick so they can be killed later."

"Like if a witness thinks they've seen or heard the person alive at a certain time," said Tempest, "but really they were already dead and it was the killer in disguise."

"Exactly. Second, it's not really a murder. This can be either an accident or suicide. But either way, the victim is the one who locked themselves in the room."

"Neither of which could apply to Cassidy."

"Agreed. Third, something deadly that's already in the room, such as a poisonous snake or a poisoned tip of a pen planted in the room."

"Which, even if something like that killed Cassidy in the first place, doesn't explain how she got into the wall. What's next?"

"Fourth, the killer didn't need to be inside the room at all to kill, even though the circumstances make it look like they did. And five, a way to lock the room that looks as if it was impenetrable, but in reality there was a way in and out."

"That last one," Tempest said. "That's what we're dealing with here. I just don't see how . . . There's got to be another way for Cassidy to have gotten into that wall that we're not seeing. Because otherwise . . ."

"Otherwise what?"

"Either I'm losing my mind, or my family curse is responsible."

"You're not going mad. Someone is messing with you."

Were they? Tempest watched the faux scenery scroll past the train car's window. So much of her life was an illusion, just as it had been for members of her family for generations.

☠.☠.☠

Tempest's phone rang an hour later, while she was immersed in the second of Clayton Rawson's four Merlini novels, *Footprints on the Ceiling*, in which the magician sleuth is able to solve the crime because of its echoes of a magic trick, and Ivy was poring over the ending of Anthony Berkeley's *The Poisoned Chocolates Case*, muttering about how they'd never know which was the true solution.

"Tempest," Gideon's voice said. "There's something I wanted to talk over with you. Can we meet?"

"Is that Gideon?" Ivy whispered. "I hear Gideon."

Tempest took the phone to the bar at the end of the train car and drummed her fingers against another book Ivy had pulled from the shelves, Paul Halter's *The Madman's Room*. "I get it that you hate phones. I promise your head won't explode because you're talking to someone on a cell phone. You can tell me now."

"In person is easier—"

"Except I'm in San Francisco right now. And I'm kind of busy." Tempest looked over the precarious stack of books.

"Will you be back in time for dinner?"

"Dinner?" She raised an eyebrow at the phone. "I suppose."

Ivy looked on with wide eyes as Tempest hung up a minute later. "You're going on a date with Gideon?"

"It's not a date. I think we've got ourselves a Watson."

Chapter 28

Gideon was already at Veggie Magic when Tempest climbed the narrow staircase in her ruby red sneakers that evening. She'd reapplied her favorite red lipstick, but otherwise hadn't changed. Gideon was seated at a round table in the corner, underneath an 1880s illustration of Hidden Creek's original Main Street. The first floor of the café was nearly packed, but the second floor, with its walls filled with old photos and illustrations from the town's founding shortly after the California Gold Rush, was only half full.

There was something comforting about the way the owner, Lavinia, had chosen to keep the café decor the same. She'd updated the menu over the years—both the food and the design of the physical menus and the chalkboard over the counter— but the rickety wooden tables, mismatched wooden chairs with colorful pillows, and artwork from Hidden Creek's history, remained unchanged.

"What's so urgent?" Tempest sat down opposite Gideon in a solid wooden chair with a rose-colored cushion and purple tassels.

Gideon placed a small, sealed plastic bag on the table. Inside was a familiar piece of black fabric.

"Why do I recognize that material?" Tempest murmured, mostly to herself.

"Because," Gideon said softly, "I'm pretty sure this is a piece of fabric from the outfit Cassidy was wearing when she died."

"Abra." It was similar to the piece of fabric she'd pried from Abra's teeth the morning before they found Cassidy's body. "Where did you find this?"

"I was at the workshop and Abra came sniffing around. I didn't know how he got out, so I brought him back to his cage. That's where I found the scrap of fabric."

"How did you know this is what she was wearing?" A creeping dread lodged itself in her thoughts. Tempest also should have put it together earlier that the fabric in Abra's mouth was part of Cassidy's outfit. She knew why she hadn't, though. Her focus had been directed entirely to Cassidy's face and hair, not her clothing. *Misdirection.* A stupid mistake. She should have paid more attention. She didn't know at the time she'd need to remember, but that's the thing with a trick.

"I went back outside to the veranda while waiting to be questioned," Gideon said. "I wanted to see what was going on, so I followed it along to the back of the house, all the way to the kitchen. I saw through the window when they had you identify her body. I wasn't close enough to tell for certain, but this is a shiny black silk fabric that catches in the light. When I saw a similar fabric in Abra's cage, I wondered if I was right."

Tempest picked up the fabric. "You are."

"Why did your pet rabbit have a piece of her clothing in his cage?"

Tempest's heart galloped in her chest. "Cassidy must have tried to come see me. That has to be it. When I found her footprint outside my house, I thought—"

"You recognize *footprints?*" Gideon gaped at her.

"Don't get your hopes up that I'm Sherlock Holmes. She used to wear these shoes with a distinctive rose pattern on their soles. It drove me crazy, because if there was dust or powder on the stage, she left a distracting mark during rehearsals." Tempest was relieved he'd interrupted her. She didn't know what she'd have confessed to him about her ghost if he hadn't.

"But you never saw her?"

"No. But this means she was skulking about my house the night before she died." *Cassidy had gone to see her. Why?*

"Meaning it's unlikely her boyfriend killed her and drove her to Hidden Creek to frame you."

"You thought I was being framed?"

Gideon shrugged. "Someone framed you earlier this summer already, right?"

"You believe me that I didn't stage a dangerous stunt for publicity?"

"You're in the public eye, so of course there will be people who try to bring you down. But that's not the main reason why I believe you. If you could see the way your dad talks about you, you'd know there's no way I could believe otherwise."

"Unfortunately, it doesn't tell me who's doing it."

"You should tell the police about the fabric—"

"I will. Can we eat first?" She'd try. But would it help? Whatever was going on was beyond the realm of police work. Like the rest of her life, this mystery spanned the globe. Whatever was happening was bigger than Cassidy being murdered and staged inside an old house in Northern California. This was also connected to Las Vegas, Scotland, and maybe even the birthplace of the curse in India.

She took three deep breaths, like she did when preparing

to go onstage, and picked up the menu. "Why'd you pick this table?"

"The hostess gave me a choice of the free tables up here, and this was the only one that wasn't rickety."

"I've made a terrible mistake befriending a stone mason. I should have known they'll always choose a straight table over a better view."

"This *is* a good view. A brick wall and in the corner so we can observe other people."

It was indeed a good spot to observe people. The restaurant's owner, Lavinia, approached, bringing them glasses of water. "Are you two ready to order?"

"Short-staffed tonight?" Tempest asked. Lavinia had owned and run the restaurant since Tempest was a kid. She often came to say hello, but didn't usually take orders.

"One of my waiters is running late." A crash sounded from below. Lavinia winced but smiled. "Another new hire. I keep telling him all he needs is confidence to lift the serving tray."

Lavinia had dreamed of opening a café even though she had no experience, so she decided long ago that anyone who was following their dreams and needed a small paycheck while they did so could have a trial run as a server. (The offer only applied to waitstaff, not cooks.) It made scheduling a nightmare, and Veggie Magic was often understaffed or overstaffed, but Lavinia wouldn't have it any other way.

Tempest ordered an iced chai to drink and a sourdough breadbasket as an appetizer. Gideon asked for a plain iced tea but needed more time with the menu.

"What's good?" he asked Tempest after Lavinia departed.

"Everything. So no need for you to study the menu." She looked from his intense gaze to the torn scrap of fabric. What had Cassidy been doing at Fiddler's Folly? How had she gone from being bitten by Abra to being stuffed inside the Knights' wall? The timing was even tighter than she thought. When she looked back at Gideon, his brown eyes were scanning the people around them.

"I feel like I should hypnotize you," said Tempest, "to see what else you remember from that morning when we found Cassidy. You're so observant that you might have seen something else."

"You can't really hypnotize people, can you?"

Tempest raised an eyebrow as she pocketed the plastic bag with the fabric. "Let's see if we can get something out of your mind without it."

"I saw you take the ripped scrap of fabric."

"I wasn't trying to hide it. If I was, you wouldn't have noticed. What else are you observing right now? I expect some seriously Sherlockian answers."

"Then you'll be disappointed. I don't know what you ate for breakfast, if you have dirt on the treads of your shoes that indicates what route you took to walk here, or if you've recently returned from Afghanistan."

"Like John Watson."

"What I can tell you is that you thought for a second that the guy in the slate gray shirt recognized you and it made you apprehensive, that you don't like tomatoes, and that your favorite charm on your bracelet is the fiddle."

"Two out of three. Not bad. You're good at observing people observing other people, but how did you know about the tomatoes? I didn't ask her to hold any tomatoes. I just ordered the sourdough breadbasket."

"You skipped ordering what was clearly the appetizer you wanted—the bruschetta—and got the plain bread instead.

Because you didn't want to be a person who was a fussy customer."

"You're good, Mr. Torres. But the fiddle isn't my favorite charm. You're right, though, that I'm thinking about it now." She hadn't been aware she'd either looked at it or touched it, but she must have, since it was definitely at the forefront of her mind. Not telling the people closest to her that she might be losing her mind was weighing on her. But now that Ivy had forgiven her, maybe she could confide in her. "Thank you."

"For what?"

"Ivy. For getting us together to make up. Oh, and that delicious *ube* cake you left for us."

His face broke into a grin. "My mom sent me home with a huge coconut *ube* cake when I visited my parents last week. She's a chef, so when she creates a new recipe, she makes it like eight different ways. My dad casually mentioned he was thinking of his sister's *ube* cake from back in the Philippines, so my mom took it upon herself to learn to bake it. She's French, and my dad is Filipino."

"I saw a classic baby blue Renault parked outside the café just now that was also near the Knights' house. Is that yours?"

He nodded. "The stone carver I apprenticed for in France when I was a teenager gifted it to me when his vision no longer let him drive. I can't imagine owning a modern car with a computer inside. It's not a practical car, and costs me way more than I can afford, but I love it."

"You grew up in France?"

"We lived for several years in both the Philippines and France before moving to California, but I was too young to remember much. I spent nine months back in France for an exchange program when I was sixteen, and secretly did that apprenticeship on the side. These days, my only languages besides English are Tagalish and Fragalog."

Tempest returned his grin. "A mash-up of Tagalog and English, and French and Tagalog."

"People in both France and the Philippines look at me like I'm crazy when I try to have a proper conversation in their language."

"My grandmother," said Tempest, "says some people don't think in language. They think in art. When she came to my show in Vegas, she told me it must run in the family. My grandfather says he doesn't get it, but he does understand the language of food."

"Sometimes when he brings lunches to the crew, I forget he's a grandfather. He seems like a young soul, and he insists on riding his bike to bring us lunch when we're on a job." Gideon paused. "I know about the curse. I know his older brother died."

"The eldest. The curse kept on following the line."

"You all kept the name. You're Tempest Raj, but it's your mom's surname."

"Indian naming conventions don't work like Western ones. At least they didn't used to, but a lot of that is changing now. My great-great grandfather didn't have what we'd consider a surname, but when he went to work for the British Raj, he added the Raj extension at the end of their names. It carried down the line."

"Did the rest of your grandfather's family keep on performing magic after he left?"

"I have a distant cousin who still practices magic with the family name, but the dynasty itself fizzled. There are more medical doctors than anything else these days. More than a century ago, that side of my family served as physicians to kings and princes in the Kingdom of Travancore—a South Indian kingdom before India gained independence and was divided into states."

"Where did the magic come in?"

"My great-great-grandfather Devaj loved magic ever since he was a boy. He was good, so he became a court magician as well." Tempest hadn't talked about this with anyone in ages. But there was something about Gideon's nonjudgmental face that made him easy to talk to.

"When Devaj went to work for the British in the north," she continued, "he took his family with him. The British asked them to perform, and their performances kept getting more and more spectacular—but also more dangerous. His eldest brother died while performing. They grieved but continued. Until Grandpa Ash's mother's eldest sister also died. Another tragedy. There were a few whispers about the family being cursed, for going to work for the British. But it wasn't really considered a full-fledged curse until Ash's eldest brother died."

She paused and took a deep breath. "And then my aunt. Grandpa Ash's eldest daughter. He'd never wanted his daughters to perform magic. But it was in the blood . . . Ash still loves magic, even though he won't perform onstage, and would be much happier if I wouldn't, either."

"I understand why you wonder if the curse is real."

"Five generations. That's it. The curse stops with me. I'm not going to let it get me. I'm going to find out what's happening."

Chapter 29

Lavinia's late waiter showed up in the form of Liam Ronan. Robbie's little brother gave them polite nods as he dropped off their teas and breadbasket. Tempest watched, impressed, as he maneuvered the heavy tray up the narrow stairs, filled with not only their drinks and appetizer, but food and drinks for two other tables of customers. When Tempest looked back to Gideon, he was looking at her with that intense yet easygoing look she was getting to know.

"You're not like I thought you would be," Gideon said.

"You're not like I thought *anyone* would be in this century. And I can't tell if we just complimented or insulted each other."

"I wasn't doing either. Just observing. And I won't judge you if you pull out your phone to look at something. I can tell you're itching to do it."

Tempest shook her head. "Only by habit. There's nothing on it for me to see anymore."

"I've gotta say, living without social media is pretty awesome."

"Only if it's by choice. Not when you're forced to do so because the media, as well as thousands of random people, including people I thought were my friends, believed I'd risk a horribly dangerous stunt for a little bit of extra glitz. It didn't take much prodding for people to say I'd only become a success because of my infamous family, or my looks, or because diversity was the 'hot new trend.'" She lifted her hands and made air quotes at the last phrase. "See? It's got me so rattled even thinking about it that I'm using air quotes. I hate air quotes."

She didn't know which accusation angered her more. She was proud of her talented family of illusionists, who happened to be a mix of cultures. But their fame and background weren't the reason she'd succeeded. "I know I'm as talented as any of the performers in Vegas. I'm not saying I'm special. I worked harder. I practiced more than anyone to get there. Still, I never fit people's preconceived notions of a magician."

"Did you even like Las Vegas?"

"That's not the point."

"So you didn't."

She didn't answer. How could she admit out loud that he might be right? After her first successful show, part of her felt like she was done, that she'd said what she wanted to say. She ditched all of the scripts she'd written for a follow-up, abandoning failed stories about the charms of her bracelet hiding gemstones, a giant tree house growing out of the sea, and a competition of magical fiddlers. They all lacked something she couldn't put her finger on.

"Perhaps," Gideon suggested softly, "Vegas isn't supposed to be part of your story. Aren't you even a little happy to be back home?"

"I miss my bed. I had the most comfortable mattress in the world, and now I'm attempting to sleep on poke-y, squeaky springs."

"That's all you've got? You miss a mattress?"

"It was a metaphor." Or at least it could have been a metaphor. But that's not what she'd meant. As her sore hip could attest, she really did miss her old mattress.

"Your dad is happy you're home. I am, too. I'm just sorry about the circumstances that got you here."

"Me too . . ." Tempest maneuvered the Houdini novelty penny between her fingers as she surveyed the café. A young man and woman at a nearby table were speaking to each other in Australian accents, drinking glasses of wine and nibbling on a pita bread and hummus trio appetizer.

She caught Gideon watching the oversize coin. "I'm sick of thinking about the past. Change the subject."

"Okay. No more talk of the past. This is the first day of your new life, Tempest Raj. Why don't you do a trick for me?"

Her eyelids hooded, Tempest's gaze bounced around the room. "All right. I've got it." She tilted her head toward the Australian couple and spoke softly. "How about I make them vanish?"

"Right now?"

"You asked me to do a trick."

"Very funny. It's not very friendly to go over and ask them to leave. If you didn't want to do a trick—"

"I didn't say that. But you need to understand something first. A trick is never just a trick. It's always a story. Always. That's the magic that makes an illusion work. I wonder which one it will be today . . ." She shook the charm bracelet on her left wrist, then focused her attention on each silver charm, one by one. "I feel the power in this one," she said finally. She held the top hat charm between the thumb and index finger of her right hand.

"Using this top hat and a bit of telepathy," she continued

in a whisper, "I'm going to make their table go topsy-turvy. I'm pretty sure it'll cause them to vanish at the same time."

"Only pretty sure?"

"One can never be too certain when it comes to the forces of nature and the universe." She winked at him and pulled a black silk handkerchief from thin air. She held it between her hands, high above the table, so the piece of cloth briefly blocked Gideon's view of the other table. "I'll let you say the magic word."

"What, like 'Abracadabra'?"

"That'll do." With a flick of her wrist, Tempest pulled away the silk handkerchief.

She turned around to see if the magic had worked. Sure enough, the table had flipped upside down, its solitary thick leg pointing toward the ceiling—and the couple had vanished.

Gideon swore. "What . . . Did you see that they were getting ready to leave or something?" He stood up and rushed to the upside-down table. "But that wouldn't explain the table . . . You were only holding up that cloth for a second or two. How—?"

"What's going on over here?" Liam set down a tray and knelt in front of the flipped table next to Gideon. The nearly empty dishes and wineglasses were resting neatly on the bottom of the table surrounding the leg, as if nothing had transpired.

"Did you see what happened?" Gideon asked.

Liam shook his head and frowned. "I didn't take those two to dine and dash." The frown turned into a grin as he looked more closely at the upside-down wooden table. "Or be big tippers." He picked up a one hundred dollar bill resting underneath an empty wineglass.

"Let me help you with the table," Tempest offered.

That snapped Gideon out of his stupor of incredulity. He helped straighten the table. "How did you do it?" He stared at Tempest with a wide-eyed expression of wonder.

She smiled enigmatically at him. "You already know," she said. "I'm the Tempest. You know what that means."

"Destruction follows in your wake."

Chapter 30

Tempest was getting into her jeep when Lavinia caught up with her.

She and Gideon had enjoyed a delicious dinner, sharing small plates of chickpea tagine, stuffed mushrooms, and veggie dumplings, only slightly dampened by the fact that Tempest refused to tell Gideon how the trick was done. But if Gideon was going to call her to an urgent meeting he refused to tell her the substance of ahead of time, of course she'd leave him baffled for a while.

"I'm glad I caught you." Lavinia handed Tempest a note.

For Tempest Raj—Meet me at Veggie Magic 9pm tonight. I know what happened.

Tempest looked around the brightly lit main street, busy with shoppers and restaurant patrons. "Where did this come from?"

"Someone called the restaurant right after you left."

"Who?"

Lavinia shook her head. "Katie took the call and wrote down the message. She said it was a bad connection, so it got cut off."

"Man or woman?"

"Is something wrong? This isn't referring to—"

"I doubt it." Tempest forced a stage smile, but really, her heart was racing and she felt her hand grip her keys more tightly. "I'd hate for a friend to think I got their message when I didn't. Could I talk to Katie?"

Tempest spoke to the hostess for five minutes, but the young woman (who happily told Tempest she was working at Veggie Magic while going to art school to become a fashion designer, after she caught Tempest noticing the multicolored folds of the asymmetrical skirt of her dress) couldn't tell Tempest much more than Lavinia had.

"Is this a joke from one of your friends?" the art student hostess asked. "Like one of those *I Know What You Did Last Summer* movies?"

"Why do you say that?"

Katie shrugged. The skirt of her dress created a rainbow of incandescent hues as it rippled. She really was quite talented. "I don't know? Like they were purposefully disguising their voice?"

"Did their phone number show up?"

Katie shook her head and pointed at the bulky black rotary phone that had been affixed to the wall next to the cash register since Tempest was a kid. The cash register had long since been replaced by a computer tablet with a slot for credit cards, but the old phone was still operational.

"They asked me to reserve a table for two," Katie added. "So if you'll be back to meet your friend, pick one and let me know? I know you just ate, but Manuel's peach pie is seriously to die for."

She'd better skip the pie.

☠☠☠

"I can't even." Ivy pressed her hands to her temples.

"It's not like I'm going to an abandoned warehouse at midnight." Tempest had talked herself out of those thoughts as she drove over to Ivy's house. "Veggie Magic is a popular restaurant that doesn't close until ten. It'll be crowded. I've reserved a three-person table in the most visible spot of the restaurant."

"Should we at least call Gideon or Sanjay?"

Tempest raised an eyebrow. "We don't need a guy to protect us."

"I was thinking safety in numbers, since they're the people who know you're investigating how Cassidy got inside the wall."

"Fair. I'll call Sanjay. You call Gideon. Unless he went somewhere on the way home, he should be there by now." She hoped. They only had a little over an hour.

Sanjay answered his phone, but Gideon didn't. Tempest gave Sanjay Gideon's address in Oakland and said to meet them there. She hoped they'd find Gideon working and ignoring his phone.

Tempest and Ivy arrived first. As she'd hoped, Gideon stood in front of a griffin sculpture in his workshop, a mallet and chisel in his hands.

"It's a terrible idea," he said.

"You'll be watching us from a balcony table. We called ahead and got you and Sanjay a reservation."

"Who's Sanjay?"

"Me." Sanjay appeared.

"We don't have time for awkward introductions," Tempest said. "Gideon Torres is the new guy working for Secret Staircase Construction, Sanjay Rai is a magician, The Hindi Houdini. You both are in my confidence that I'm looking into how Cassidy Sparrow came to be inside that wall."

"He is—?" both men said over each other. "I thought I—"

"We don't have time for this." Tempest pinched the bridge of her nose. "I need you two to be immediate best friends. You'll be our eyes and ears at Veggie Magic when Ivy and I meet someone who has information about the crime. We're perfectly capable of doing this ourselves, so the only question is whether you'll be our backup."

The two men sized each other up, then nodded grudgingly.

Sanjay and Gideon traveled to Veggie Magic separately, and Tempest and Ivy went in Tempest's jeep. "Let's take a quick detour back to my house," Ivy said. "It won't take long, since it's nearby."

"Why do we need to stop?"

"I've got pepper spray at home."

"We'll be in a public restaurant," Tempest pointed out. "Do we really need a weapon?"

It turned out it wasn't an option. Ivy threw another stack of clothes onto her bed from the dresser, then flopped down on top of them. "I swear it used to be in here. Why can't I find it?"

"It's fine. Remember, public place."

When they came down the stairs at Ivy's house, Tempest pulled them back.

"It's Preston." Tempest groaned. The bow tie he was wearing with a short-sleeved, bright yellow dress shirt could have served as comic fodder and ingenious misdirection if employed by a more skillful magician than Preston the Prestidigitator.

"Your Stan?"

"Yup, my stalker-fan's jeep is blocking mine."

"He has the same car as you?"

"He thinks it's a form of flattery."

"We can't get to your jeep without talking to him." Ivy grinned.

"Then why are you smiling?"

"I've got another idea."

They circled the back of the house to the other side, where Ivy's scooter was parked. Ivy tossed her an extra helmet and they jumped on the scooter. The engine sputtered to life, and they took off at the breakneck pace of twenty miles per hour.

At the slow pace, Tempest's laughter could be heard above the wind on their faces.

"I hope that's hysteria. I can't have you laughing at the Pink Princess." Ivy didn't need to shout to be heard.

"I don't think he saw us. He was too focused on my jeep. We're safe."

"We're not, though." Ivy brought them to a stop after they turned the corner. "I'd feel better if we had that pepper spray."

"I have an idea. How long will it take the moped to get to Robbie's house?"

☠.☠.☠

Robbie opened the door before they knocked. "You're in luck. I forgot Liam was working late so I put too much food on the grill. Want some dinner? No, that look on your face tells me you don't want dinner."

"Life is too weird right now, Robbie," Tempest said. "Could we raid the backyard?"

"Comfort browsing to feel like you're one of the Three Investigators, like when you were young?" Robbie asked as he led them around back.

"Not exactly," said Tempest. "Do you still have the mace you bought at an estate sale several years ago?"

Ivy's face crinkled. "He bought pepper spray at an estate sale?"

Robbie laughed. "She means a different kind of mace."

Robbie collected all sorts of cast-offs that he found at salvage yards, antique markets, and junkyards. In anyone else's hands, the items would certainly be junk. But to Robbie, they were treasures that could be repurposed into magic. He'd collected so much over the years that it looked like the backyard salvage yard of the fictional Jupiter Jones's uncle in the kids' books Tempest was still reading when Robbie came into her life. She'd loved to visit his house for the magical items she'd find hidden in the towering stacks in his backyard.

Tempest had last been there about a year before, at a summer barbecue when she was home for a visit. She recognized some of the items he hadn't yet found a use for. He had some cool new things, too, including a vintage tailor's mannequin and a clawfoot bathtub. She doubted Secret Staircase Construction would be hired for any bathroom renovations, but maybe he thought it would come in handy someday.

Robbie rummaged through the heap of junk that wasn't exactly junk until he found a rusty box. He lifted it out and removed a spiked metal ball attached to a wooden handle.

"No way," Ivy whispered.

"I've never found a use for it," Robbie said. "I almost forgot about it. Why do you want it? Is Darius working up a plan for a medieval dungeon secret room?"

"Something like that," Tempest murmured. "Could I borrow this? And do you have a tote bag it'll fit inside?"

With their makeshift weapon in hand, they headed out to meet their mysterious host.

Chapter 31

The Veggie Magic hostess, Katie, greeted them with a smile and led them to the table. A glance to the second floor confirmed that Gideon and Sanjay were seated upstairs with a view that included Tempest and Ivy's table.

"Good thinking to reserve a table," Katie said to Ivy. "It's crowded tonight. Oh, and I think there's something wrong with your phone? Or you were somewhere with the worst signal?"

"She thinks I'm the creeper who called?" Ivy whispered to Tempest once Katie left them with the colorful menus.

"I don't like this," Tempest said, staring at the empty third seat.

A shy waiter she didn't know fumbled with their menus before taking their orders. Tempest wondered if he was the same one who'd broken dishes the other day, or if Lavinia was giving multiple clumsy waitstaff a try.

Half an hour later, they'd finished their tea and were nearly done with dessert. It was half an hour until closing time, and their mysterious host still hadn't arrived.

"Do you think they spotted Sanjay and Gideon?" Ivy asked.

"You can't miss them. That was the point." But it had been

a terrible point. In assuring their safety in multiple ways—picking a central table, carrying a large bag with a medieval weapon, and inviting their friends to look after them—they'd scared their informant away. Tempest yawned. "I'm ridiculously tired."

Ivy snorted. "That's all we need. The murderer doesn't show up, and we end the night falling asleep. Dr. Fell would be terribly disappointed in us."

"We're terrible heroes, aren't we?" She yawned again. The ghostly fiddler was wreaking havoc with her sleep.

She jerked awake.

"Is she okay?" Lavinia stood over the table, speaking softly to Ivy.

Ivy laughed. "Can we get the check? Looks like it's past her bedtime."

"I'll send Stanley over with a dishrag, too. Looks like Tempest got some cherry cobbler on her wrist."

"I don't know if sitting on the back of my moped is the best idea," Ivy said. "Let's get Sanjay to drive you home."

Tempest could barely keep her eyes open.

She wasn't merely tired.

There was something wrong. Numb. Unable to move.

She was falling.

Deeper.

Into darkness.

The eldest child dies by magic.

Chapter 32

Tempest wasn't at the bottom of the sea when she woke up. She was in her bedroom. And she wasn't alone. In the stillness of early morning, she heard the sound of breathing that wasn't her own.

Sanjay was asleep, fully dressed aside from the absence of his shoes, curled on his side on the beanbag next to the bed. His bowler hat covered half his face, shielding his eyes from the bright sunlight streaming in through the window. His lustrous black hair didn't have the decency to have a single lock out of place after sleeping on a beanbag. An urge to run her fingers through that hair nearly overwhelmed Tempest. Instead, she tossed off the covers and kicked his foot. He grunted awake.

"Why are you in my room?"

He rubbed the sleep from his eyes and grinned at her. "Don't you remember?"

She hadn't thought to look at herself before waking him up. She flung her arm out to grab the sheet, but stopped when she caught a glimpse of her clothes. There was no need to cover up. She was still dressed in jeans and a T-shirt.

"You were so tired that I wasn't sure you could make it up

the stairs on your own." Sanjay scratched the stubble on his chin. "And you were rambling about ghosts and curses, so I thought it would be a good idea if I stayed."

"Thanks." She stepped across the key outline on the hardwood floor and disappeared into the bathroom, and immediately felt much more herself with clean teeth and cold water splashed on her face. She was glad to see Sanjay had made himself at home, using an extra towel and toothbrush from the supplies under the sink. Her left arm felt strange. *Huh.* She must have slept on it.

"How much sleep have you gotten in this past week?" Sanjay asked when she emerged. "And what's the deal with the new guy? You had *dinner* with him last night?"

Tempest stretched her shoulders. Something still felt off about her left arm. It wasn't the usual tingling sensation you'd feel if you'd slept on top of it. "Sanjay. Something's wrong."

"Of course something is wrong if you haven't slept in a week and you're going on dates with a strange man you hardly know."

"It wasn't a date. And even if it was, that's not what's wrong." True, she was still tired, but felt more well-rested than she had in days. Yet she was more and more certain something wasn't right.

Her bracelet.

She held up her arm.

"So many things are wrong," said Sanjay. "Starting with last night's wild goose chase."

"This isn't my bracelet," she whispered as the charms brushed against her skin.

"Now I'm certain you haven't been sleeping. That looks exactly like your bracelet. I know. You haven't taken it off in years. Are you having nightmares about nearly dying—?"

"We're *not* talking about that. I'm telling you something's wrong right now—"

"Stop changing the subject. I'm sorry. I didn't know how bad you were feeling, but it looks like you really need to talk about what happened."

"You know what happened." Tempest was vaguely aware she was beginning to shout. "I was nearly killed in a stage accident, most likely caused by a woman who's now dead. I'm only alive because an anonymous person helped me avoid drowning in front of a thousand people. And furthermore, my mom's ghost appears to be haunting me."

As the words she'd been holding back slipped from her mouth, a heavy weight lifted along with them.

Sanjay gaped at her. "This is more serious than not sleeping."

"I've been hearing her play the fiddle. But if you tell me I need to see a therapist, I'll scream." Maybe she did need to, though. The burden she'd been carrying felt so much lighter after having admitted what she'd seen and heard to Sanjay.

"Actually," he said, "I was thinking it means the killer is still trying to get at you. Which worries me more than anything."

Tempest stared at Sanjay for six seconds before bursting into laughter and jumping into his arms. They fell backward into the beanbag. "That's exactly what I needed to hear."

"You didn't think you were going crazy, did you?"

She let go of him and turned away.

"You did," he whispered. "You really thought—"

"Now that we can agree I'm not crazy, you have to listen to me about something else. I know why I was so tired last night. Someone drugged me."

Sanjay folded his arms. "Not very effectively."

"It worked well enough for them to steal my bracelet."

"Just because you're not crazy doesn't mean there's something wrong with your bracelet. It's identical—"

"Because this is the plastic reproduction we made as a prop for Cassidy."

Sanjay unlatched the bracelet and held it up to the window. The charms caught in the light like her original bracelet, but from the way he was lifting it up and down, she knew he could tell it was lighter than it should have been.

Tempest flopped down onto the bed and put her head in her hands. "That means *Lavinia* is the killer."

"Who's Lavinia?"

"The owner of Veggie Magic. She was the one who was concerned about cherry cobbler on my bracelet as I was falling asleep." Tempest groaned as she sat up. She'd known Lavinia since she was a kid.

Sanjay handed her bracelet back to her. "You really don't remember?"

"Remember what?"

"You were so tired you fell out of your chair. Several people helped you up."

"We were waiting for either a murderer or an informant," Tempest growled, "and I was so messed up that I *fell out of a chair,* and you didn't think to consider that I'd been poisoned?"

Sanjay scratched his stubble. It was clearly bothering him. She'd never seen him anything but clean-shaven. "In retrospect, I see your point. In our defense, we all knew you'd had a rough week—and a rough summer."

Tempest avoided his gaze as she inspected the plastic bracelet. It was a near-perfect replica, since she needed it to look the same from the stage. "You don't think someone killed Cassidy to get her copy of the bracelet, do you?" It made no sense.

Sanjay flipped his bowler hat into the air. It landed perfectly on his head. "The features of this custom hat took me years to perfect. It's a work of magical art." He removed the hat, and a second later the seemingly empty hat started to shake. An orange tree began to grow from the emptiness. Thirty seconds later, the tree was eight inches high with three branches of leaves and a full-size orange.

"Even something this magical isn't worth killing over." He tossed her the orange.

She caught the fruit. It was real. "Not to a rational person."

"Even an irrational person didn't need to kill her to get her bracelet. She didn't wear hers all the time like you do, right? Only on the stage. And why steal hers just so they could steal yours? They could have gotten your bracelet last night even if they didn't have the replacement."

"But then," said Tempest, "I would have known it was gone."

"You do know it's gone."

"But would they know I'd realize it was switched?" Was she overthinking things? "Maybe this whole thing is misdirection."

"Forget about the swap for a second, in that case. Get back to your bracelet itself. Why would someone want it?"

"Nobody else would want it. It only has sentimental value." *Her inheritance.* That's what her mom had called it.

Sanjay twirled a purple flower between his fingertips. "Are you sure about that?" As he spun the stem, the purple petals transformed into red ones. "Things right in front of us aren't always what they first appear."

Chapter 33

After Sanjay left to meet his team for a rehearsal before a show that night, Tempest called Detective Blackburn, only to learn that the detective was no longer involved in the Cassidy Sparrow case at all, since Las Vegas had been determined to be the crime scene. She was transferred to the detective at Vegas Metro, which did no good. He was still convinced Isaac was guilty, and that drama queen Tempest's stolen bracelet—if it really had been stolen, which he seemed loath to believe—was none of his concern. Neither was the scrap of fabric. It wasn't related to his nearly completed investigation.

Meet me at Fiddler's Folly? she texted Ivy.

"I can't believe I didn't realize you'd been drugged," Ivy said after she arrived.

They were in the secret room above Tempest's bedroom. Tempest stood with her hands on her hips as she looked at her idols and friends, immortalized in framed posters on the wall. What would Adelaide Herrmann do?

"It was probably a crazed fan," Ivy said. "Right? What about that Preston guy we saw at my house?"

"How would he know to call Veggie Magic to get me that message?"

Ivy considered the question. "He found my house. Maybe we didn't lose him after all."

Abra had been scampering around underfoot. He was currently happily curled up on Ivy's lap, and was displeased when she eased him off and stood up. He expressed his displeasure by chomping her shoelace.

"Bad bunny," Tempest scolded.

"Everyone knows this famous bracelet," Ivy said. "Maybe someone needed it so they could impersonate you."

"Don't make me say how far-fetched that is."

"Did you tell the police we saw Preston hanging around earlier?" Ivy asked.

"I told the Vegas detective, but he's not concerned about a fan who wanted a bracelet." Tempest wriggled the fake bracelet on her wrist. "The silver one is so much heavier. How could they have not realized I'd notice the difference?" She unlatched the bracelet and set it on the floor. Abra came over and sniffed it, but quickly grew bored.

"They really do look identical, though."

Tempest lifted the chain in her hand. The eight charms brushed against each other. The top hat, Janus-faced jester, handcuffs, lightning bolt, selkie, book with the title *The Tempest*, fiddle, and smallest of them all: a key.

"Why did they need my charm bracelet?"

She turned from the window and held them up against her classic magic posters in the background. So many of the charms were replicated in the posters . . . Spotting Nicodemus the Necromancer in his top hat, she pried apart the clasp of the top hat charm.

Ivy placed her hand on Tempest's. "Hold on. You're taking it apart?"

"I never would have done it to my real one, but this? This I can break. The only time I took off the other one longer than for a quick cleaning and polishing was when we made a cast so Cassidy's plastic stage replica could be identical. Because details matter. That's why I'm hoping my anal retentiveness has come in handy. If this is identical enough . . ."

"You think your mom might have left a clue for you."

"She referred to it as my inheritance. What if she meant it literally?"

Tempest lined them up, keeping the charms in the order they'd been placed on the bracelet before she pulled it apart. Top hat, Janus-faced jester, handcuffs, lightning bolt, selkie, *The Tempest*, fiddle, and key. "Not alphabetical."

"What if it's a cipher?" Ivy grabbed a pen and paper, and wrote the first letter of each word. "T. J. H. H. S. T. F. K. No vowels . . . but I didn't think it was a straight anagram anyway. But if they correspond to different letters, we just need the key."

Tempest held up the key charm. It was the smallest of them all. Strange, since a key was what her mom had always talked about.

"You know what I mean," Ivy said. "The *substitution* key."

"But if it's this type of clue, why would the person who stole it need the bracelet at all? *Either* of the bracelets. And if they wanted to take it away from me so I wouldn't figure it out, why give one of them back to me?"

As Ivy scribbled, Tempest rearranged the charms on the floor. She picked them up one by one, thinking about what her mom had always said. *This is your inheritance.* That was just one of her mom's stories, wasn't it? A way to remind Tempest that she was a key that could open any door to fit in anywhere she wanted to go and be anything she wanted to be.

She picked up the first two charms, the top hat and the two-faced jester. "The magician's hat would have looked good on you," she said, placing the top hat onto the head.

It snapped into place.

She gave it a tug and it immediately popped out, but she hadn't imagined the perfect fit. She popped it back on. The crown of the jester's hat fit perfectly into the grooves of the inner circle of the top hat, even in the plastic material.

Heart beating faster, she picked up each charm. The selkie's seal tail twisted in a circle. Tempest had always thought it was a stylistic choice, but what if . . . she tested the rod of the bolt of lightning. It twisted perfectly into the loop of the selkie's tail.

But what else could the lightning bolt fit into? She pressed it into the base of the jester's neck, but it fell right out. Was that because it wasn't the original bracelet? No, it just needed something else to hold it in place. The handcuffs, which were a mirror reflection of each other, two closed loops that looked like the hilt of a sword. They popped onto the top of the lightning bolt to hold it in place underneath the jester.

That left the key, *The Tempest* book, and the fiddle. The top of the book snapped into the bottom of the selkie's tail. The fiddle, the fiddle . . . Could it fit into the ridges of the closed book? Sure enough, the left half of the fiddle popped into the book, leaving the right half exposed. With the cut-out shape of a fiddle, it resembled the grooves of a skeleton key.

The charms themselves formed a key.

Ivy looked up from her scribbles and gasped.

"It's a key," Tempest said. She never would have known if she hadn't been willing to take the pieces apart. But now, she couldn't believe she'd been so blind.

You're a key that can open any lock, her mom had said. *This is your inheritance.* Words she had always thought her mom meant symbolically, because the charms were each related to things they shared. But what if it was more than that? The twenty-first birthday card her mom had given her five years ago, shortly before she vanished, didn't mention the charm bracelet leading anywhere.

But it did.

Emma hadn't planned on vanishing. She hadn't planned on not getting to tell her daughter the secrets of the charm bracelet key.

"It's real," Tempest whispered. "My inheritance is real."

"Your mom never told you anything about this?"

Tempest shook her head. "I don't know what it opens. Someone killed Cassidy to get her copy, so they could get my key without me knowing. The killer is ahead of me in getting to whatever this opens."

"Of *us*," Ivy corrected. "They're ahead of *us*."

PART II

The Key

Chapter 34

Tempest jumped onto the bed and traced the star constellation on the ceiling with her fingertips. The springs
squealed underfoot. She must have looked up at the
familiar key-shaped constellation thousands of times.

"What are you doing?" asked Ivy.

"We need to start searching somewhere. Maybe one of the
stars is a lock."

Ivy leapt onto the bed and snatched the key from Tempest's
hand. "You can't shove a plastic key into the lock, wherever
it is. It could break off. Let me make a cast with the materi-
als in the workshop."

"That'll take too long."

"A day." Ivy wrapped her hand around the key. "And you
can have the plastic version back in a few hours."

"Let me show my dad first. He might know—"

"I bet he's already gone for the day."

"I thought you weren't resuming work yet."

Ivy shook her head. "I think he didn't want to tell you, but
he's still repaying the favor of the guys he borrowed the fencing from."

Tempest let go of the key. She texted her dad to ask if he

could meet her at home for lunch as she followed Ivy to the workshop. While Ivy prepared the wax, Tempest took photos, just in case anything went wrong.

Ivy frowned at a message that popped up on her phone. "I need to get to work, but I can finish this later today."

"I'm sure my dad will let you stay—"

"It's not Darius. I really do have to go. Don't be *TSTL* before I get back."

Tempest couldn't help smiling as Ivy disappeared out the sliding door of the workshop. She'd try her best not to be Too Stupid To Live before her dad got home.

As it happened, she didn't have long to wait. Darius pulled up in his truck minutes after Ivy left. She tugged the workshop door shut behind her and met him in the driveway.

"Early lunch?"

"Your text made me nervous."

"Good. Tell me what this is." She held the plastic key in front of her father's face, but didn't hand it over.

"Is that a key?"

"You don't recognize it?"

"It looks vaguely familiar, but not exactly, you know? Where did you get it?"

"Tell me what's different about me." She spun into a pirouette and stopped with her arms outstretched and the key clasped in her left hand.

"That you're scowling at me. You never scowl at me. You know better than that."

"I'm not scowling." She stopped scowling.

"Got it. You took off your bracelet."

"Someone stole it when I was out with Ivy last night. They replaced it with this one."

"Who—?"

"I don't know who did it. It's complicated." She held up the key in her palm. "What's important is that the pieces of the charm bracelet form this key."

Her dad was silent for nine seconds as his gaze remained locked on the key. "I'll be damned. That's why Emma was so secretive when she made the charm bracelet for you."

Tempest blinked at him. "She was?"

"Let's get inside." He was silent until they reached the living room. Darius plunked down in front of the fireplace, looking like he'd just completed a marathon. "I thought she was distant because she was close to finding her sister's killer. I didn't know she made a charm bracelet that was also a key."

"Does it open a secret drawer with her research into who killed my aunt?"

The color drained from Darius's face. "You can't tell anyone else about this key." He took her hands and pulled her onto the couch next to him.

"You believe she was right, that Aunt Elspeth didn't die in a stage accident," Tempest whispered. She breathed in a new world, seeing her father in a new light. "I thought you were only humoring her. That you never believed—"

"I never knew what to think." He ran a hand across his face. "Coincidence? Murder across generations? A curse? I've never been superstitious. You know that. The premature deaths of your ancestors always sounded to me like accidents. They were performing dangerous stunts. I was never convinced there was a curse, or a personal vendetta against her family—until Elspeth's accident. Then I started thinking more seriously about it. A decapitation with a guillotine is macabre. It's also personal."

Tempest shivered as she thought of the guillotine falling on her trapped aunt's neck.

"That accident," Darius continued, "convinced your mom that someone was taking advantage of the legend of the curse to kill her sister. Because Elspeth never would have created a guillotine illusion herself."

"Because the Selkie Sisters would never perform any illusions with violence against women. No sawing a lady in half. No decapitations. No guillotines."

Darius shook his head. "But your mom hadn't been close to her sister for two decades. People change."

"Mom never told you what happened between them?"

"She didn't like to talk about it."

"You must have pressed at some point."

Her papa's gaze fell to his ring finger, where he still wore his wedding band. "Whatever happened," he said softly, "it's all in the past. I didn't want her looking for her sister's murderer. If Elspeth really had been murdered, it was too dangerous, and I told her that. That's why she stopped telling me about it. I should have been more supportive. I thought by trying to protect her that I was protecting you, but—" He broke off and wiped his eyes. "But that's all in the past. After she . . . after what happened that night when your mom disappeared, you were all I had left. I couldn't risk anything happening to you. That's why I encouraged you to throw yourself into magic to heal, instead of repeating her mistake of looking into who killed her sister."

"You knew more than you told me."

"I believed what I told you," Darius said. "I still don't know what's true, and what happened that night she disappeared."

Tempest thought about how they both always said her mom had "disappeared," not that she'd died. Even though they both knew that she had.

"What do Grandpa Ash and Grannie Mor think? Have they been lying to me, too?"

"None of us are lying. We're saying that the most important thing is keeping you safe. Whatever happened, we've all still got each other now."

Grandpa Ash always said that even though he and Morag had lost their daughters, they'd gained a son and a granddaughter. Tempest studied her papa's face, still moist around the eyes. "You're not going to help me figure out where this key leads?"

"I don't think I ever want you to find out."

"You're scaring me, Papa."

"Good."

She forced a laugh, but it fell flat. "What have you done with my cheerful, fatherly papa?"

"Promise me," Darius said. "Stop trying to figure it out. And tell no one."

Tempest stopped herself from telling him she'd been with Ivy when she discovered the charms formed a key. She knew she could trust Ivy, so there was no need to give her dad more to worry about than he already had. "How can I pretend I never realized the charms form a key?"

"I lost the love of my life to this curse—whatever it is. So *no*, I don't *want* you to let it go. But I *need* you to. I couldn't bear it if I lost you, too."

"Nothing is going to happen to me."

Darius ran a hand across his face and shook his head. "I thought the same thing when I was your age."

"I really will be careful. I just need to figure out where to begin."

"This isn't one of your plays you performed in Las Vegas. You're not doing anything else about the murders and the curse. Let it go. Promise me you'll let it go."

Chapter 35

Tempest promised her dad she wouldn't leave Fiddler's Folly. She wasn't lying to him. After all, there was a good chance the key led to somewhere here at the house. Had Emma Raj left something in the mysterious hidden nooks and crannies of Fiddler's Folly for Tempest to find?

From the fireplace that led to a reading nook to the grandfather clock that led to the secret flower garden, she searched the house from top to bottom. She wanted to identify the hiding spot as soon as the stronger cast of the key was ready.

She searched more mundane locations as well, looking for anything that remotely reminded her of a key or any of the individual charms. A knot of wooden paneling resembled a bolt of lightning (sort of); a crack on the ceiling looked a bit like handcuffs (although she was pretty sure that crack had formed after an earthquake which was more recent than her mom's disappearance); and there was a copy of Shakespeare's *The Tempest* on two of the bookshelves in the house. A whole shelf in the secret reading nook was devoted to books on Houdini, but they were regular books, and nothing in the wooden shelf itself could serve as a lock for this key.

More realistic possibilities were the purposeful key shapes

that she and her mom had made together, from the stars on the ceiling of her room to the key-shaped segments of wood in the floor. But there were no apparent locks there, either. What was she missing?

Tempest knew, in truth, that she was missing a lot. There was no reason to believe the key opened something at Fiddler's Folly. She was grasping at straws. She'd searched the house because the opportunity presented itself, and she needed to rule it out. But she knew too little about what was happening.

She took a deep breath and spun on her heel. Her inheritance, which she had always thought was symbolic, might have been more than that. She touched off for a second spin. The repeated pep talk Emma always gave Tempest, telling her daughter she was a key that could open any lock. Another spin. The family curse that stole both her aunt and her mom. *The eldest child dies by magic.* Tempest came to an abrupt halt. She possessed the first physical clue to the mystery of the family curse, her only tangible clue.

Her mom had wanted to tell her something. But what?

Chapter 36

I shouldn't be awake for several more hours," said Tempest. "This isn't natural."

Darius shook his head at his daughter. "Getting up with the sun is the most natural thing in the world."

"In the Dark Ages."

"Hey, I gave you coffee."

Tempest took a sip from her travel mug. They hadn't woken Ash to make jaggery coffee, but Darius had heated milk to make her a café au lait.

"How is this even worth it?" Tempest asked. "The sun *sets* over the ocean on the west coast, so we don't even get an ocean sunrise. And we could have driven most of the way here instead of walking."

"Patience."

He'd timed it perfectly. They passed the wishing well she hadn't thought of in years and reached the crest as the dark sky ticked up a notch into soft light.

They stood in silence as the sun rose, filling the darkness with light. Feeling the warmth of the light and the power of the force so much bigger than herself caused her to forget to keep time. She had no idea if she stood basking in the first rays of dawn for ten seconds, ten minutes, or anything in between.

Tempest turned her head, but her papa was no longer next to her. She set down the mug of coffee and did a back-bend into the sun, then went to look for him after her feet touched the earth.

She found him sitting on a bench, finishing his coffee. She sat down next to him. The wood slats were dry, but cold through her jeans.

"You going to tell me the sunrise story again? Or is this your apology for being a dictator about me not investigating?"

"Maybe. Or maybe it's my way of keeping an eye on you until I can convince you I'm right. My command can't convince you to do anything. It never has. You have to convince yourself."

"Fine. Are you going to tell me the sunrise story or not?"

"I've told you enough times."

"I know. But it's a good story."

He kissed the top of her head and began the story Tempest had heard so many times she knew it by heart.

"When I was just starting out in construction," Darius began, "I was working a job in the Hollywood Hills. It was right before dawn, and I was the first one who arrived. I was leaning against my truck, drinking a cup of overpriced coffee, since I hadn't yet figured out it was smarter to bring what you needed. The sky had barely turned from darkness to a hint of light. But I swear it looked as if a spotlight was shining on her face.

"A lone woman, with lush black hair down to her waist, walking in the middle of the street. I didn't mean to go over to her, but it was as if I was compelled, like she was a siren on an asphalt sea. Her smile lit up the world when she saw me.

She told me she was lost, and it was incredibly important she reach the top of the hill with the Hollywood sign by the time the sun rose. She feared she was running out of time.

"I'd never met anyone from Scotland before, but of course I knew the accent from TV and movies. My first thought was that she was an actress coming down from a high from some Hollywood Hills party the previous night. I mean, what could be so urgent about a sunrise? But something made me believe her urgency. That it was real.

"I told her she wasn't going to make it by sunrise on foot, but she should get out of the winding road filled with drivers who took the turns too quickly. 'Is that your truck?' she asked. 'Will you drive me?' The guys would be there any minute, I knew, but I couldn't refuse her. Still, I told her it wasn't safe to get into the trucks of strange men. She said first of all I didn't feel like a stranger, and second and more importantly, that she'd been the one to ask me for a ride. She would have refused if I'd been the one to offer.

"So off we went. I took a couple of wrong turns—since your mom and papa grew up in the Dark Ages before GPS was common—but we made it as the sun itself appeared on the horizon. She knelt on the wet grass and ran her hands through the droplets of dew. I momentarily wondered if that first thought I'd dismissed had been right and she was feeling the effects of some drug, especially when she ran her wet hands across her face, as if she was washing it.

"When she caught my eye, my expression must have been obvious, because she laughed and laughed. When she'd recovered her breath, she told me the story of Arthur's Seat, the cliff above Edinburgh where legend says if you wash your face in the dew of the grass at dawn, you'll find your true love. It had backfired for her and her sister in Scotland, but she was hoping it would work better in her new adopted country. 'The legend applies to a king's hill in Edinburgh,' she said, 'and this was the closest to American kings I could think of.' She nodded toward the looming letters of the Hollywood sign.

"She introduced herself and I swear it felt like we were only talking for a few minutes, but in reality, it was hours. By the time I got back to the job site, I was fired. Emma felt terrible. She had no idea I was only a workman at the house. She thought a guy who looked like me could have lived in that house. She bought me breakfast as a first step in making it up to me. It was nearly lunchtime by then, so we went to an all-day breakfast place. She thought it was harsh for them to fire me for being late one day, so I confessed I was already a problem employee for wanting to do things my own way.

"We didn't come up with the idea for Secret Staircase Construction on the spot at that diner, but in the blur that was the first month of our relationship, we had it. Her getting me fired was fate, she said."

"Fate," Tempest whispered. Was that what was happening now?

"We need to let her go. We had her for more than twenty years. That has to be enough. In some form, the curse is real. *The eldest child dies by magic.*"

As the sun rose and brought warmth to her face, Tempest couldn't bring herself to tell her dad that the curse had already come for her.

"I didn't take it seriously," Darius said, "and neither did your mom. But she tried to tempt fate, so it came for her. She wasn't the one who was supposed to die. You're not either—unless you mess with the curse."

Chapter 37

When they got back to the house, Grandpa Ash and Grannie Mor were on their way out to the supermarket to get food for a dinner party that night.

"What dinner party?" Tempest asked.

"There was so much sadness last week," Ash said. "Your gran and I were thinking the best remedy is to bring people together."

It turned out they'd invited everyone on the Secret Staircase Construction crew, plus Ivy's sister's family, so Dahlia would be coming with Vanessa and Natalie. Natalie asked if her new friend Justin would be there, so the guest list was expanded to include the Knights as well.

"It'll be a proper ceilidh," Grannie Mor had said with delight. A ceilidh, pronounced "kay-lee," is a Scottish social gathering. But that description only scratches the surface of its true nature. There would be music and storytelling in addition to food.

There was no way Tempest could talk them out of it without telling them she was convinced the police had the wrong man and she was investigating.

But now, before the ceilidh preparations began, was

Tempest's chance. Her dad had to get to a job site, and her grandparents would be gathering enough groceries for a feast. For at least an hour, she'd be alone on the entire property, not just the main house. Ivy had finished the stronger replica of the key that morning, so Tempest could search the rest of the structures for where the key led.

An hour later, her grandparents hadn't yet returned with groceries, but there was nowhere else Tempest could think to look. She lifted the wing of the dragon who granted her entry into her bedroom. She slid the soles of her sneakers slowly along each step, wondering if she was missing something, or if this was a wild goose chase.

One step before she reached the top, she froze as a solitary fiddle began to play.

The notes began so faintly at first that she wondered if she'd imagined it. Five seconds later, there was no mistaking the mournful ballad filling the air.

Tempest stumbled on the top step, catching herself with her left hand, and looked sadly at its charmless, naked wrist. She winced in pain as she pushed up with her wrist and stood in the center of her room. The music swelled.

Where was the ghostly fiddler? The mournful ballad was both everywhere and nowhere.

Cold dread thudded in her heart, spreading fear further into her body with each beat. She reached for her phone to make sure the music wasn't coming from there. But even before she looked at the screen, she knew it wasn't.

It wasn't even noon. The light from a bright summer sun shone through the trees. The darkness of night was half a day away. The ghost, or whatever it was, didn't care. It was emboldened.

"Stop it!" she screamed. "Or show yourself!"

The ghost fiddler did neither.

That was it. She wasn't going to sit passively by and wonder what could be done. She was going to get the truth out of her family about the family curse. They'd always been evasive about certain elements. She knew it hurt them to talk about it, so she hadn't pressed. But she needed to know.

Chapter 38

Tempest grabbed a deck of bicycle cards and fanned the deck. Cardistry wasn't exactly magic, but a magic-adjacent style of misdirection that created beauty out of playing cards, manipulating the cards into movable art that looked impossible. She was rusty, but the repetitive motions helped still her mind as she waited for her grandparents to return. It worked for a short time, until the flourishes became easier. That's when the thought crept back into her mind that the way they'd discovered Cassidy's body was a trick. The question was whether the body was supposed to be Tempest, or if it was staged there for her to find.

Grandpa Ash and Grannie Mor returned from the market not only with enough food to feed dozens of people—but also with Liam Ronan in tow. Ash had decided that Liam had a lot of potential, so he'd be helping with the cooking. Confronting her grandparents for details about the secrets they'd been keeping about the family curse would have to wait.

Tempest considered storming off to fend for herself in the main Fiddler's Folly kitchen, but who was she kidding? Now that her grandparents lived in the tree house, her dad never kept anything stocked in the kitchen at the main house. The last time she'd looked in her dad's fridge, she'd found two jars of pickles, a mason jar of Ash's homemade yogurt, a carafe of oat milk, half a *dosa* wrapped in foil, and five bottles of local craft beer. The kitchen cabinets held several boxes of cereal and bags of chips. If she'd planned on staying, she would have stocked up. But every day she stayed was a day longer than she'd intended.

Glancing at Liam, Tempest considered heading to Veggie Magic or simply making herself a bowl of cereal, until Ash said lunch would be freshly made tortillas, homemade refried beans, guacamole made in his mortar and pestle with extra jalapeños, and salad greens from the farmer's market. A "simple affair," he said. Tempest's mouth watered in the fragrant kitchen, so she decided she'd put up with Liam. As he served her a heaping spoonful of the caramelized onion refried beans with a smile, she was pleasantly surprised that Robbie's younger brother had flipped back to the good side of his personality she'd briefly witnessed. As long as he was in a kitchen, Liam seemed happy.

After lunch, she retreated to her secret staircase while Ash and Liam got cooking, and Morag went to her art studio to practice a couple of songs on the fiddle she planned to perform at the dinner party.

Tempest wished she could believe as they did, that everything was resolved. From her grandparents' perspective, if the police had made an arrest, then obviously the matter of Cassidy's death was settled. But Tempest knew that even if they were right—which they weren't—that didn't lay the family curse to rest, clear her name from Cassidy's sabotage, or save Secret Staircase Construction from financial ruin.

In her haphazard unpacking, she hadn't yet found her box of half-used notebooks. She hoped she hadn't lost them in the frantic move. But those story ideas wouldn't do her any good now. What she needed was a blank notebook. She found one in her old desk and spent the rest of the afternoon scribbling possible solutions. None of which made any sense. She was three pages from the end of the notebook and feeling a cramp in her finger when her phone buzzed with a message that guests were arriving.

Calvin and Justin were the first to arrive. Tempest took Justin to meet Abracadabra while Calvin followed Darius to the tree house deck.

"Natalie's Mamma Vanessa read us *Bunnicula*," Justin told Tempest as he pet Abra. "It's about a vampire bunny. Have you read it?"

"It was one of my favorites when I was your age."

"It's not fair that Natalie has two moms and we don't have *any* anymore."

"Life isn't always fair, but do you know what's *the best*?"

He shook his head.

"You and I," she said, "are both are lucky enough to have the best dads on the planet."

Justin was silent for a moment before a smile crept to his lips. "Can I have a glass of water?"

"Of course." Tempest put Abra back in his hutch and led Justin toward the tree house. Because of the thick trees and slope of the hillside, it wasn't clearly visible from the tower. She pointed. "The kitchen is in the tree house."

He ran ahead of her, kicking up dirt behind him. "Is this a puzzle too?" he asked at the tree house front door. The gargoyle knocker grinned down at them.

"Far too easy for you."

In the kitchen, he asked her for a container of sugar along with the water.

"There's fresh apple juice if you'd like something sweet."

Justin shook his head and laughed. "No, silly. I need the sugar. You'll see. Our moms were like this sugar. You can see them when they're alive, and their love for us is the sweetest. But then—" He set the glass and jar on the counter and scooped a spoonful of sugar into the water.

As the crystals dissolved, Tempest saw where this was going. Someone had taught her this lesson when her aunt died. At sixteen, she'd been too old to appreciate the sentiment, but it made her smile to see the happiness on Justin's face. The stainless-steel teaspoon clanged against the edges of the glass as he swirled the sugar into the water.

"After our moms died, we couldn't see or touch them anymore, but they're like the sugar. They're still there with us, but their sweetness is diverse."

"Diffuse?"

"I said that, Ms. Raj!" Justin giggled and handed the glass to Tempest. "Taste it."

She sipped not only the faintly sweet liquid, but the memories of her mom that were now living through her. She smiled as her grandmother joined them in the kitchen. Like Tempest's mom, Morag had a pixie-like countenance. It wasn't only their small size, but something mischievous in their eyes.

"I hear you like riddles, young man," said Grannie Mor. "Do ye ken the faerie folk?"

Tempest was never sure if her grandmother's Scottish accent grew thicker on purpose when she began to tell a story, or if it was unconscious, absorbed from her childhood experience of hearing her elders telling her the same stories she was now telling herself.

Justin nodded. "Faeries are like Tinker Bell."

"Faeries from my homeland are much, much bigger. And

much more mischievous as well. It was a particularly mischievous faerie who's in the riddle of the bridge."

Justin's eyes grew wide. "The riddle of the bridge?"

Morag nodded and looked wistfully into the trees. "In a land far away, where trolls and faeries roam the land, and selkies swim in the sea—"

"What's a silkie?"

"Ah! A selkie is a beautiful woman, but she's also a seal when she's in the water. She's drawn to both the land and the sea. So in this far-off land, faeries have magic, but they *didnae* give away their magic for free. People have to give them something in exchange. In a small town, much smaller than Hidden Creek, the townsfolk needed a wee bridge. One of the builders, he *wasnae* so experienced in laying bricks. He uttered a curse, which is a dangerous thing to do! With his curse, he accidentally asked the help of the faeries. A faerie complied, but you know faeries never give away any of their magic for free. In exchange, if ever more than three people crossed the bridge at the same time, their souls would be taken to the land of the faeries."

Justin gave Grannie Mor the side-eye. "Only three people?"

"Only three. So here's where the riddle comes in. One night, a blacksmith, a baker, and a candlemaker crossed the bridge. They were claimed by the faeries. Why?"

"That's only three people," Justin said slowly. "So . . . one of them was carrying someone."

"Smart lad." Grannie Mor's eyes crinkled as she grinned. "But no, none of them were carrying another person. Keep thinking."

The dinner party was far bigger than expected. Tempest shouldn't have been surprised, since her grandmother had called it a ceilidh. The guest list was too big for everyone to fit on the deck, so the crowd split up into smaller groups. Calvin, Gideon, and Dahlia learned they were all history buffs, and when Calvin learned about Gideon's sculptures, Darius suggested they show him the workshop, which still had one of Gideon's creations that would be given to a client soon. Robbie volunteered to help Grannie Mor with a broken easel, so the two of them disappeared into her downstairs art studio. Ash was chatting with Ivy and Liam in the kitchen, and Vanessa was watching the kids in the breakfast nook.

Tempest stood alone at the gnarled tree-branch railing of the deck, listening to the laughter and chatter. A figure stepped into the trees—a figure holding a violin.

Tempest held her breath, but it was only her grandmother.

Morag lifted her bow to the strings, and Tempest let out her breath in relief that the song was nothing like her mom's ballad the ghost had been playing. Her grandmother's fingers were knotted with age, but you'd never know it from the beautiful music or the powerful paintings that emerged from those fingers.

Robbie joined Tempest on the edge of the deck. "You look tired, Twirls."

Tempest rested her head on Robbie's shoulder. "It's been a long week."

"She plays beautifully. Like your mom."

Even though the song was so different from that of the ghost, Tempest couldn't help but be transported back to her room, where she'd seen her mom's image out of the window and heard her mom's fiddle. She knew it couldn't be real. What she didn't know was whether she'd imagined it all, or whether someone was trying to unsettle her.

Vanessa found Tempest and Robbie out on the deck. "Have you seen the kids?"

"I thought they were inside the kitchen with you," Tempest said.

"I left them in the breakfast nook for a minute when I went to the bathroom. When I got back inside, they were gone."

"It's a nice night with good music," Robbie said. "They probably went outside like the others did when Morag began to play the fiddle."

The three of them headed downstairs. Tempest wasn't the least bit worried—not until she reached the bottom step.

She knelt and scooped up a toy that had been abandoned on the step. Justin's robot. Next to it lay a joker playing card.

The kids were gone, leaving behind the playing card Tempest had given Justin to fight monsters.

Chapter 39

The party disbanded as everyone searched for Justin and Natalie. Rationally, Tempest knew their disappearance wasn't connected to the curse. Yet the sight of the joker card lying abandoned on the step made her fear the worst. Shaking off the unhelpful thought, she reminded herself what it was like to be that age. They were most likely playing a game.

Tempest searched the main house, in case they were playing in any of the secret passageways. Ivy investigated the nooks and crannies of the Secret Staircase workshop. Grannie Mor checked the tree house. Outside, Justin's and Natalie's parents went in different directions in the woodland hillside, while Liam and Robbie followed the fencing to look for any gaps. Ash and Darius went to knock on doors of nearby houses, since they knew the neighbors.

Tempest ducked her head as she stepped from the empty secret garden through the cherrywood grandfather clock. Setting foot in the kitchen, she found herself face-to-face with Liam.

He held Abra in his arms. "I found this little fellow. Do you know if he knows how to follow a scent?"

"That's not a bad idea," she grudgingly admitted.

They found Justin's robot for Abra to sniff, then set him down on the doorstep. Abracadabra looked from Tempest to Liam, then hopped inside the house, toward the fireplace.

"Is there something behind there?" Liam asked.

The hearth looked like any other dormant fireplace, though perhaps a bit large for the small living room. A brick backdrop and a few logs were visible beyond a fire screen, which was flanked by plaster plinths and a mantel with crown molding. For the entire time Tempest had grown up in the house, they'd never once lit a fire. Because it wasn't really a fireplace. Instead, when you pushed aside the fire screen, you might notice that the bricks were only a painting of bricks on lightweight plywood.

Tempest lifted the rearmost log. The left side lifted, but the right side stayed firmly affixed. Its lever activated, the faux brick panel slid open and revealed a secret room. Normally the sight of this particular room gave her a delightfully nostalgic feeling. Now, all she felt was anxiety. Had the kids made their way here?

Abra hopped over the stack of logs and scampered inside.

"Wow." Liam bent forward and followed the bunny.

If you used standard measurements, this was the smallest secret room in the house. Only six feet wide in each direction, but the walls stretched two floors high, up to a slanted skylight that let in natural light. Bookshelves lined two of the walls from the floor almost the entire way up to the ceiling twenty feet above. A built-in ladder rested in the corner between the two shelves, and two comfy armchairs were tucked into the opposite corner, with a small table between them, large enough for two cups of tea.

"Empty," Liam muttered. "Bad bunny."

"Natalie?" Tempest called. "Justin?"

"I get it that this is a magical house, but there's really no-where they could be hiding in here. Unless there's a secret-secret room beyond this." He kicked the claw-foot leg of the closest armchair. "Is there?"

"Not exactly." Tempest bolted up the steps of the ladder. Higher and higher—until she disappeared.

Liam swore. Abra thumped his foot in protest of his agitated voice.

Tempest poked her head over the side of the bookshelf on the left. "They're not here." On top of the bookshelf on the left was a recess of about four feet. The nook she'd named "Hag's Nook" after a classic mystery novel had been one of Tempest's favorite hiding spots. She leaned back from the edge as she sneezed. A layer of dust covered the area. Nobody had been up here in years.

Or had they?

Tempest hadn't made a second set of tracks through the dust with her hands and knees, had she? She'd climbed over the edge so quickly that she hadn't been paying attention to the layer of dust.

"The bunny is on the move again," Liam called from be-low. When she looked over the edge again, both he and Abra had vanished.

By the time Tempest reached the floor, neither one was in sight, but a moment later she heard Liam's voice coming from the kitchen.

"I don't think Abra is cut out to be a drug sniffing rabbit." Liam was crouched in front of Abra, who was scratching at the grandfather clock with his fuzzy gray-and-white paws.

"I bet he smells some of the things that grow in that back garden. This idea was a bust."

"Hey, I tried."

"I didn't say you didn't."

"You could at least be civil."

Tempest took two deep breaths. "We're wasting time. I already searched the rest of the house. We should get back outside to help the others."

As they stepped outside, Tempest's heart sank. A pile of clothing lay a few yards away. Liam was the first to reach it.

"A bedsheet?" He held it up.

"There's a spot of paint. I bet it's one of the sheets my grandmother uses to cover things in her art studio."

"Then why are you still standing there if it's not a real clue?"

Tempest tossed the sheet to the ground. She could see Calvin and Robbie from where they stood a few dozen yards away, close to the fence where the property line ended and the hillside turned into even steeper woodland. "What did I do to offend you? Abra is usually a great judge of character, and he likes you. I did, too, when you came to my show a couple of years ago."

His expression was more resigned than malicious. "You always had everything handed to you."

She stared at him. He was serious. "What are you talking about?"

"The fame. The show. You're from a famous family. Even your house has a name instead of a regular street number! Who *does* that? It's not fair for the rest of us to have to start with nothing. You had everything handed to you, but you still got greedy for more."

It wasn't the first time she'd heard that the only reason she'd gotten a headlining show was because of her infamous family. The assertion certainly had a kernel of truth.

Her family had been wrung through the press because of their personal tragedies.

If that made people inclined to give her a chance, she'd take it. It's what you did with an opportunity that mattered. Tempest worked harder than anyone: perfecting her moves, spraining countless joints, and working herself past the point of exhaustion.

"If a producer thought my mom's disappearance would be good publicity, then sure, I wasn't going to turn down an opportunity to let people find me and the story I wanted to tell them about my mom and aunt. You've seen my show. You know the whole *point* is not that I wanted to tell the world my mom's story—but to give her the happy ending it doesn't seem like she'll ever get."

Liam snorted.

"I never wanted Vegas. I wanted my mom back. If I couldn't have that, then at least I could do what I do best in a way that let me share her story with the world. Now if you're done being petty, let's go help the others."

They climbed the hillside in silence for a few moments. "I didn't do those things they accused me of this summer, you know," Tempest said.

"I know. My brother believes you, so I do, too."

"You do? I thought—"

"You thought that's what I meant that you got greedy? Nope. You got greedy when you rewrote your first successful show—the one I saw—to make it even bigger."

"That's not why I changed it. I was under contract to write something new. The first new script I wrote was about my charm bracelet—before realizing I was falling into the same pattern of writing a story about my mom. She was still the center of the new script, even though this one was fiction.

A story about rubies hidden inside of the silver charms." She laughed without humor. "I based it on a real treasure one of Sanjay's friends found that was linked to both Scotland and India, so I liked the idea of fictionalizing those rubies. But even though it was only a made-up story, it involved my mom too much . . . Liam, are you okay?"

He stumbled over the root of a tree.

Refusing her offer of a hand, he brushed the dirt off his knees and kept going. "I'm just worried about the kids."

They'd nearly reached the others.

"There's a gap in the fence right here," Robbie called. "Big enough for the kids. Maybe Ivy can fit through here?"

He was at the top of the property, the section of chain-link fencing leading up the hillside. There was no path, so when Tempest walked up to the top of the hill, she'd go around to the side of the house to meet up with the proper path. But Robbie was right. There was a gap in the fence big enough for two little kids to fit through. Everyone aside from Darius and Ash, who were still canvassing the neighborhood, congregated at the spot.

"I can fit, too," Grannie Mor said. "The rest of you take the path."

Tempest was already leading the way, while texting her dad where they were heading. "See you on the other side."

Three minutes later, the group converged on the path hikers used to climb to the top of the hill. Using their cell phones as flashlights, they continued up the hill for five minutes, calling for the kids.

"Mamma V! Mommy D!" Natalie's voice carried through the trees.

They found the kids at the wishing well. Natalie was showing Justin how to throw a coin into the well and make a wish. Tempest texted her dad to let him know they'd found the kids safe and sound and they could stop knocking on neighborhood doors.

Vanessa scooped up Natalie in her arms, and Dahlia hugged them both. Calvin fell to his knees and hugged Justin tightly.

"Why did you run off?" Vanessa asked. "You could have showed Justin the well another time."

Natalie wriggled in her mom's tight embrace. "We were following the ghost."

Chapter 40

The kids had seen the ghost, too. Tempest wasn't losing her mind.

"We thought we should follow him," Justin explained.

"*Him?*" Tempest repeated. They were standing on the hillside next to the well. Tempest's red sneakers were muddy, matching Justin's hands and Natalie's knees.

"You don't follow strangers, J," Calvin said. "You know better than that."

"We thought he was part of the riddle," Natalie said, as if that explained everything.

Justin nodded. "Aren't there ghosts in faerie lands?"

Grannie Mor stifled a sob. Tempest knew she'd never forgive herself if her riddle had led to something bad happening to the kids.

Ivy caught Tempest's eye. "Should you tell—"

"What was he doing?" Tempest asked the kids, ignoring Ivy.

They looked at each other. "Dunno," Justin said. "Haunting?"

"We were playing in the kitchen with Mamma V," Natalie said, "but she went to use the toilet."

"Natalie, honey," Dahlia prompted.

Natalie smiled and looked from Dahlia and Vanessa to the

crowd hanging on her every word. She was clearly enjoying the spotlight. "We looked out the window and saw the ghost walking over to the big house."

"It was just like in a book," Justin said. "She ran down the stairs, so I followed."

Tempest knelt next to him. "Why did you go into the hills if the ghost was heading toward the house?"

"When we got outside," Justin said, "we only saw his ghost light."

"He was walking up the hill on the other side of the tree house," Natalie added.

Justin frowned. "But I think we were wrong. When we found a spot to get through the fence, we looked for his light again. We found it, but it wasn't the ghost light."

"We only found these." Natalie pointed up at one of the street lamps lighting the hillside path.

"You weren't scared?" Dahlia asked them.

Natalie giggled. "He wasn't *really* a ghost, Mommy D."

"How did you know that?"

"Because ghosts aren't *real*." She giggled again. This time Tempest was pretty sure it was because Dahlia was tickling her, trying to make sure she wasn't scared.

"Only closet monsters," Justin added. "They're real. But the ghost was wearing a Halloween costume."

"Did you recognize him?" Calvin asked.

The kids looked at each other, then shook their heads.

"You sure you're okay?" Dahlia brushed a lock of Natalie's hair out of her face.

"It was an adventure!" Natalie said. She wriggled again. Dahlia set her down and rubbed her lower back.

Justin nodded in agreement. "Natalie ran too fast, so I couldn't go back to get my robot. I think I dropped him on the stairs of the tree house. Did you find him?"

"We did." His dad handed him the sturdy toy. "But we really need to understand why you'd run off. That's not like you."

"He was in a costume, and we're at a party. It was part of the party. Wasn't it?"

"Did anyone dress up as a joke or something?" Calvin asked. "We won't be upset. We know you didn't mean for the kids to follow."

Nobody admitted it.

"One of your deranged fans must've leapt over the fence," Morag said. "We need to call the police."

"How do you know it was a man?" Tempest asked. "You kept calling the ghost a 'he.' But you never saw his face."

"He was really tall," Justin said.

"Can you tell me more about the costume?" Tempest asked.

Justin looked confused. "We already told you."

"You did?"

Natalie nodded. "He was dressed like a ghost. Mamma V, stop fussing!" Vanessa was inspecting Natalie's dirty knees.

"Do you mean a white bedsheet?" Dahlia asked.

The kids nodded in agreement.

A white sheet? Was it the abandoned sheet they'd found? What kind of costume or ghostly apparition was that? A bed sheet didn't fit the pattern.

☠☠☠

"A ghost!" Morag shook her head, sending a perfectly coifed strand loose. All of the guests had departed, and the family was alone in the tree house kitchen. "Kids have the most marvelous imaginations."

"But we don't know if he was harmless," Darius said. "I'll strengthen security and let the police know."

"That won't help," said Tempest. "I've seen it, too."

Her father and grandparents stared at her for six long seconds before anyone spoke.

"A ghost?" Her dad flexed his muscles, as if readying himself to fight an invisible force. "You've really been seeing ghosts?"

"Just one. And it's mainly the fiddle music. Mom's fiddle music."

"You didn't think to tell me?"

"I did—"

"You said it was an intruder."

"Because I know it has to be. Someone is messing with me. They didn't physically harm me, so I didn't want to worry you more than I already had."

"You didn't want to *worry* us?" Ash sputtered.

"This conversation isn't about me," Tempest insisted. "We've all been keeping secrets from each other. All of us. That stops now."

She took a deep breath, shook out her big hair until it swayed around her like the windswept tendrils of a mythical selkie, and stood with her shoulders squared. She was The Tempest.

"It's time," The Tempest said, "to talk about the family curse. No more secrets. We've all lost too many people we care about. Something is going on, and we can only figure it out if we all tell each other what we know about the curse. I need to know what you're not telling me about my mother."

Chapter 41

I t was now after eleven o'clock. Moonlight shone through the swaying branches of the walnut, oak, and eucalyptus trees at Fiddler's Folly, telling stories in shadows on the sloping hillside. Ash had brought them all together over a midnight snack. They'd stuffed themselves at the dinner party, and this was set to be a tense discussion, but still, her grandpa couldn't resist feeding everyone.

The string of lights installed for the dinner party still hung from the outdoor deck, illuminating the yard. Because of the sensitive nature of their discussion, and the knowledge that someone had been spying on them, they weren't meeting outside. Instead, they were gathered in Morag's art studio on the first floor of the tree house.

Aside from two floor-to-ceiling windows flanking the front door, the windows were placed high on the walls, allowing light to filter through the trees and hit the studio differently at every hour of the day. Beneath the windows, one wall was lined with storage shelves, one with racks for paintings, and one with mounted paintings. Grannie Mor's workspace was made up of two massive wooden tables in the center of the studio, one of which rested against the back of the stairs.

Her fiddle rested on a section of the larger table that wasn't covered in paint. There weren't enough chairs for everyone, but Tempest and her dad had too much nervous energy to sit still anyway.

"We've all been keeping secrets," Tempest said. "Not just me. Tonight, we get everything out into the open. I'll tell you about the ghost. But first, I need to know about the curse you've been lying to me about."

"Oh, the curse is real," said Morag. "But not in the way you think."

Ashok took her hand in his, and nodded for her to continue.

"You know the facts that can be written in a family tree. Ashok's grandfather—your great-great grandfather—was born in 1880. Devaj was a physician from the Kingdom of Travancore. He fell in love with magic, and got his siblings interested in it as well. Wishing to see more of the world, as a young doctor he went to work for the British. He was good. He performed magic shows for the British and received invitations for more. He brought his wife, his elder brother and wife, and his unmarried younger brother, to perform with him. It went well for several years, until—"

"*The eldest child dies by magic,*" Tempest whispered.

"That's where it began. But nobody thought so at the time. This was the first generation of Raj magicians. Unlike magicians who came from families with a tradition of performing magic, they had nobody to learn from. They were still learning the craft."

"Making mistakes."

Morag nodded. "Your great-grandmother was born in 1919. Her eldest sister was born several years before. Wanting to be seen for a talented person, not a woman who should be married off, she tried to replicate the same dangerous trick that had killed her uncle."

"I've never heard this."

"My mother told me one story," Ash said, "but other relatives told me others. It was true that my aunt had been killed, but I never learned exactly how it happened. It was covered up, because it was too ghastly to share."

"That's why I made these paintings." Morag nodded toward the wall with paintings of dangerous acts, her blue-gray eyes shining brightly. "The trick itself is inconsequential. The point I'm getting at is that Devaj's eldest brother died in an accident. His eldest daughter fought convention and tried too hard to distinguish herself. She knew she'd never have a good marriage because she was too dark-skinned for a good match—so she risked too much."

"And killed herself?"

"We don't know if it was on purpose," Ash chimed in, "but she clearly took a risk. That much I know. The family didn't want to believe such a thing was possible."

"Which is when the legend of the curse was born," Tempest said.

"Then Ash's older brother Arjun died mysteriously by magic," Morag said. "That was the only unexplained death— until . . ." Her lips tightened.

Darius squeezed his mother-in-law's shoulder and said, "Until Tempest's aunt Elspeth."

Morag laughed as a tear escaped and rolled down her cheek. "Elspeth was the impossible child. There was no controlling her spirit. She was always going to do what she wanted. Much like you, Tempest. It was the hardest thing in my life to lose her and your mother, but it was the greatest joy of my life to have them briefly. Elspeth didn't die of a curse."

"I thought," Tempest cut in, "Grandpa Ash believed—"

"He lost his brother when he was a teenager," Morag snapped. "It's natural that he believes in the curse."

"It's a curse," Ash said. "I don't pretend to understand the universe, but there is some sort of curse."

"Elspeth didn't die from a *supernatural* curse," Morag said. "She was murdered. I thought at the time that she'd died in an accident, reckless like her great aunt who'd died in India. Tempest, *your mother* was the one who believed it was murder. And she was right. That's why your mother was killed. Because she found out. That's why she'd been acting secretive leading up to her disappearance. That's what she was going to reveal that night she disappeared at the performance to honor Elspeth. She was going to name your Aunt Elspeth's killer. *They got her first.*"

Tempest felt as if the room was spinning around her. Her mom hadn't taken her own life. Her aunt hadn't died in an accident. They'd been murdered.

Chapter 42

Your mom and aunt's deaths don't have to do with a Raj family curse that originated in India five generations ago," Morag said to Tempest. "It's only the curse of two unsolved murders. It took Elspeth and Emma. It nearly took your life in Las Vegas when your show was sabotaged."

Tempest's lungs felt as if the surrounding oxygen was evaporating. Her limbs felt as if she was underwater. "You believe the sabotage to my show was related?"

"I don't know. But we can't take any chances with your life. That's why you need to stop looking for answers."

"You can't be serious. I can't stop—"

"You're going to stop." Morag stared at her coldly.

"I can't just let whoever killed Cassidy and sabotaged my show go free. Even if the story of the curse has been warped, it's still—"

"Why," said her grandmother, "do you think I'm so hard on you, Tempest? I love you more than anything. I can't lose you, too. None of us can."

Tempest saw her prickly grandmother in a new light. Morag was only cold to her when she was worried. Why hadn't she seen that before?

Was the current attack on Cassidy and Tempest related to her aunt's death and her mom vanishing? They all knew she was dead, but it was still so difficult to say the word out loud, even to herself.

"Eat," her grandfather said, holding up a platter of her favorite cardamom shortbread cookies under her nose. "You need energy."

She accepted a cookie only because she was shaking. He was right. She felt life flowing back into her as she chewed the sweet and spicy cookie. It grounded her and brought her back to the present.

"Now tell us about the ghost," Morag said.

"Not yet," said Tempest. "That's not the whole story. Nobody has ever told me why my mom left Scotland for California. There was a vague reference to a love triangle, but you all contradicted each other about the details. I knew it wasn't the real story."

Morag closed her eyes and took a deep breath before speaking. "Emma began to play the fiddle when she was young," she began. "They were both natural performers. Emma idolized her big sister. But she also believed her father's story about the curse. She wanted the Selkie Sisters show to be storytelling with music, but Elspeth knew that adding the story of the curse to a program of stronger illusions would draw crowds. Elspeth was the one who told the public about the curse."

Tempest had never considered it before, but of course someone must have told the press about it. "None of you ever told me that."

"Your mom didn't want us to," Darius said. "She wanted you to believe the simpler story that there was a love triangle that made her leave and come to California, not that she left because she didn't want to perform on a program that included the curse. She didn't want your life to be about the curse. Only when Elspeth died did everything change."

Morag looked out the window at the flapping tree branches before turning back toward her granddaughter. "Please, Tempest."

Tempest held up the charm bracelet key.

Her grandmother gasped. The lines on her face deepened. "Where did you get that?"

"You know what it's for?" Tempest's heart sped up.

Morag looked as if she'd seen a ghost herself. "No. But I've seen it before. It appeared in one of my old paintings I'd given her years before. Only . . . I didn't paint that key myself."

Morag rushed to her stack of paintings, flipping through the canvas sheets so quickly that one of them crashed to the floor. She didn't make a move to retrieve it. She stayed focused on the paintings until she found what she was looking for.

Pulling out a two-by-three canvas oil painting of the ocean, with shaking hands she set it onto the larger worktable. The painting depicted a lighthouse tower at the edge of a cliff. Morag pointed to one of the waves. A key had been painted into the water. *Tempest's key.*

"I saw this after your mother vanished," Morag said. "I didn't know what it was."

Tempest's mom had left it for her to find.

"This key is made from the charms of my bracelet. She *wanted* to tell me something. She joked that it was my inheritance, but what if it wasn't a joke?"

"What are you saying?" Darius asked.

"Did she rob a bank in Edinburgh? Is that why she had to flee? And the gold is waiting for me somewhere this key leads?"

"If your mom had wanted to rob a bank," Morag said, "I have no doubt she would have been successful. She could always pull off the impossible. Just like you."

"I'm going to do it, Gran. We can't keep living under the shadow of the curse. We can't keep hiding from this. It's time to lay the curse to rest."

Her grandmother nodded and wiped a tear from her eye.

"It's time," Darius said, "for you to tell us about this ghost. That's why you got me up the other night when I thought we had an intruder? You thought you were being haunted?"

She did, but that wasn't it at all. "Someone wants me to think I'm losing my mind. A person who doesn't want me to learn the truth about what happened to Cassidy."

"Cassidy?" Ash repeated. "The police arrested her boyfriend. The terrible man tried to get you implicated by bringing her body here, but he failed."

"That's the *easiest* explanation," Tempest said. "But it overlooks the most important thing."

"We never figured out the wall," Darius murmured. He began to pace. It must have been bothering him, too. He'd inspected the crawl space.

"Doesn't matter," Ash insisted. "That boy is a magician."

Tempest shook her head. "He's magician adjacent. It's not the same thing at all. He's a stagehand at a theater who gets other people to do most of his work. Gran? Grannie Mor, where are you going?"

Her grandmother walked stiffly away from them, her fingers gripping the edges of the canvas. She stopped at an easel with a lamp above it and clicked on the light.

"You can see the paint is different in another spot as well." Morag pointed at the key hiding in the waves. "This is a watercolor painting, but the key is oil. And look, so is the lighthouse tower's spotlight."

"Is it a location in Scotland?" Tempest asked.

Morag shook her head. "I painted this scene out of my imagination. It doesn't exist. I don't see how it could tell you where to use the key."

Or could it? Why did the shape of the lighthouse and its spotlight look familiar?

Chapter 43

Tempest didn't bother trying to get to sleep after that. She knew she'd just lie awake waiting for the ghostly fiddler to return.

Instead, she set off for Las Vegas.

Her manager, Winnie, would have a fit if he knew what she was doing. He and the lawyers were adamant that she wasn't supposed to talk to Isaac. Because of the threat of the lawsuit, she wasn't supposed to be in contact with Cassidy, Isaac, or anyone else who'd been involved in the show. At least not without an attorney present. But Tempest didn't want a lawyer here for this conversation. Not that she could afford one anyway. Just talking to Isaac would probably cost her as much as her jeep was worth, the one thing she'd never sell.

The drive south on Highway 5, cutting east at Bakersfield, would take about eight hours. It would give her time to think.

The closer she got, the more that night came back to her. How close she'd come to joining her ancestors. *The eldest child dies by magic.* It had shaken her more than she wanted to admit. That was the reason she hadn't fought harder to clear her name. When the first lawsuit against her was dropped and the insurance company paid out, she stopped fighting.

She lost her house because it was overly mortgaged and her producers had canceled the show.

She knew she'd prove them wrong and get back on her feet eventually, but as the distance between her and Las Vegas grew shorter and shorter, her foot eased off the gas pedal. What was she rushing toward?

She knew her family wouldn't realize she was gone until they noticed her jeep was missing the next morning. They would assume she'd gone to bed like they had.

Her dad must have noticed the jeep missing after he got up, because her phone began to ding as she drove through the Mojave Desert, at six thirty in the morning. She thought about ignoring it, but she didn't want Darius to call the police. She stopped for coffee and gas in Barstow, and texted him back while she sipped weak coffee that tasted even worse with the background smell of gas filling her car. *Safe and sound. Went for a drive to clear my head. Don't worry if I stay out for the day.*

Call me, Darius texted back immediately.

"You think someone kidnapped me and stole my phone?"

"After last night, I don't know what to think."

"I promise I'm fine."

"Where are you?"

"I told you, I went for a drive. Please tell Ash and Mor that I'm fine."

"I didn't tell them you were gone. Didn't want them to worry."

"And I don't want you to worry. Love you, Papa."

The skyline of the city she'd called home loomed on the flat horizon for a dreaded twelve minutes before she reached the jail.

She felt a confusing mix of emotions as she passed the

billboard announcing glitzy shows of all kinds. This was a fantasy world. Treasure Island. Venice. Paris. But it was all a veneer. A façade. Once you scratched the surface, it all fell away. Just like her "friends" had.

There *was* real magic here, though. Not only stage magic, though there was plenty of that. The magic of some of the happiest moments that had happened here. Brilliant performers transported their audiences, including Tempest, into a world where magic was possible. A world where Tempest's mom and aunt hadn't died. A world where the Raj family curse was only make-believe. That's what she wanted to give people. And she *had*. This place had enabled her to do that.

Isaac Sharp had shrunk since Tempest had last seen him earlier that summer. Taking a closer look, she realized he hadn't actually changed physically. His light brown hair was still cut in a more expensive haircut than he could afford. He hadn't lost his toned muscles from his daily trips to the gym. His crystal blue eyes were still hooded with that classic teen heartthrob look. But now, dark circles shadowed those eyes, his perfect posture had been replaced by slumped shoulders, and his hair was unkempt.

"I thought you weren't supposed to be talking to me," he said.

"You helped Cassidy wreck my show." She'd said it to him before, back when everything had gone down. But that was all a blur.

"I didn't." But his gaze didn't meet hers. He was lying.

"Why'd you kill her?"

"I didn't." He looked her in the eye now, and she believed him.

"You're an abusive jerk and a liar, Isaac, but I'm going to help get you out of here."

He scoffed, but held her gaze for the first time since she'd arrived. "Didn't you hear? I'm being held without bail."

She turned on her scowl. "I wouldn't bail you out even if they set bail." She didn't add there was no way she could afford it these days anyway.

"So you're going to make me magically disappear? Maybe fit me under your skimpy little jacket to stage a vanishing act from the Clark County jail?"

"I meant, you jerk, that I believe you that you didn't kill Cassidy."

His slumped shoulders straightened. He blinked at her, bewildered. "You do?"

"You're not the one haunting me."

"What?"

"Never mind. If you want my help, tell me what you know about my bracelet." She held up the plastic charm bracelet that had been swapped for her real one.

Isaac smirked.

"You know something."

"Maybe." He pressed his thin lips together.

Why had she ever thought he was the least bit attractive? The legs of her uncomfortable chair squealed on the concrete floor as she stood up. "Fine. If you don't want my help—"

"Wait, you're serious? You're, like, investigating?"

"What do you know about this bracelet?" She dangled it in the air in front of the glass.

His shoulders slumped even further. "I don't know anything beyond what Cassidy told me. How you were always saying it was your inheritance. It was a daily reminder of her jealousy that she didn't come from a rich and famous family like yours."

"My dad runs a construction business." A struggling one that she could no longer afford to help.

"Your mom's family was famous. That's how you got your shot. Not like me and Cassidy."

"That's why she wanted the bracelet? To hurt me?"

"What? She didn't want your stupid sentimental jewelry. She wanted the—" He stopped himself.

"I'm leaving if you're wasting my time."

"She wanted your show."

"I knew it!" That wasn't the answer she was expecting that moment, but it was the one she'd been waiting to hear for months.

"Cassidy thought she was as talented as you. She was pretty good. She could have done it through sheer will . . . God, I can't believe she's gone."

Tempest held her tongue and didn't say she knew he'd hit Cassidy. She needed him to open up, not shut down. "You knew about her plan to sabotage my show?"

"I didn't have anything to do with it. I'm not legally responsible. You can't blame—"

"If you had nothing to do with it, I can't very well blame you."

"But I could have come to you." He held her gaze. Was that genuine remorse she saw in his eyes?

"Why didn't you?"

"Why do you think? She was going to be rich and famous. We'd picked out a house. Much more tasteful than yours. White picket fence and everything. We were going to move in together."

"After she wrecked my show and got it for herself."

"That was the idea. But we didn't mean to—"

"You didn't mean to *what*?"

He placed his palm on the scuffed glass. "She never meant the stunt to kill you. Or anyone else. Trapping you underwater while the fire started . . . You have to believe me. That was never supposed to happen. She only wanted you to be delayed long enough so you couldn't put out the fire. Not to drown."

A white cold descended over her. The same cold she remembered from that night, soaking wet, only escaping because someone had realized she was still trapped in the water chamber. *Freezing cold, but surrounded by fire.*

Cassidy had impersonated Tempest and bought fireworks meant to start a fire, attempting to show how irresponsible Tempest was to add an unapproved and illegal stunt to such a carefully choreographed show. Cassidy had also tampered with the locks of the water chamber built to look like the ocean. Tempest should have been able to escape within seconds. Instead, she was under water for one minute and thirty-seven seconds. Until two strong arms had flipped open the lid and pulled her out.

As she stood soaking wet on the stage, encircled by flames, her savior had disappeared. Tempest had asked herself several times if he'd been there at all or if she had imagined him. None of her crew had stepped forward to claim responsibility for the heroic act, and a couple of members of the audience said they thought they saw someone from the audience jump up onto the stage when the fire began. But the person was never found.

The flames that ripped through the curtains were quickly extinguished, and the only injuries in the crowd were from people shoving each other, but those ten minutes had ruined her career.

"Are you really going to help me get out of here?" Isaac pressed his hand more firmly to the glass.

"No. I'm not going to help you. I'm going to help myself,

like I should have done when you two ruined me. But just like before, you'll do nothing but be swept along for the ride. So yeah, you'll get out of here because of my actions. But I'm not doing it for you."

"That's my girl. The Tempest I remember."

She turned her fiercest scowl on him. "I'm not your girl, and I never was. But there's one thing you're right about. The Tempest is back."

Chapter 44

Tempest climbed to the top of Hidden Creek Hill at sunrise. Her dad wasn't forcing her to do so this time. She hadn't even set an alarm to wake up. She'd simply awoken as the first rays of sunlight streamed through her bedroom window.

She'd slept for a few hours in a casino hotel room that was cheap because they expected customers to gamble away their money, before getting back on the road home, arriving in the late evening and assuring her family she was safe and sound.

The wind was working its magic, bringing the sound of the hidden creek to her ears. She paused at the old wishing well. This time, she'd remembered to bring a penny with her.

The copper coin came from the piggy bank in her childhood bedroom, a wooden puzzle cube her dad had built. Her muscle memory was rusty, and it had taken her a few minutes to work out the right order to push the slats of wood to open the box and reward the patient puzzle master with its treasure. Seventeen dollars and thirteen cents spilled out onto the hardwood floor of her bedroom. She selected the penny that rolled to the darkened wood slats in the shape of a skeleton key.

Now she clasped the penny in her left hand and ran her right one across the stones that formed the low well. If she hadn't met Gideon, she wouldn't have stopped to consider what type of stone this was. Smooth on top, but rough along the edges. More peach than gray, which surprised her. Her first instinct was to reach for her phone and download an app that could tell you what type of stone it was. She stopped herself. What was the rush? Why was she always in a rush? Why couldn't she stop running? She was alone in a peaceful spot, feeling the soft gray-green moss growing on the edges of the stones, listening to the faint sound of babbling water, watching the expansive sky transform from night to day. She closed her eyes as she squeezed the penny, made a wish, and dropped it into the well. Less than two seconds later, the coin clinked, having found a home with the countless wishes people had dropped into the well.

She ended the silly superstitious gesture by twirling in a pirouette. One frivolous gesture deserved another. They both brought a smile to her lips. Everything in her life had been so overly rigid for the last few years that she'd forgotten some things were worth doing for no reason at all. She spun once more, not bothering to check if she was still alone. The rubber soles of her red sneakers left an imprint in the soft dirt as she came to a hard stop facing the top of the hill. She breathed in the sea-like scent of the moss, the peaty dirt that reminded her of the Highlands, and the lemony fragrance of the walnut tree nearby, then kept walking up.

At the top of the hill, she was rewarded by the sun hitting her face. It was the start of a new day. Anything was possible.

Two other people were there. They'd driven up the back way, where you didn't have to walk. A week ago, she wouldn't have thought twice about driving up, instead of walking the ten-minute hike up the hill.

Wanting to be alone, she walked away from the unobstructed view and found a spot to watch the sunrise through the branches of an oak tree. There, she spread out the simple picnic she'd made for herself. Shredded jackfruit carnitas on fresh-baked San Francisco sourdough bread with ploughman's chutney. She needed to calm her mind, and this was the perfect spot to do so. She bit into the delicious sandwich that was a mash-up like her.

It was Grandpa Ash who'd taught her one of the biggest lessons on being comfortable being herself. It was the summer when she was seven years old and spending the summer in Edinburgh. An unfortunate little boy made fun of her looks and the food she was eating (unfortunate because he'd ended up with nasty scrapes on his knees after he was seen talking to Tempest at the park, though he'd adamantly refused to tell his parents what had happened).

"There's a Tamil proverb I'd like to teach you," Ash had said. "*Yaathum urae, yaavarum kaeleer. Vaalha, Vaalha.*"

Tempest repeated the lyrical words she didn't understand. She liked the vibrations they made on her tongue.

"It means," he said, "*I belong to every country, let everyone hear. Live. Live.*"

Tempest remembered the grand smile on his face, the one he must have used when he had good news for a patient who'd been expecting bad, when he'd paused before saying, "You're a citizen of the world, Tempest. Don't ever forget that. Not everyone will understand you. That's the way of the world. You don't ever need to run from yourself, because you're at home anywhere you have people who love you. And you have many people who love you." He'd rested his hand on his heart before adding, "Now, have you eaten?"

Leaning against the cool bark of the oak tree, Tempest polished off her mash-up sandwich.

A nearby twig snapped loudly.

Tempest didn't think much of it at first. This was a public park, and the sun was rising. She hadn't expected to remain alone all morning. Yet . . . there was something off about the sound. In the silence that followed, she knew what it was. It had only been a single sound, not the usual noises you'd hear if a person or animal walked by. And it hadn't come from the trees above.

"Hello?"

No answer.

Maybe it had just been a twig breaking off of a nearby tree. The wind could also alter the perception of where a sound came from, as she knew well in this town with its hidden creek. That must have been it.

Her mind, however, was now far from calm. She'd been fooling herself to think a tranquil breakfast could solve her problems. She was misdirecting her own mind. She didn't know the first thing about investigating a crime. What she knew about was misdirection. She knew she could solve the trick. The answer was at Calvin Knight's house. And she was going to find it.

Chapter 45

Sanjay was still asleep when Tempest called him.

"I should have turned off my phone. Why do I never learn? I'm hanging up on you now, Tempest."

"You want me to investigate alone?"

Sanjay swore.

Forty-five minutes later they were ringing the doorbell at Calvin Knight's front door. In the bright daylight, what had once reminded Tempest of a Scooby-Doo haunted house looked more like a fairy-tale castle.

Justin waved at Tempest through the living room's bay window, and she heard him run to meet his dad at the door. Tempest had called ahead to make sure it was all right for them to come by.

"You really think you've got it figured out?" Sanjay asked her.

"We were all looking for something to open up a secret passageway. But if I'm right, everyone missed it because there wasn't a single answer."

"Misdirection," Sanjay murmured.

"Is there going to be a magic show?" Justin asked.

"Maybe in a few minutes," Tempest said, knowing Sanjay would have at least the basics in his truck.

"Why don't you go upstairs to practice your piano lessons, J," Calvin said.

Justin scrunched up his face, certain he was about to miss something good—which, in all fairness, he was. Hopefully. But after four seconds and a look from his dad, he got a running start and slid across the smooth wooden floor of the foyer, bringing himself to a stop by grabbing the balustrade. With one look back at them, he ran up the stairs.

Tempest, Sanjay, and Calvin left the sunny foyer and walked through the kitchen, into the walk-in pantry.

"We expected a team of people to find a secret passageway," Tempest said, "but we were looking at things the wrong way around. Many people looking for one secret lever. Something like what Secret Staircase Construction would create. But if this was meant to be a *real* secret, it wouldn't be so easy."

Sanjay groaned. "It would need multiple levels of misdirection."

Tempest nodded. "We didn't need multiple people. We needed multiple mechanisms."

Calvin ran his fingers along the decorative cornice that framed the doorway. It was clear how much he loved this house. "Without someone to tell us what we're looking for, how will we find it? You already searched the hidden closet. Your dad's crew and the police investigators also looked."

"We were all thinking about the problem at hand," said Tempest. "How Cassidy got into the wall. We weren't thinking about *why* the house had a secret passageway in the first place."

Calvin shook his head. "I already told you about the history of when it was built. They weren't on the run because of the Fugitive Slave Act."

Tempest grinned. "Can we take a look at the sliding book-shelf my dad built?"

"Tempest." Sanjay clicked his tongue. "I love a good per-formance as much as the next person, but we're wasting Cal-vin's time—"

"We're not."

Calvin activated the bookshelf lever by pulling the spine of *Invisible Man*. The small room was the same as Tempest remembered from the first day she visited the house. Most important, the window. She pointed at the decorative high window in the shape of a wine bottle with a corkscrew that she'd assumed also served as a security bar.

"You think that's the lever?" Sanjay asked.

"It's the key."

Sanjay reached up to grab the corkscrew, but Tempest put her hand on his arm.

"A figurative key," she added. "This symbol is what tells us what to look for. When I reviewed the plans of this house, a sketch from 1925 didn't match up with the original. What was happening in 1925?"

Sanjay narrowed his eyes at her. "My great-grandparents were hanging out in Rajasthan."

Calvin grinned. "Prohibition."

Tempest nodded, and they hurried back to the newly dis-covered storage area behind the wall they'd cut open.

"I don't know exactly what we're looking for, but if they were up to what I think they were, we're looking for a spot that isn't necessarily easy to open, like you'd need if you were running away."

Two minutes later, Calvin pointed to the base of the shelf with the glass jars. "Is it just me, or does that notch of wood look an awful lot like a jug?"

"And that little hole in the middle doesn't look like it was made by a critter," Tempest added.

While Tempest and Sanjay pushed and pulled at the section of wood, Calvin disappeared. He returned less than a minute later holding a corkscrew. "Try this."

They twisted the corkscrew into the hole and pulled. The panel of shelving swung open, revealing a one-foot storage closet—filled with old bottles. A Prohibition-era hiding spot.

"This is amazing." Calvin couldn't stop beaming.

From a historical perspective, it was. But it wasn't a secret passageway. They were still no closer to finding out how Cassidy had gotten inside.

☠☠☠

"Do you know what this means?" Sanjay asked Tempest as they walked down the driveway thirty minutes and three magic tricks for Justin later.

"That if Calvin decides that hiding spot is of historical significance, my dad doesn't have a single job lined up?"

"This is truly a case of misdirection."

"We already knew it was a trick." Tempest instinctively felt for the handcuffs charm on her bracelet before remembering that it wasn't there.

"You thought you saw Cassidy fall out of the wall, but you must not have. Whose car are we walking back to?"

Tempest shook her head. "We really did see her, though. Me in particular. I was there to catch her. We even saw her in that first crawlspace through the hole in the wall." Tempest thought back to that day. "Ivy was the first one who spotted the body inside the wall."

Sanjay spun his keys around his index finger. "That doesn't mean she put it there."

"But it does tell us something else . . ." The glimmer of an idea flickered in Tempest's mind, but went out again.

Sanjay shoved his keys back into his pocket and declared, "I know who it was."

"You do?"

He stopped as they reached the sidewalk, and instead turned around and jogged back to the side of the house. Tempest followed. He pointed at the wraparound porch. "The veranda stretches the whole way around the house, right?"

"It does."

"While the rest of you were inside the house, captive in your respective rooms, who was the person who was on the outside wraparound porch?"

"Gideon," Tempest whispered. He'd told her as much when he said he'd seen the clothes she was wearing.

Sanjay nodded. "Exactly. The new guy. Who you know nothing about."

That wasn't quite true. But without knowing it, Sanjay had given her the clue she needed. She didn't have quite all the answers yet, but she now knew the biggest piece of the puzzle. Sanjay had given her the answer without realizing what he'd done.

"Do you have a show tonight?" she asked.

"Not tonight. Why?"

"Good. I need your help to catch Cassidy's killer."

Chapter 46

That raven looks like he's watching us." Tempest raised an eyebrow toward the stuffed black bird perched atop the bookshelf in a corner of the Locked Room Library. After leaving Sanjay, Tempest had driven straight there to meet Ivy.

"Valdemere is creepy, I admit." Ivy wriggled her nose at the raven. "His sensor is watching us, to caw if we walk by."

"Seriously?"

Ivy shrugged. "I'm just glad he's not in the train car meeting room."

"How'd you know the raven's name?"

"I'm working here part-time now," Ivy said. "Mostly over the weekend, when the regular staff is off. But I fill in other times when I'm free. That's why I'm here today and couldn't go with you to the Knights' house earlier."

"My dad didn't tell me you were doing this."

"Darius doesn't know. It feels like I'd be betraying him if I become a librarian."

"This is where you've been going when you said you had something else you were working on."

Ivy's cheeks turned bright pink.

"If going to library school is what you want to do, he'll be thrilled for you."

Ivy's blush intensified, but she smiled. "We can talk about that later. I'm guessing you didn't ask me here to be my career counselor. And you could have filled me in about the Knights' Prohibition discovery via text message. Why did you want to meet?"

"You don't need to get back to work?"

"I told Enid I was taking my lunch break when I saw you arrive. Want to get some privacy in the train car?"

Ivy unlocked the train car meeting room and clicked on the moving scenery. "Now spill."

"First, you need to understand why I think my idea works."

"The idea you haven't yet told me."

"Bear with me. Dr. Fell has his locked room lecture that looks at all the possible permutations of an impossible crime, including nuances of various types of locks. Ivy Youngblood has her own variation on the possibilities, a simplified version—"

"It's not exactly *simplified*," Ivy grumbled.

"How about streamlined. Is that a better word for it?"

"Definitely."

"The Ivy Youngblood method of analysis relies not on specific mechanisms," Tempest said, "but concepts for how something seemingly impossible can really be true. A time shift, where the victim is thought to be alive when they were actually dead, or the opposite. A death that's not really a murder, but an accident or suicide. A trap hidden inside the room that kills. A way to kill from outside the room. And a way to lock the room to make it look like the killer couldn't have gotten out, yet they did."

"You were paying attention." Ivy smiled and settled into a

seat in which she could watch the faux scenery go by. "I'm impressed. But only by you. Not myself. My methods, and those of Dr. Fell, might apply to fiction, but they clearly don't translate to real life. Neither tells us how someone got Cassidy into that wall. It doesn't matter if she was still alive when she was put there, if someone pretended to be her, or whether she was killed by a mechanism or a person—or even if she killed herself. I haven't done you any good this week."

"You have, Ivy. The ideas from our childhood that you've continued exploring are what have gotten me this far. They just needed a little tweaking—along with some decisive action. The more I've thought about it, the more I've realized all impossible crimes can be summed up in one word: 'Misdirection.'"

"Is this the Tempest Raj Locked Room Lecture?" Ivy asked.

"I hadn't thought of it like that, but I suppose it is. So here goes. There are endless variations on how a supposedly impossible crime can be made possible. John Dickson Carr's detective discussed seven concepts, plus five general types of locks, for a total of twelve. By having so many variations, he lulled us into a false sense of finality, making the reader believe it was possible to list all the permutations. I know, I know, Dr. Fell said there were infinite variations. But by listing more points than we can count on two hands, he made it feel like an exhaustive list. Like it *should* give us all the answers. It doesn't.

"You narrowed it down to five broad concepts. Which is more in the right direction. Five makes it clear they're just broad strokes. General ideas to help hone our ideas. But really, at their core, it's all about misdirection.

"What I do—or rather, what I *did*, on the stage—is misdirection. Pushing and pulling attention exactly where we want it to go. Leaving nothing to chance. An intricate balance of what's real and what's physiologically *thought* to have been seen. It's a puzzle on multiple layers, because we can't trust any of our senses. There's what really happened versus what we experienced. It's a puzzle to figure out which is which."

"These puzzle plot mysteries fell out of favor after the Second World War," Ivy said, "when psychological elements became all the rage—the *who*dunnit moved on to the *why*dunnit. Of course, lots of authors continued writing puzzle plot whodunnits, and lots of authors were already writing psychological explorations long before the balance shifted. Agatha Christie did both brilliantly. It's why she's the one who's most remembered now."

"Agatha was right," Tempest said. "The *why* is as important as the *how*. They're intertwined. That's the other element that can get us to the solution. We can't look at the trick independently, like I thought. At first, I thought the solution of the impossible crime of how Cassidy's body got into the wall would tell us everything we needed to know. But it doesn't. Not quite."

"Which brings us to the reason you wanted to talk?"

"I know how it happened."

"You know how Cassidy got into the wall?"

"I know the trick. But I don't have proof. Which is why I need your help." Tempest told Ivy her plan.

Chapter 47

The door barely made a sound as they pulled it open and stepped into darkness.

"I used to be disappointed that the front door doesn't creak like a spooky old door," Ivy said, "but tonight, I'm glad of it."

It was a few minutes before ten o'clock that night. The Locked Room Library had closed hours ago, but Ivy had gotten permission to use the library for Tempest's plan. Their helpers would be joining them shortly.

When the lights came on, Tempest was startled to find herself standing in front of the knight's suit of armor that stood at the information desk. She'd seen him before, but he looked different at night. Different enough that she automatically thought of the shiny armor as a "he" instead of an "it." She peered into the knight's helmet. Not that she actually thought someone would be inside. But with everything that had happened this past week, she wouldn't have been surprised.

They had enough light to walk to the train car meeting room, but Ivy must have felt the same way as Tempest, because she turned on the lights for the rest of the small library as well.

"Do you really think this will tell us the answer?" Ivy asked.

"Aren't you the one who's supposed to say, 'Once you eliminate the impossible, whatever remains, however improbable, is the solution'?'"

"To quote from the Sherlock Holmes story, 'The Sign of the Four,' 'When you have eliminated the impossible, whatever remains, however improbable, must be the truth.' But Sherlock is no Dr. Fell. Really, 'whatever remains'? How does that even mean anything?"

Tempest's cell phone buzzed. She hoped her plan would work.

An hour and twenty minutes later, everything was in place. At ten minutes to midnight, the Secret Staircase construction crew had all arrived. Darius, Robbie, Gideon, and Ivy gathered around the narrow table in the train car. At five minutes to midnight, Sanjay joined them.

"Cutting it close," Tempest commented.

"If you'd told me what this was about, I could have known what to prepare for." He flipped his bowler hat into his hands. "Besides, I presume you'll be starting at midnight on the dot?"

"No need. We're all here, so let's get started."

Sanjay slipped into a free seat and nodded.

"The mystery of what happened this week comes down to misdirection." Tempest lifted a paperback book from the table and watched as their gaze fell from her eyes to the book. This wasn't a book from the library, but a copy of Shakespeare's *The Tempest* she'd brought with her from Fiddler's Folly.

"All of you except for Sanjay," she continued, drumming her fingertips on the book, "were at Calvin Knight's house when Cassidy's body was discovered inside the wall. You all have different pieces of information, so I'll begin with a short recap of the three most important questions that explain why we're here tonight. First, was Cassidy's death supposed to be mine? She was thought of as my doppelgänger, after all. Which she used to her advantage when she wrecked my show. And I'm the one with a family curse that's been going strong for five generations."

Her dad ran his hand across his face. Tempest gave him a warning glance and continued. "Second, do we have a truly impossible crime? Somehow, she got inside that wall that hadn't been opened in a century—I know, I know, probably more like half-a-century, since that outer wall was sheet-rock. But still, there was no way for her to have gotten inside. Third, a ghost has been seen and heard at Fiddler's Folly this week. Is someone pretending to be a ghost? If not, that again brings us back to the curse."

"And why," Gideon asked, "are we in a closed library at midnight?"

"You're all here," Tempest said as she ran her fingers over the cracked spine of the book she held in her hands, "because I know who's behind all of this. To prove it—" She closed her palms over the book. When she opened them, *The Tempest* was gone. "—you're all going to help me vanish."

PART III

The Trap

Chapter 48

Tempest looked from one shocked face to the next. "I need to vanish to catch the killer."

They all began to speak at once.

"Absolutely not," Darius growled.

Gideon nodded. "Giving them a taste of their own medicine?"

Ivy zipped her puffy pink vest until it covered half her face. "I knew my life would be turned upside-down when you came back, but I really had no idea."

"That's a bad idea, Twirls. I won't be part of it." Robbie spoke as he got up and walked toward the door. He dipped his head as he stepped through the train car door.

"I'm going to do it with or without you," Tempest said. "It'll work a lot better if you help me."

Darius ran his hand across his face. "Who are we trying to catch?"

Tempest took a deep breath. "I can't tell you."

"This. Is. Insane." Each word Ivy spoke grew louder and louder.

Darius put his head in his hands and sighed. "What do you need from us?"

The piercing caw of the raven caused their voices to cease. Robbie had walked far enough into the library that he'd activated its sensors.

Tempest leapt up and chased after Robbie. She found him pacing next to the Gothic section. The raven's obsidian-colored plastic eyes seemed to follow her as she went. "I can't do it without you."

"You don't need me—"

"Are you making that sound?" Tempest squinted her eyes at him.

"What sound?"

Thump THUMP. The faint thumping of a heartbeat.

"You hear it too?" Tempest was relieved to see him nod nervously. "It's not my imagination."

"Where's it coming from?" Robbie whipped his head around. He rushed to the wall and pressed his ear to it.

Tempest pointed at the faux brick door a few feet from Robbie. "There." She approached it cautiously as the others watched.

"The Door to Nowhere," Ivy had called it. From the title of a controversial John Dickson Carr novel—controversial because it included both a rational ending *and* a supernatural ending.

The bricks were rough and cool to the touch. "It's not real," she whispered. "We wouldn't hear a real heartbeat this far away, through a wall."

"The Tell-Tale Heart." Ivy picked up a slim volume of Edgar Allan Poe stories from a nearby shelf. "The Poe story, where it's guilt that makes the murderer think they hear a heartbeat."

Thump THUMP, thump THUMP, thump THUMP.

"But we all hear it." Gideon's voice was softer than the

rhythmic pounding of the heart that lay beyond the wall. "And it's getting louder. I didn't believe you about the family curse, Tempest. But now—"

"It's not the first time a ghost—or whatever this is—has appeared to me." Tempest's voice was barely louder than Gideon's. "The curse has come for me. The curse—"

"The curse," Darius growled, "isn't claiming my baby."

Ivy and Robbie both jumped as his fist smashed into the bricks. Tempest's exterior remained calm, but inside, her own heart was thudding just as loudly as the heartbeat inside the wall. With arms stronger than Tempest had imagined, Gideon pulled Darius back. Blood dripped from Darius's fingertips.

"We need a better way to get into that wall," Gideon said.

"Already on it," Sanjay strode into the room. The others hadn't seemed to notice that he'd left. In his arms he was carrying what looked like an oversize vintage medical bag. Tempest recognized it as the bag of tricks he kept hidden behind the front seat of his truck, which went anywhere he did.

Sanjay knelt in front of Darius and Gideon, close to the brick door to nowhere. Was it Tempest's imagination, or was the beating heart growing louder? The sound of the bag's opening zipper was drowned out by the rhythmic *thump THUMP, thump THUMP, thump THUMP.*

Sanjay tossed a gauze bandage up to Darius, who caught it in his uninjured left hand. "I'm nothing if not prepared." The next thing he removed from the bag was a dagger.

Ivy gasped.

Sanjay rolled his eyes. "I'm not the killer. We can get out the bricks with this. Um, right?" He looked to the Secret Staircase Construction crew.

Ivy gasped again. "We really need to ask Enid before we destroy her library."

"No time." Sanjay poked at the mortar between two bricks.

"Ivy's right." Darius didn't look up as he wrapped the roll of gauze around his knuckles. He flexed his hand and grunted. "Enid lives above the library."

"I'd forgotten about that." Robbie was still pacing. He'd moved from the Gothic section to modern locked-room mysteries, which were further away from the thudding heart. "How can she sleep through this noise?"

"She can't." The librarian Tempest had met earlier that week pushed open a white door marked *Private*. Her bright red matte lipstick and 1940s outfit were nowhere to be seen, replaced by a ponytail holding her long brown hair on top of her head and a matching set of purple pajamas. Instead of peep-toe pumps, her feet were adorned with fluffy white slippers with bunny faces on the toes. But standing with her hands on her hips, she projected the same sense of authority.

"What," she continued, "is that noise?"

Thump THUMP, thump THUMP, thump THUMP.

"'The Tell-Tale Heart'?" Ivy answered.

Enid frowned. "Ivy, when I gave you permission to use the meeting room after hours, I didn't think you'd be throwing a murder mystery party. If that was your intent, I'm terribly offended you didn't invite me." She grinned. "Is there room for one more? Let me go throw on some clothes."

Ivy bit her lip, and it was Sanjay who spoke. "It's not a party. It's either a family curse that's come to claim Tempest, or a murderer who's messing with us. We need to break open this brick wall and see what's inside."

Thump THUMP, thump THUMP, thump THUMP.

Enid blinked at him, momentarily speechless as she stared at Sanjay's outstretched arm, which was still holding the dagger. Her eyes opened wide, and she clasped her hands together. "Marvelous!"

"Um, Enid?" Ivy touched the librarian's arm. "This is real."

"Then let's get on with it. Is that dagger all you've got? I'm pretty sure I've got a mallet somewhere."

"Have you all gone insane?" Robbie asked. "You don't know what's in there."

"Which is exactly why we need to open it." Enid marched in her bunny slippers over to Sanjay and took the dagger from his hand. "Goodness, that sound *is* rather loud."

Thump THUMP, thump THUMP, thump THUMP.

"Yes," Enid continued, "I think a mallet will be better."

"Quicker," Gideon said. "But more invasive for your wall."

Sanjay rummaged through his oversize bag. "Pickaxe?"

"Why do you have a pickaxe?" Tempest asked. "What illusion could it possibly be used for?"

Sanjay handed the pickaxe to Gideon and whispered the answer in Tempest's ear. Gideon grimaced as he broke down the wall. Tempest stood with her father, who was nursing his hand. Ivy and Enid stood back, looking on. Robbie was still pacing and shaking his head.

The pickaxe thudded nearly as loudly as the beating heart as it dropped from Gideon's hand and crashed to the floor. He'd only opened a one-foot square.

Thump THUMP, thump THUMP, thump THUMP.

Tempest rushed to his side and looked into the wall. The sound was almost deafening now. "No. No, no, no!"

"It's happening again," Gideon whispered.

"What are you talking about?" Robbie snapped.

"See for yourself."

Tempest stepped aside and made way for the others. A body in a sack was crammed in the one-foot-wide crawl space.

There was no mistaking it. Long brown hair overflowed out of the top of the bag. Now that the wall was open, a metallic scent filled the air. Shining a flashlight into the hole in the bricks, the source of the scent was clear. Where the hair met the scalp, it was thick with dark red blood.

Chapter 49

et me through." Darius pushed Gideon aside and began smashing bricks in earnest.

Sanjay put a hand on his shoulder, but Darius shrugged it off. "Shouldn't we call the police?"

Thump THUMP, thump THUMP, thump THUMP.

"She might still be alive." Her father's voice made Tempest shiver.

"Oh God," Robbie whispered.

With one last smash, the bricks opened enough to allow the camouflage-colored canvas sack to fall forward. Darius caught it in his arms, the brunt of the weight falling onto his wrapped hand.

His lips moved as if he was saying a silent prayer. He shook his head. "She's dead."

The thumping stopped.

They stared at each other in silence for seven seconds, waiting for the sound of the heartbeat that never came.

"Everyone into the meeting room." Darius gingerly rested the body onto the floor. "Now. Tempest, that means you, too. No investigating. We don't know if this was another attempt to get to you."

Darius's cell phone was at his ear before they reached the train car. "I found a dead body," he said into the phone, and gave his name and the address.

He turned to the group after hanging up. "Apparently if it's a new dead body they take it much more seriously. Someone will be here in a few minutes."

"You guys?" Ivy said softly. "Where's Enid?"

"Probably off throwing up." Robbie looked like he was about to do the same.

Ivy shook her head. "I haven't seen her since you opened the wall."

Sanjay jumped up and was out the door before anyone could say anything. A string of Punjabi swear words escaped his lips.

"Whoever has a weak stomach shouldn't come out here," he said.

"Why not?" Tempest pushed past him.

"Because," Sanjay said, "the librarian we just met, who runs this little library, is the dead body that fell from the wall."

Tempest's ruby red sneakers came to a stop a foot in front of the body. This wasn't how they'd left things. The drawstring on the army surplus sack had been pulled back, as if the dead body inside had tried to crawl out.

Enid's body, dressed in purple pajamas, was facedown on the floor. The back of her skull was caved in and coated with blood. Her right arm was outstretched, as if she'd clawed at the floor. But with the wound on her head, Tempest's dad was right—there was no way she could have been alive.

Thump THUMP, thump THUMP, thump THUMP.

The sound of the beating heart was back.

"This isn't happening." Robbie fell to his knees.

"It certainly *looks* impossible," Sanjay said.

Robbie wiped his eyes with a handkerchief from one of his multitude of pockets and looked up at them. "How can you all be so calm?"

You did this, a disembodied voice whispered.

"Don't you hear that?" Robbie croaked.

You did this to me, Robbie Ronan.

"No," Robbie whispered. He pushed himself up and stumbled backward. "Tempest, don't you hear that?"

"Hear what? Are you feeling okay, Robbie?"

Robbie crashed into a bookshelf. A paperback copy of Clayton Rawson's *Footprints on the Ceiling* fell to the floor.

Thump THUMP, thump THUMP, thump THUMP.

"Make it stop!" Robbie shouted.

Thump THUMP, thump THUMP, thump THUMP.

"This isn't happening!" Robbie held his hands over his ears.

Tempest walked up to Robbie and pulled his hands from his head. "Is there something you want to tell me, Uncle Robbie?"

His eyes were still transfixed on Enid's body. Tempest followed his gaze. "Poor Enid."

At the sound of Tempest's words, Enid's outstretched hand began to quiver. Her fingers curled, and her fingernails scraped the hardwood floor like claws.

Robbie began to shake. "That's impossible. How is she . . . Do the rest of you see that?"

"Don't look so horrified, Robbie," Tempest said. "You know that none of this is real. Just like when we found Cassidy in the wall. This is exactly how you did it, isn't it?"

Robbie's attention snapped from Enid's writhing body to Tempest's disappointed face. "I'm sorry, Twirls. I'm so sorry. This all got out of hand. I never meant for any of this to happen. None of it."

"You could have been a great illusionist, Uncle Robbie. It took me a long time to work out how you did it. And I needed my dad and friends to pull it off." She felt a lump in her throat as she spoke the words. It had been so long since she'd relied on anyone. Since she'd felt she could trust anyone.

"Can I get up now?" The corpse sat up.

Chapter 50

"Y ou bringing us here to help you vanish was just a trick?" Robbie was sitting at the end of the long, narrow table in the train car meeting room, bound to the table with galvanized steel shackles from Sanjay's bag of tricks. The group stared down at him as if he was the suspect that he was.

"More like a trap." Tempest stood at the opposite end. Her dad was to the right of her, the librarian to her left. Enid held a wet towel to her head. The fake blood had been on a wig, but some of it had seeped through onto her own hair.

"How did you fake this?" Robbie's voice cracked as he spoke.

"I think," Tempest said, "you already know."

"She worked out how you did it." Darius flexed his muscles as he stared down at the man he'd trusted for so many years. The bandage was now gone from Darius's hand, the fake blood having washed off his skin more easily than it had from Enid's hair.

Tempest rested a firm hand on her dad's shoulder, fearing he'd leap up to throttle Robbie at any moment. He squeezed her hand and nodded for her to continue.

"There never was a body inside the wall at Calvin Knight's

house," she said. "Everyone was right that the wall hadn't been opened in decades. There was nothing false about the walls. There were no secret passageways. No false panels. What you all saw was something that looked like a body: a tailor's dummy. The tailor's dummy left behind in an old storage room at the house where a dressmaker and tailor lived."

The metal-framed dressmaker's mannequin that Tempest had used for tonight's illusion was now seated at the table between Gideon and Robbie, opposite Ivy and Sanjay. Gideon kept inching away from it, as far as he could get without sitting in Darius's lap. The mannequin really was rather creepy.

"It's my fault," Ivy said. "I'm the one who said it looked like a body."

"But Robbie," said Tempest, "is the one who took advantage of the ambiguous situation to create enough misdirection to hide a real body."

The combined scowls of Tempest and Ivy were directed at Robbie, who kept his gaze downward, looking at the manacles that bound his hands.

"I still don't see how he did it," Gideon said, bumping Darius's elbow as he scooted further away from the mannequin. "I was there that terrible morning. I saw everything. I'm good at noticing details. But I still don't understand how he got Cassidy into the bag. When you told us about your plan tonight, I went along with it because I trust you. But unlike Enid, who's alive and could remove the tailor's dummy and replace it with her own body, Cassidy was already dead."

"Misdirection." Sanjay spoke for the first time since they'd moved into the train car meeting room. He spun his bowler hat in his hands and tossed it into the air. They all turned toward him, even Robbie, as it brushed against the low ceiling and landed back on his head. "Isn't that right, Tempest? Um, Tempest? Hey, where did she go?"

The group looked back to the other end of the table—but Tempest had vanished.

Sanjay grinned. "We couldn't resist."

Darius roared, so Tempest sped up her entrance and poked her head back into the room. She'd been hiding right outside the train car, listening.

"We wanted to demonstrate that complex props aren't always needed," she said. "A combination of psychology and timing can do the trick. I should have seen it sooner, and suspected Robbie from the start, but I'm used to thinking of misdirection as something that needs to be practiced thousands of times to get it just right. But here, we had misdirection created by someone we all know can adapt within moments. Robbie is the member of the crew who thinks on his feet. Whenever the Secret Staircase Construction crew has a problem they didn't count on, Robbie has a solution within minutes—often within seconds. We all know this. He can pull anything out of that vest of his." He hadn't been wearing his workday vest that night or she would have taken it from him before they shackled him to the table.

"You're not going to tell me he hid Cassidy in his vest." Gideon shuddered.

"No," said Tempest. "But think about who suggested you didn't have the right tools with you to fully open up the wall."

Ivy smacked her forehead.

"It was Robbie," Tempest continued. "That was his excuse to go back out to his truck."

Gideon groaned.

"Cassidy's body must have been in his truck already," Tempest said. "Is that right, Robbie?"

Robbie gave a slight nod as he continued to avoid Tempest's gaze.

"His pickup truck is always stuffed with useful junk," Tempest continued, "so it would have been a relatively safe place to hide a body until he could figure out what to do with it. Maybe he even thought he'd have a good excuse if her body was found in the bed of the truck, since it's not like it's locked, or even enclosed. But now I'm just speculating. What I do know is that Robbie did one more thing besides move her body into his oversize bag of tools—he cut off her hair."

Robbie looked up at Tempest, but didn't speak. A combination of sadness and admiration lit up his eyes.

Tempest wound a lock of her long black hair between her fingers. "He cut off Cassidy's hair because he needed a heap of black hair to appear on top of the sack when it came out of the wall. He didn't yet know what was inside it, but he, like the rest of you, agreed with Ivy that it looked like the shape of a body. Robbie was the one who said they needed a bigger tool, the one who sawed open the wall enough for the sack to fall out—which even I know is more of a rushed job than is good practice—and the one right there as it fell. As he pretended to fumble with the sack, he placed the lock of Cassidy's hair he'd cut off on top—which he must have held together with a rubber band or other type of tie from his vest—so it looked like a head of hair was inside it. We were all convinced by then that it was a body, so my dad took charge and ordered everyone out so we could call the police. If he hadn't called them, Robbie could easily have done so. He needed us to get out of that room."

Gideon swore. "I remember what happened next. Robbie said he wanted to take his bag of tools from the pantry back to his truck so the police wouldn't keep it as evidence."

Tempest nodded. "That's when he switched the body. What he had originally carried *in* was a heavy bag supposedly filled with an assortment of tools he might need for opening the wall—but it really contained the one saw he needed, plus Cassidy's body. What he carried *out* was a bag with the tailor's dummy."

Robbie stopped fiddling with the shackles and looked up at Tempest. When he spoke, his voice was dry and broken. "I didn't even feel like it was me who was doing it. I know that's not an excuse, but it's the truth. My mind is always racing. Always spinning wacky ways to solve problems. It's the only thing I've ever been good at. So when Ivy said there was a body inside the wall, that part of my brain took over. I'm sorry, Tempest. So very sorry. I never meant for any of this to happen."

"Why did you kill her? That's what I've been trying to work out. You met her once, I think, when you visited me in Vegas and came backstage before one of my shows. But that was years ago, for five minutes."

"But that's the thing," Robbie said. "I didn't kill her."

Chapter 51

really didn't kill her." Robbie looked at Tempest pleadingly. "I was framed. Her body was left at my house, so I panicked and moved the body. It was stupid, I know . . . I didn't even think about Isaac, until he was arrested. I met him backstage as well as Cassidy, when I visited you. He must have remembered my name, because my house is where he dumped her body."

"You made us think someone was going to kill my baby girl," Darius roared. "How could you do that to her?"

Robbie shrank back. He looked as if his whole body had shriveled in the last hour, as he tried to disappear from them and himself. "I didn't think through the implications. I acted on instinct. Like I always do when trying to fix things."

"Did you even consider Calvin and Justin Knight?" Darius's large body loomed over the table. "You put a dead girl's body in the home of a Black man who's also a single father."

"I wasn't thinking! I was scared, because I knew I was being framed."

"You're not the same man I've considered a friend as well as an employee for fifteen years." Darius leaned back and shook his head. The muscles of his jaw pulsed, and he spoke through gritted teeth. "You had a choice when you found her body, and you screwed up unbelievably."

Gideon gaped at him. "You don't actually believe him that he didn't kill her, do you?"

"No," Tempest said. "Because he was also the ghost."

Ivy gasped. Darius swore. Robbie said nothing.

Enid stood up. "Anyone else need a drink?" She scooted past the group, unlocked a cabinet behind the train car's bar, and held up a bottle of Irish whisky that was three-quarter's full. Everyone nodded except Tempest, who wanted to keep a clear head. She never drank before a performance. And that's what this was. She was the one standing before them, telling her story, and coaxing Robbie's out of him.

"You don't get one." Enid looked down her nose at the shackled Robbie. She passed small glass tumblers to everyone else seated at the table. Gideon glanced nervously at the mannequin as he accepted his glass. Enid's smile lingered a moment too long on Darius's face as she handed him his glass. It was a look Tempest was used to seeing single women between the age of thirty and sixty give her dad. He tried to discourage them by continuing to wear his wedding ring. It didn't work.

"Ivy." Tempest closed her eyes and thought back to the beginning of that week, which felt so long ago. "The day after Cassidy's body was discovered, you and Robbie went to check up on a job in Marin. Kids had broken something you needed to fix."

"That's right."

"But before that . . ." Tempest thought back to that day. "I went over to your house to tell you I didn't believe Isaac was guilty. I was still worried Cassidy's death had to do with me and the family curse."

"I remember."

"Did you tell Robbie?"

"We spent the whole afternoon together. Of course I—" She broke off and put her head in her hands. "I yet again handed him the information he needed."

"Robbie knew Isaac wasn't guilty, because he'd killed her himself. He knew Isaac would be cleared at some point during the investigation, so he had to confuse the issue even more. Once Isaac was cleared, suspicion might fall back to me and my family curse. If Robbie made sure it stayed that way, no one would pay any attention to him. That was the cruelest thing he did. Teasing me to make me think my dead mother had come back to me as a ghost."

"I'm sorry," Robbie whispered. "I realized how cruel that was. That's why I didn't bring her image back a second time. Only her music."

Tempest blinked back tears. She'd known it was a trick, but part of her had still wanted to believe it was her mom.

"Pepper's Ghost?" Sanjay asked Robbie.

Tempest smiled. Sanjay's words brought her back to the present.

Robbie blinked at him. "Who's Pepper?"

"That famous illusion is way too complex," Tempest said. "Robbie couldn't have pulled it off on his own, especially in that setting outside my window. All he had to do was throw me off balance. He used the most basic tricks imaginable, but Robbie had psychology on his side. For the ghost's first appearance, he was simply projecting a video he'd taken of my mom playing the fiddle. She always played at the parties we had at the Folly when I was a kid. I wasn't expecting a ghost to appear, so the illusion could be crude. I saw her from my bedroom window, which was far from the oak tree where her image appeared. After that, you abandoned bigger theatrics and focused on sound."

Tempest paused and held up a small speaker and a smaller microphone in her palm. "You're one of the very few people who have complete access to Fiddler's Folly. I didn't find these when I searched my room, because you hadn't gone inside my room itself. I found them in Hag's Nook, the little nook high above the reading room. That's why the dust had already been disturbed when I climbed up there."

A low growl sounded in Darius's throat and he started to rise. Tempest put a hand on his shoulder to keep him seated. "Just a few more minutes, Papa. I need to understand why he did it."

"I'm so sorry for the things I did," Robbie said, "but I didn't kill that girl."

"Stop. Lying. I know Isaac is innocent. I went to see him—"

"I knew it." Darius ran a hand across his face and half groaned and half laughed. "That's where you went when you disappeared the night before last."

"I knew you'd stop me if I told you what I was doing."

"Where were you when you called me back?"

"Barstow?"

"What did he—"

Sanjay cleared his throat. "I believe The Tempest has the stage."

"I'm nearly done." She turned to Robbie and spoke softly. "Uncle Robbie. How many times have I said those words?" She closed her eyes and counted to three. Exploding at him wouldn't get her the final answer she needed.

"There's just one last piece of the puzzle," she continued once she had control of her emotions. "My charm bracelet key. I understand the scattershot misdirection of the ghost, but I don't understand why you'd steal my charm bracelet. And why at Veggie Magic? You could have stolen my bracelet much more easily anytime since I've been home. Did you kill Cassidy to get a replica of my bracelet? Did you really think I wouldn't notice the difference? And did you not realize the plastic version would still form this key?"

Confusion washed over Robbie's face.

Tempest dangled the key from her fingertips. "Do you know what this key opens?"

Robbie's confusion intensified, but four seconds later, his face transformed into a blank slate.

The same cold dread Tempest had felt when the ghostly fiddle played in her ear earlier that week crept up her body. She shivered when it reached her shoulders. Robbie had realized something. Or come to some sort of decision.

"Why," she whispered, "would you wreck your life over Cassidy Sparrow?"

"I confess," Robbie whispered back. "I killed her."

Darius put his phone to his ear. "I'm calling the police for real this time." He stepped out of the train car into the main library as his call was answered.

The rest of the people at the table glanced awkwardly at each other and their drinks. Gideon gave one last sideways peek at the mannequin prop at his side before standing up and following Darius.

"Why?" Tempest said across the table to Robbie. "Why did you need to kill her?"

Robbie stared out the train car window. The faux scenery now showed a scenic coastline. They sped past the rocky shores of a tempestuous ocean.

"You endangered the kids, too," Tempest continued. "You put Justin and Natalie in danger."

Robbie shook his head and met Tempest's gaze. "That was

the kids' imaginations. I wasn't the ghost that night. I know I screwed up beyond what's forgivable, but I'd never hurt a child. I was searching for them with the rest of you."

"After they'd already vanished."

Robbie kept shaking his head. "I was with you beforehand, remember? I was with you on the deck when the kids were still in the kitchen."

"You had a party?" Sanjay asked.

"Same time as your show," Tempest answered without looking at him. She was still staring at Robbie. She knew she couldn't trust her emotions to read his regretful expression accurately. She'd gotten him to confess, so why did she feel that something was completely wrong. *The timing.* Robbie wasn't lying. He couldn't possibly have been the ghost that night. Someone else was involved.

Chapter 52

Something isn't right." Tempest paced beneath her magic posters in the turret above her bedroom, twirling the key between her fingers.

The police had taken Robbie into custody. He waived his right to counsel and said he was guilty and turning himself in. Sanjay had recorded the whole conversation at the Locked Room Library, in case it would be necessary, but with Robbie's confession, it might not be. Which was for the best, since California's privacy laws were strict about recording people without their permission.

Tempest's dad had gone to bed a little after two a.m., and promised he'd get up early to tell Ash and Morag what had happened.

Now Sanjay, Gideon, and Ivy had joined Tempest in the turret above her bedroom. They'd raided the kitchen, but in the main house that meant slim pickings. They took a bag of tortilla chips and a container of guacamole upstairs.

Gideon yawned. Sanjay glared at him as he twirled his bowler hat in his hands.

"Sorry." Gideon shook himself. "I'm not a night owl. And these beanbags are surprisingly comfortable."

"I agree with Tempest," Ivy said. "It doesn't quite fit, does it?"

Gideon extricated himself from the plush beanbag and studied a collage of Tempest's old photos mounted on the wall underneath the poster of Nicodemus the Necromancer. "You've known Robbie since you were a kid?"

"Since I was eleven." Tempest looked out the window. It was a dark and silent night.

"And I've worked with him since I was sixteen," Ivy added, "when I started working for Darius part-time. I had the biggest crush on Robbie." She reddened, though it was unclear if it was from embarrassment or rage. "I thought he was my very own MacGyver. He'd always built silly little contraptions for me, to distract me when I was going through a terrible year at home. I can't believe he'd do this."

"Don't our Agatha Christie and John Dickson Carr books tell us it's the person we least suspect?" Tempest took the framed collage off the wall and tapped the glass over Robbie's goofy grin.

"There are people," Ivy said, "who I suspect less than Robbie."

Tempest flung the frame aside, not caring whether it broke. "He absolutely was the ghost and the person who set up the impossible crime with Cassidy's body. But drugging me, stealing the bracelet key, and killing Cassidy? Those pieces don't fit."

"Of course it fits." Ivy scowled at Tempest. "He's a two-faced traitor. He—"

"Stop bickering, kids." Sanjay stepped between them and plucked the key from Tempest's fingers. "This key is still the key."

"Very punny." Ivy giggled.

Tempest sighed. "Look what you've done, Sanjay. You've broken Ivy."

Ivy zipped up her puffy pink vest until half her face was hidden beneath the collar. "Aren't the rest of your brains broken? This has been the strangest week of my life, and I've had some pretty eventful weeks. It's nearly three o'clock in the morning, Tempest has been living through a haunting, one of the few people in my life I thought I trusted just confessed to murder, and there's still a mysterious key from Tempest's mom."

Sanjay said, "You forgot about the fact that a social media rumor started that Tempest herself had died, that she was worried the curse had come for her, and that her creepy superfan has been lurking about."

"My list wasn't meant to be all-encompassing," Ivy grumbled.

"What made Robbie confess?" Tempest asked.

"You were incredible," Sanjay said. "You had it all figured out. He saw that—"

"I *didn't*, though. I solved the impossible crime and the fact that the Raj Family Curse is a series of explainable events. I figured out it was Robbie who got Cassidy's body into that house to be discovered, and Robbie who haunted me after he learned I didn't believe Isaac was guilty. Except for being the ghost on the night of the party. After admitting to killing a woman, why not admit to being the ghost one last time?"

"Because he put my niece and Justin in danger that night," Ivy said. "It's one thing to kill a grown woman, but quite something else to hurt a child."

"The more important point," Tempest said, "is that I have no idea *why* he would have killed Cassidy and stolen my original charm bracelet key."

"The key could be a red herring," Ivy suggested. "Simply a thoughtful gift to remind you of your shared love of magic and how she always said you were a key that could open any lock, like Houdini."

"Then why did Robbie steal it?" Tempest held the key up to the window. "On a personal level I hate to think of him as a killer, but I know I can't look at this only with my heart. I can't think of him as Uncle Robbie. But *logically*, it really makes no sense for him to steal my bracelet—and definitely not in the way that he did. That's the biggest reason I feel like we're missing something, and maybe we should believe his original confession—the one where he only admitted to moving the body."

"I saw a coffee maker downstairs," Gideon said. "Should I make us a pot so we can keep talking?"

"You'll never get back up here by yourself. You don't know the secrets to get into either my bedroom or this upper room."

"I'll go with him," Sanjay said. "That way I can keep an eye on him, too."

The two men climbed down the steep, ladder-like stairs hidden in the wall. As they descended, Tempest heard Gideon say, "I wanted to ask you about a vanishing act Tempest performed at Veggie Magic, making two customers disappear and their table vanish. Do you know how . . ." Tempest couldn't make out the words after that, but she knew Sanjay wouldn't reveal the secret.

"I'm with you," Ivy said. "I really don't see Robbie as a killer. But I have no problem admitting it's because of my heart. When you left, he helped me a lot. He was never close to his family when he was younger. He had a lot of anger at his dad for leaving."

"I'd forgotten about that," Tempest said.

"But he still remembered his dad and missed him. Like I missed the man my dad was when I was really little, before his life didn't turn out the way he wanted and he began taking it out on us. I don't care that this is the logical explanation. I hate that Robbie is guilty. I hate it." Ivy slunk further into the collar of her puffy vest.

"Robbie is definitely guilty of covering up the crime and of messing with my head. But why did he all of a sudden confess to murder? I *didn't* have evidence there, or even a very good argument. He confessed when I went back to saying Isaac wasn't guilty . . ."

Ivy poked her whole head out. "I know that look."

"He's protecting someone. And you gave me the answer of who it is."

Chapter 53

Tempest flew down the stairs, Ivy close behind. They skidded to a halt in the kitchen. An empty kitchen. Sanjay and Gideon weren't there.

"Didn't they say they were going to make coffee?" Ivy whispered.

"They were." Tempest picked up the remains of a spilt bag of coffee beans.

Ivy's hands flew to her mouth.

Tempest was about to wake her dad (and his baseball bat) when she heard faint voices coming from another room.

"That's a terrible idea," Gideon's voice murmured.

"Have you got a better one?" Sanjay whispered back.

Tempest and Ivy found the guys in the living room. The room was dark, and the two men were peeking out the front window.

"You scared us to death." Ivy flipped on the light.

Sanjay was at her side in less than two seconds to flip the light switch back off. "There goes our element of surprise."

Ivy's hand flew to her mouth again. "Is someone out there?"

"Listen," Tempest hissed. It was the faint sound of a horn. No, a buzzer. "It's the doorbell on the outside fence gate that my dad never fixed to be louder." They wouldn't have heard it at all if they hadn't been awake already. Tempest lifted the lid of a bronze lamp on the side table. The mechanism triggered a hidden coat closet to slide open. She grabbed her red jacket and shrugged it on.

"Um, what are you doing, Tempest?" Sanjay moved quickly to block her path to the door.

"Oh no!" Tempest's eyes opened wide with horror as she pointed to the side window.

While Sanjay and the others rushed to the window, Tempest slipped out the front door. She heard Sanjay groaning behind her. "I can't believe I fell for that," he muttered.

The night air was cold enough that Tempest could see her breath. Her footsteps were silent as she followed the stone path. Outside, the sound of the buzzer was louder, but still quite faint. And their visitor more impatient.

Gideon was the first to reach her side. "Are you sure this is a good idea?"

She paused and smiled at him. "You think I'm going to confront a killer and you're still here at my side? That's very brave of you, Gideon Torres."

His expression was difficult to gauge in the darkness.

Sanjay and Ivy caught up to them as Tempest headed not to the gate that was just beyond sight, but to the workshop. She unlocked the sliding door and headed for the corner closest to the front of the property.

"The periscope." Ivy nodded her approval. "Does that thing even still work?"

"We're about to find out."

"You guys have a periscope?" Sanjay looked around the workshop in wonder.

"Long story." Tempest lifted her hands above her head and

yanked the curved handles of the colorfully painted PVC piping hanging above a worktable.

"I thought that was a piece of art," Gideon said.

"Functional art." Tempest put her eyes to the viewfinder and spun around. A street lamp halfway down the block illumined the figure standing at the gate. She nodded in satisfaction.

"You see them?" Ivy asked.

"You don't look surprised," Gideon commented.

"I'm not." Tempest pushed the periscope aside. "After Ivy helped me realize who Robbie was protecting, I was going to visit him myself. But now I don't have to. Liam Ronan is pacing at the front gate."

Ivy pulled her back as Tempest headed for the door. "Robbie's brother is the killer? You can't go out there."

"He's unarmed," Tempest assured her. "That's what I wanted to check."

"Ivy's right," Sanjay said. "He could be hiding a gun."

"Cassidy wasn't killed with a gun. If he has a bludgeon in his pocket, it's four against one. Besides, he's standing patiently outside a fence he could climb if he really wanted to get inside, ringing the sickly doorbell instead. I don't think he's coming for violence."

"Then why's he here?" Gideon spoke softly, yet they all stopped and thought about the question.

"That's what we need to find out." Tempest slid open the workshop door.

"Why do I put up with this?" Sanjay muttered as he followed them toward the front gate.

Liam had stopped pressing the buzzer, but was pacing back and forth in front of the gate, as if trying to decide what to do. His brown leather jacket had slid off his right shoulder, and the laces of his left sneaker were untied. He scrambled back, nearly tripping over his shoelaces, when he spotted four people walking toward him. He recovered quickly and ran forward to grab the bars of the gate.

"They've arrested the wrong man," he said through the bars. "My brother is innocent."

"He called you with his one phone call?" Tempest asked.

Liam gripped the gate so tightly that his fingertips were turning white. "I think they were recording it, or at least he was worried they were, because so much of what he said was in riddles." He glanced nervously around the dark and empty street. "Can I come in to explain?"

"We don't usually let murderers into Fiddler's Folly."

Liam jerked back, as if the gate had electrocuted him. "You think I—?" He shook his head furiously. "You've got this all wrong."

Gideon stepped forward. "Take off your jacket."

"What?" Liam stammered.

"If you're not a killer and not here to hurt Tempest, you won't mind handing us your jacket and letting us pat you down to make sure you're not carrying any weapons." Gideon's voice was calm and steady on the surface, as it always was, but Tempest detected the slightest tremor in his voice.

Liam hesitated for only the briefest moment, then tugged off his jacket and tossed it over the gate, where Sanjay caught it. He also turned out the pockets of his chinos, revealing a slim wallet, a cell phone, and a squished pack of gum.

Sanjay nodded. "His jacket is clean. Good enough for us to pat him down inside. Go ahead and open the gate."

Tempest did so, and Liam stepped forward—just as Sanjay slapped a handcuff onto his right wrist. Liam was too stunned for the crucial next second in which Sanjay spun him around and handcuffed his left wrist, leaving his hands cuffed behind his back.

"Hey!" Liam protested. "I'm the one who came to you. Who *are* you, anyway?"

"Apologies." Sanjay tipped his bowler hat. "The Hindi Houdini, at your service. No, not that last part. You want to talk to Tempest, this is how you do it."

"Nice," Ivy murmured. "None of us are TSTL."

Sanjay gave her a questioning glance.

"She's saying we're not Too Stupid to Live," Tempest clarified. "Good call on the handcuffs."

"Why do you people even *have* handcuffs?" Liam squirmed in the cuffs.

Sanjay held tight. "Where are we taking him?"

"Workshop," Tempest answered.

"This is kidnapping," Liam cried.

Tempest raised her eyebrow at him. "We can call the police right now."

He remained silent.

"Workshop it is." Tempest led the way.

"You've stopped yawning," Ivy whispered to Gideon as the two of them walked behind Tempest, Sanjay, and their prisoner.

"I need to remember that the adrenaline of capturing a killer does more for one's alertness than a whole pot of coffee."

Chapter 54

anjay handcuffed Liam to the leg of a metal table bolted to the floor in Ivy's corner of the workshop. They offered him a chair, but he declined. It was a countertop-height table, so he could stand without difficulty. The only thing he couldn't do was move from that spot.

"I'm only putting up with this brutality because I think you can help my brother." He tugged at the cuff, but only half-heartedly.

"You could do that yourself by confessing to the police." Sanjay stood alert at the far end of the table, watching Liam's every move, as if he expected him to magically free himself from the handcuffs.

"Why would I come to you if I was guilty?" He shook the cuff and looked up at the high ceiling. "Robbie confessed because he thinks I'm guilty. I have an idea why, but he wouldn't tell me enough for me to understand if I'm right."

"Why are you talking to us and not the police?" Ivy crossed her arms and scowled up at him.

"Because," Liam's gaze bore into Tempest, "I know something that Tempest will have a better idea about than the police."

"My bracelet." Tempest felt the naked spot on her wrist

where the charm bracelet from her mom had kept her company for the past five years. "When we last spoke, you got all weird when I was telling you about my bracelet. You know something about the last piece of the puzzle. Do you know why my bracelet was stolen?"

Liam swallowed hard. "Cassidy called me a little over a week ago."

Tempest heard someone next to her gasp, but she couldn't take her eyes off of Liam.

"You knew Cassidy?"

He shrugged. "Not well. I met her backstage at your show two years ago. She was a flirt. We exchanged numbers and hooked up that weekend, but I hadn't talked to her since then. She wanted your address. She said you'd stolen something of hers when you left Vegas. Something she needed to get back."

"What did she say I'd stolen?"

"She wouldn't say at first. I thought it was weird she'd ask for your address rather than your new phone number, so I knew something was wrong."

"Couldn't she just look it up?" Sanjay asked.

Tempest shook her head. "I use a different last name than my dad. The property is listed under his legal name, Darius Mendez, but she didn't know his name. We keep it that way because I like my privacy."

"When I wouldn't give her your address," Liam continued, "she called to tell me more. She told me you'd swapped her bracelet for yours before you left, because you knew she'd hidden a gift from an inheritance she'd received inside the charms on her bracelet."

"You've got that the wrong way around," Ivy cut in. "Tempest's mom made that charm bracelet for her, for her twenty-first birthday."

"Cassidy confided in me," Liam said, "that Tempest had stolen that story from her, and hired Cassidy as her stage double to keep her close and make sure she wouldn't reveal the secret."

"That's ridiculous!" Tempest exploded.

Liam shrugged. "How was I supposed to know which one of you to believe? She told me she'd give me one of the valuable rubies from her bracelet if I helped her. She said she was coming to California to see you, so I gave her my address if she needed a place to crash. But she never showed. When I heard she'd been killed, I knew why she didn't."

"You didn't tell the police she'd contacted you?"

Liam held up his free hand. "First I heard was when they'd already arrested her boyfriend. It had nothing to do with me."

"There are rubies hidden in the charms?" Sanjay asked. "That's why you never took it off and were so upset when it was stolen? You could have gotten a safe deposit—"

"There are no rubies hidden inside the charms," Tempest snapped. "It was a script I wrote for a follow-up show. I was contractually obligated to write a new show after two years. I couldn't think up a different story, so the show continued for an additional year, but my manager, Winnie, kept on me for a new show. It always starts with the story, so I kept trying to write a worthy follow-up. One of my ideas was inspired by that ruby treasure your friend Jaya discovered. Since four of the eight charms are big enough for gemstones to be theoretically hidden inside, if they were silver-plated instead of silver throughout, I toyed around with the idea of a hidden treasure inside the charm bracelet. Since my mom had always said it was my inheritance . . ." Tempest groaned. "Cassidy thought it was real?"

Liam nodded. "She must have. Did she have any way to have read that script? Did you share it with her?"

Tempest groaned again. "No, but a couple of my notebooks are missing. I thought I'd simply misplaced them, since I haven't really unpacked yet. But if I left any of them behind at the theater, she could have read it. I didn't do the best job packing up my things."

Tempest's head throbbed. Fatigue and anger surged and made it difficult to think. She'd wanted to get away from everything so badly. She hadn't stopped to think about what she'd left behind. Running away, like Ivy said.

"So Cassidy wanted to steal what she thought was a ruby bracelet?" Ivy said. "But she was already long dead when someone did manage to steal it."

"Apparently my brother thinks I was her partner." Liam balled his hand into a fist and rattled the cuff. "Robbie must have seen her text messages—I wouldn't put it past him to snoop on my phone, since he's always bugging me about getting my life together. How could he believe I'd kill someone? I mean, I know we didn't grow up together since he's so much older than me, but really? I don't know why he's so convinced—"

"Liam," Tempest stopped him. "He didn't tell you where he found her body?"

Liam shook his head.

"She was *at your house*. Well, Robbie's house, but you're staying with him, so you know what I mean."

Liam swore. "That's why he was acting so strangely that day. And why all of a sudden he suggested asking Ashok to mentor me. I thought it was because he'd seen a dead body—which would freak out anyone. But then he told me he'd taken care of everything, and I didn't need to worry. I thought he was just being emotional because it was someone around my age who had died. But he really truly thought I killed her?" Liam banged the cuff against the metal leg again.

"Robbie is an idiot to confess," Tempest said, "but he loves you so much that he'd go to prison for the rest of his life to protect you."

"Can you take this thing off now?" Liam rubbed his wrist. "Doesn't what I told you prove Cassidy and her boyfriend wanted to steal what they thought was a ruby bracelet, and the police had it right the first time with Isaac? My brother can claim temporary insanity or something, for his confession."

Tempest shook her head. "Isaac was in jail when my bracelet was stolen. Her killer is still out there . . ." She sucked in her breath as she watched Liam's face. A face that looked so much like his older brother. A face she'd seen multiple times that summer because of his new job. "You're the one who drugged me at the café to get my bracelet!"

"I didn't," he stammered, slinking back.

"That's the worst poker face I've ever seen," Sanjay said.

"Maybe," Gideon said softly, "we should see if he has more to say with this hand in the jaw of the lion." He tilted his head toward the stone lion, which Tempest knew didn't have a movable jaw.

Liam stumbled backward so forcefully that the heavy table jumped an inch, screeching as it scraped across the concrete floor. "You people are crazy! You can hardly call it *drugging*. It was an over-the-counter sleeping pill. Nothing illegal. Nothing dangerous."

Tempest groaned. "You don't know where the charm bracelet key leads, then."

"What key? Do you mean the tiny key charm? I didn't touch that one. I knew that one was too small to hide a ruby."

No. *No, no, no.* "You broke the other charms, looking for the rubies?"

Liam kept his gaze focused on the floor. A welt was already growing on his wrist from when he'd pulled the handcuff forcefully enough to move the table. "Not all of them," he whispered. "I didn't destroy all of them."

"You were the ghost the night of the party!"

"I thought that was Robbie," Sanjay cut in.

Tempest shook her head. "He was the ghostly fiddler, but the night of the party, someone put a sheet over themselves, so the kids thought it was someone dressed as a ghost as a game." She turned to Liam. "You tossed it on to go between the tree house and main house, to search for another bracelet?"

He nodded. "I didn't know the kids would think it was a game. I didn't mean for them to go running off. But I thought if the bracelets I had were only stage props, the real ruby bracelet must've been in your room. I didn't make it that far, though. I came running back as soon as I heard shouting that the kids were missing."

He hadn't stolen the bracelet to use it as a key. Tempest's charm bracelet inheritance, whatever it was, was forever beyond her reach.

Chapter 55

It took half an hour of arguing to decide what to do with Liam. In the end, they agreed they'd first drive him back to his house so he could give Tempest the remains of her bracelet. Then they'd proceed to the police station, where Tempest would file a report about her stolen bracelet, and Liam would tell the police what he knew.

It was possible Liam was lying about not having seen Cassidy, but from how he reacted to being accused of stealing her bracelet, Tempest didn't think so. Which meant the real killer was still out there. Hopefully with the information Robbie and Liam could give the police, they'd figure it out quickly.

When Tempest, Ivy, Sanjay, and Gideon emerged from the police station, the sky was transforming from black to orange. They'd been up all night.

Back at Fiddler's Folly, Tempest went to the Secret Fort tower to check on Abra. She smiled to herself as she looked at the crooked lettering. Stepping through the doorway, she found the fluffy gray bunny curled up comfortably in a stack of hay, his floppy right ear draped over his eyes.

"Sorry I left you alone for so long. At least you didn't escape your hutch last night like the other day."

Abra sat up and wrinkled his nose at Tempest, then turned his tail to her. She would have taken it personally if she hadn't seen him munching on some hay. She must have woken him up. It was only dawn, after all. She never checked on him that early.

"I'll get you a real bunny door just as soon as I get a pen set up so you can have a safe place to play." She frowned as she studied the door to his hutch. So much had happened the past week that she hadn't taken time to examine the hutch more carefully after his escape. She'd assumed the hutch's lock had been damaged on its trip from Nevada to California. But what if something else had broken it?

After being up all night, Tempest's alertness was beginning to wane. Now her fatigue vanished as adrenaline surged. *On the night Cassidy was killed, someone had let Abra out of his hutch.*

Abra had a chunk of ripped fabric in his mouth the morning after his evening exploration, and another ripped piece in his cage that Gideon had discovered. He was a good watch rabbit. He wouldn't have been happy with a stranger taking him out of his cage.

"Cassidy wasn't coming to see me," Tempest whispered to the bunny. "She was trying to break into the house to steal my bracelet. She was looking for a way in, and saw the key-shaped handle of the hutch. She knows about our family's love of hidden keys. She wondered if it was a real key. That's why it's broken off."

Her killer might have been there that night, too. Cassidy could have been killed right here at Fiddler's Folly.

Tempest had no time to consider the disturbing question, because heavy footsteps crunched on the leaves behind her.

"I'm surprised you're awake," her dad said.

She relaxed as he stepped through the unfinished door of Secret Fort. "I haven't gone to bed yet." She rubbed her eyes.

"Come over to the tree house with me," her dad said. "Their light is on, so you can help me fill in your grandparents before you get some sleep."

"Yeah . . . some updates happened after you went to bed."

Darius ran a hand across his face. "How—truly, how?—could there have been updates?"

"We could both use some coffee. I'll fill you in along with Grandpa Ash and Grannie Mor."

An hour later, Tempest was ensconced in the cozy tree house breakfast nook between her dad and grandmother, drinking her second cup of jaggery coffee as she finished explaining everything to her dad and grandparents.

Ash handed Tempest a plate of *appam* with wild blueberry preserves on top. "You're trying to give an old man a heart attack?"

The skillet-cooked breakfast dish of ground rice, coconut milk, and jaggery was a symphony to Tempest's tired senses. She loved the texture of the soft, fluffy pounded rice that formed a pancake, with decadent richness from the full-fat coconut milk and light sweetness from the jaggery. And the addition of blueberry preserves? Brilliant. That one was Morag's recipe, from when she used to pick wild blueberries growing up as a child. Tempest was glad Ash had insisted sustenance was called for after she began her story.

Ash returned to the stovetop, glancing back at the breakfast nook with a shake of his head as he stirred the baked beans Morag had requested. The beans were comfort food from her childhood. The nostalgic mood was going around.

Darius was tossing fistfuls of a sugary dry breakfast cereal into his mouth.

"They seemed like such nice young men," Ash said.

"I'm going to wring Robbie's neck," Morag added. She was the only person Tempest knew who could look so elegant in a robe. The vibrant color of the royal blue silk looked like it was plucked from one of her paintings.

Tempest set down her fork to avoid shoveling the whole creamy rice pancake into her mouth. "I expect he'll have to serve some time for obscuring the investigation."

Morag clucked her tongue. "As he should."

Grandpa Ash snatched the box of sugary cereal from Darius's hand and handed him a plate of *appam* and baked beans. For Morag, he fixed a bowl of the tomato-y beans with extra stewed tomatoes, with two triangles of buttered toast sticking out on top.

"Sit down with us, Dad," Darius said.

Ash nodded and fixed himself a plate. A sad smile crossed his face as he joined them in the breakfast nook. He steepled his fingers together and rested his elbows on the wooden table, ignoring his food.

"From everything Tempest has told us," Ash said, "I'm not convinced Liam is guilty of murder. Sleeping pills and theft are quite different. We still don't know who killed Tempest's stage double."

"Or where the key leads," Morag added. "And why our daughter painted it into one of my paintings of the sea. What did she want you to find?"

Before taking a bite of his own food, Ash stood back up and darted out of the kitchen. He returned fifteen seconds later. Pushing aside his plate, he set his box of business cards on the table. He counted in Tamil as he flipped through the cards—counting was the one thing he still found easiest to do in his first language—until he came across what he was looking for. He handed the card to Tempest.

"A private investigator?" She handed the card back to him. "We don't need a private investigator. How did you meet a private investigator? Don't tell me he's another fan of your cardamom shortbread cookies."

Ash chuckled. "In spite of clearly being in pain from a dislocated shoulder, he was the one person who offered to help carry my bike when the escalator at the BART station was broken. I learned he didn't have health insurance, so I snapped it back in for him."

Tempest shuddered. "We especially don't need a private investigator who does things that get him a dislocated shoulder."

Darius took the card from her hand. "Maybe we do. A man like that, who helped an elderly man and isn't afraid of violence, could at least serve as an extra bodyguard for Tempest until we figure out what's going on."

Tempest raised an eyebrow at the two men as Ash nodded. "I don't need a bodyguard. I need to figure out who left Cassidy Sparrow's body in Robbie's house."

"Exactly," said her papa. "There's a killer in your orbit. I don't like that one bit. I'll make some calls to get added security around Fiddler's Folly."

"You can't afford either that or the private investigator bodyguard."

"Doesn't matter. I can take more jobs helping out other contractors who've got standard projects lined up. Or take out a mortgage on the house to pay for it."

There was no way Tempest was going to let her dad mortgage away his home—*their* home that belonged to all of her family.

"It's six o'clock in the morning," Tempest said. "Far too early to call anyone. Give me a few hours."

"A few hours for what, dear?" Grannie Mor brushed an unruly lock of Tempest's hair out of her face.

"To solve this."

Chapter 56

Three hours.

With zero hours of sleep, Tempest had three hours to figure out what was happening before she'd be held prisoner by her well-meaning family.

It was likely that Cassidy had been the intended victim because of the plot to steal what she thought was a valuable bracelet. Tempest thought back on what she knew about Cassidy's motives and actions.

Cassidy thought she'd figured out a good way to claim what she saw as rightfully hers—taking over selfish Tempest's show, since she saw herself as just as talented. So she pretended to be Tempest when she bought some equipment to add fireworks to the show.

Opening night of the new season, the sabotage went off as planned, but the aftermath didn't. The first part of Cassidy's plan worked, and Tempest was blamed for the accident, and ousted from the show. Her contract and financial backing were pulled. She had to repay a bunch of money, so she lost her house and her savings.

Cassidy stepped in, saying she could continue the show. She didn't realize it wouldn't be that easy. Isaac had convinced her it would be easy, since he always told Cassidy she was more talented than Tempest.

Cassidy was angry that even though she'd gotten even with Tempest for undervaluing her, her plan didn't have the outcome she wanted. On top of not being a headliner, now she was out of work.

Worse yet, that's when Isaac must have hit her. He'd done it before, so how would he have reacted when their plan for Cassidy to seize control of the show failed?

Desperate, Cassidy must have thought she could get her hands on Tempest's bracelet, which Liam confirmed Cassidy had mistakenly believed concealed gemstones. So she tried to find Tempest's address, and when she couldn't, she began calling people who might know. Liam gave it to her and offered to let her stay with him. Cassidy drove to California. Her shoe print and ripped fabric that Abra had bitten off proved she'd tried to come and see Tempest, with evidence pointing to her wanting to sneak into the house.

That's what Tempest knew from what she'd seen, what Isaac had told her, and the police evidence of Cassidy's blood in Isaac's car.

If Tempest had been in Cassidy's place, after failing to get into the house and being bitten by Abra, what would she have done next?

She needed caffeine to think. Her dad and grandparents' worries would distract her too much if she stayed at Fiddler's Folly, so she called Ivy to tell her what was up and ask to meet her at Veggie Magic.

The café had just opened for the day when Tempest arrived. The hostess said she could grab any free table, so Tempest took one by the window while waiting for Ivy.

Three minutes later, Ivy slid into the seat opposite Tempest, and a waiter immediately dropped off menus.

"We're just here for takeout," Tempest said. "Double Americano for me. Actually, make it a triple."

"Ditto," Ivy agreed.

The waiter left to put in their drink orders.

"Two hours and twelve minutes until your time is up," Ivy said. "You need to focus."

"I know."

"There's hardly anyone here, so we could stay here instead of getting the drinks to go."

Tempest shook her head. "Then we'd have to be careful watching for who's listening in once it begins to get crowded."

"If you had any ideas about where we should go next, I'd agree. But . . . we don't have any ideas." Ivy bit her lip. "Do we?"

"Not exactly. I was thinking we could take our drinks up the hill to the spot where we found Justin and Natalie the other night."

"Returning to the scene of the crime."

"That," said Tempest, "is also why I wanted to come to Veggie Magic, even though we're only here for takeout coffee. I keep thinking back to the night that Liam gave me a sleeping pill. There was something else that night . . . I just can't remember, because I was so tired."

The waiter brought them their drinks, and Tempest handed him the one credit card she hadn't chopped to pieces. When he handed it back to her, his smooth fingers brushed against hers.

The last piece of the puzzle.

She looked up and locked eyes with the waiter. "Preston?"

He smiled. Not the shy smile Tempest was used to seeing,

but the self-satisfied grin of a far different man than the one she thought she knew.

"Where?" Ivy whipped her head around, scoping out the quickly filling café. She stood up so hastily that her chair overturned, giving Preston the opportunity he needed. He bolted out the front door.

"Follow that waiter!" Tempest shouted back to a stunned Ivy.

Chapter 57

Tempest paused for a second on the sidewalk, long enough to see Preston dart into an alley across the street between a pub and a stationery store.

She sprinted across the street, ignoring the blare of two horns and narrowly avoiding one bumper. Behind the row of storefronts was a narrow road for deliveries. She didn't see anyone except for a man unloading kegs of beer, so she thought she might have lost him. Then a movement at the end of the storefront road caught her eye. Preston.

He disappeared around another corner, but she followed and found herself on the winding road that led to the top of the hill. A few cars drove by, and two pedestrians who couldn't possibly be Preston were taking a stroll on the opposite sidewalk. Ivy was nowhere in sight, but she couldn't wait.

The sound of pebbles crunching caught her attention. On the hillside above her, someone was running on the hiking trail. She couldn't see for certain that it was Preston, but the footfalls were moving at a more rapid speed than a casual jogger. Tempest took off on the trail. She'd left her takeout coffee in the café, but even after being up all night, she no longer needed the caffeine for energy.

The path switched from dirt and gravel to a flight of steps on a particularly steep section. She was going so fast she tripped on the first step, but caught herself. Like so many things she'd done this week, she'd been moving too quickly to see the truth. At the top of the fifty-fifth step, she paused to catch her breath. Preston stood several yards in front of her.

Waiting for her.

He'd wanted her to follow.

Preston smiled and took off running again. Again, she followed, helpless to resist. She needed to know the truth. She knew, now, that she'd been looking for the wrong connection. There had been multiple acts of misdirection that had obscured the truth. Robbie had been protecting his brother, so he'd moved the body and played the role of the ghost to obscure the truth he thought the police were sure to discover eventually. Cassidy and Liam had both been after the bracelet. She wasn't killed for someone to get her bracelet. Cassidy had been killed *to protect Tempest*.

Tempest never lost sight of Preston for more than a few seconds, but she didn't catch up to him until eleven minutes later. They'd reached the spot near the top of the hill where she'd had her sunrise picnic.

"You." She paused both to gather her thoughts and to catch her breath. "You were the person I heard while I was here."

Preston leaned against the tree she'd been sitting under while eating her jackfruit-and-chutney breakfast sandwich. He shrugged and gave her that confident grin that looked so strange on his face.

"You killed her to protect me," Tempest whispered.

"Of course. I'll always protect you, Tempest. It's a good thing I was in the front row on opening night."

The smooth hands and strong arms that had lifted her out

of the water. Her heart was still thudding from running up the hillside. Now it felt as if it was going to burst from her chest. "I know."

"I'm only sorry I didn't have proof that Cassidy was the one who sabotaged your show. I thought about staying in Vegas to gather evidence against her, but when you left . . . my selfish desire to be close to you won out."

"Preston the Prestidigitator . . . You're nothing like him."

He laughed. "If I showed people how good I was, they'd remember me. But if I'm a hapless amateur? Preston the Prestidigitator is an easy idea to remember but a difficult man to recognize. What color are his eyes that barely meet your gaze? How tall is he underneath that slouch? But I have to say, it took all my willpower to flub my audition at the Castle."

"You're an actor."

"Of course. So are you. I was playing a role, just like The Tempest, The Hindi Houdini, and Nicodemus the Necromancer. We're not so different, you know. I was waiting for the right moment to show you that. I admit I hadn't counted on it being today, but it'll do."

Tempest recoiled as he took a step toward her.

He sighed. "I'd have thought my previous actions have proved you have nothing to fear from me."

"You killed a woman."

"I saved your life. Twice."

"I was about to get out of the water chamber myself." She was fairly certain that was true, but not entirely. "And Cassidy wasn't going to kill me. She only wanted my bracelet."

"For all of your world travels, you're surprisingly naïve. She came to Hidden Creek with a drug a lot more powerful than Liam's sleeping pills inside her travel bag. Chloroform. It's not nearly as harmless as television would have you believe. Who knows what would have happened to you if she'd given it to you to steal your bracelet."

"How did you—" Tempest broke off, unsure what she wanted to say next. How did he kill her? How did he find her? How did he know Cassidy had chloroform with her?

"I can see this is a lot to take in. Perhaps I should start at the beginning." Even Preston's voice was so different than she remembered. "As soon as you came back to Hidden Creek, I got the job at Veggie Magic to be close to you. Giving Lavinia the name of Stanley was a nice touch, don't you think?"

Stanley, for Stan—the slang for stalker-fan.

"Liam was so rude to you the first time you came into the café after returning home," he continued. "When I needed to figure out what to do with Cassidy's body, framing him was perfect. I was so surprised when her body turned up somewhere else, though. But I'm already getting ahead of myself."

"You're skipping over Cassidy's death."

"It wasn't planned, but I'm not sorry. I never will be. As I mentioned, I'd already come to Hidden Creek so we wouldn't be apart. I was angry at Cassidy for taking your show away from me and the world. But not angry enough to kill her. But one night when I was holding vigil outside Fiddler's Folly, just for a short time to wish you good night from afar, I saw her leaving. What had she been doing at your house? I got in my jeep and followed her.

"It was quite late by this time, so she must have noticed a red jeep was following her. I trailed her to a residential street and saw her pull up into a long driveway next to a high fence. I was all the way down the street, parked apart from the houses. I was contented for the time being to know where she was staying, so I was preparing to drive back to your house to make sure you were all right, when she surprised me." He shook his head. "I'm not usually so careless. But she worked in the world of magic as well. She knew the importance of surprise. Before I realized what was happening, she was screaming at the jeep, calling me *Tempest*."

"The jeep. You have the same red jeep as mine."

He nodded. "In the dark, she thought it was you who'd followed her home. I couldn't have her screaming and drawing attention to us, so I got out with the intention of putting my hand over her mouth to quiet her. That's when I saw she had the same intent—only instead of an empty hand, she was holding a cloth soaked through with chloroform. You can guess what happened next. No guesses? I'll keep it simple. We fought. I won."

"Most fights don't end in a death."

"You need to realize I didn't know what she'd already done to you. I was upset. She was dead before I knew it. I hadn't planned that, but I needed to figure out what to do with her. I made sure that none of the lights in the houses down the street had turned on. Once I was certain they hadn't, I walked up to the house where she'd parked. She was staying with Liam! I couldn't believe my good fortune that was handed to me."

"Wait, she was already staying there?"

Preston smirked. "Did Liam lie about seeing her to protect himself?"

"That explains why Robbie was so sure Liam was guilty. He'd already seen Cassidy."

"I checked on you next—that's always my first priority. When I saw the light on in your room, which you then turned off shortly after midnight, I knew you were safe. Then

I dumped her car—careful with gloves and all that—knowing I'd stage her body in their house once they both left for work. I admit I was quite confused by how that played out. Until I realized Liam's brother was protecting him. Love is what makes the world go round, you know. Liam's brother protecting him. Me protecting you—"

"You were at Ivy's house before Liam drugged me."

"Again, I was trying to protect you. I heard him make that call from the alley behind the café, so I knew he was up to something. I wanted to warn you."

"If you're not going to hurt me, then you won't mind that I've already called the police." Tempest held up her phone. "They heard everything and are on the way."

Preston grinned. "I'm so glad. It saves me from calling them myself. I figured it was time for me to turn myself in."

"You did?"

"What other choice do I have?" Preston smiled and held up his hands as the crunch of shoes on the dirt path grew closer.

The Cheshire cat smile on his lips unsettled Tempest. Yet he didn't try anything when the officer handcuffed him and led him to the back of his patrol car.

An hour later, Tempest learned that Preston never made it to the police station. When the officer pulled up in front of the station, the back of the car was empty.

Chapter 58

With Preston's confession recorded on Tempest's sleight-of-hand 9-1-1 call, both Robbie and Isaac were released. A warrant was out for Preston's arrest, but Tempest wasn't hopeful they'd find him. Not with how well he'd fooled her for years.

The following afternoon, Tempest's phone rang with an unknown number.

"Tempest, is that you?"

"Winnie?" If her manager, Winston Kapoor, was calling her, this couldn't be good.

"I missed the sound of your voice, my girl."

"You don't have to pretend to care, Winnie. You can come right out and tell me how bad the lawsuit is."

"Lawsuit?"

"I assume that's why you're calling."

"You have it all wrong. I'm calling with good news. Isaac came straight to me after he was released from jail. He confessed his role in enabling Cassidy to sabotage your show. I knew that girl was trouble from the start. How soon can you get back here?"

"Where?"

Winston paused for three seconds. She imagined him adjusting his favorite purple tie as he stared at himself in the mirror he kept next to his desk. "Vegas. To your show. Where else?"

"I don't have a show. I don't have a house. You told me I was lucky I didn't have four separate lawsuits filed against me."

"Tempest, always so dramatic. But I suppose that's why your shows were so phenomenal. And will be again."

"What are you talking about?"

"The producers are groveling for you to come back. Aggrieved parties can sue the dead girl's estate if they want, but they can't come after you or the funders. They want you back."

Tempest imagined exactly how it would be. She knew she could put in the hard work again. That there would be moments of joy as she brought wonder to people. But she'd already told the story she wanted to tell. She loved what she was able to accomplish, but she could now do what she should have done a year ago.

"You can tell them I said no. I'm out."

Silence. This time for ten seconds. "Sorry, I think the signal must have cut out. It sounded like you said you didn't want to come back." He laughed nervously. "But of course that couldn't have been what you said."

"I've always wanted to bring magic and a sense of wonder to people's lives."

"That's my girl. I knew you—"

"It's something I can do here in Hidden Creek. I see that now."

Winston coughed. "That famous Tempest Raj sense of humor—"

"I'm not kidding. They should hire Carisa or Kayla for the venue. I don't know if they'd take it, but either one of them would be amazing."

Through all of the events of the past week, Tempest knew she didn't actually want to get back to Vegas, like she'd thought she wanted. Her producers had wanted something new, so the new show opening the night of the sabotage wasn't the one that had brought her joy and made her famous. She loved her family and friends here in Hidden Creek. She would still bring magic to life by being the new magic creator for Secret Staircase Construction. It was a similar role to what her mom did, but her own. Using her skills at story-telling and misdirection, she'd get the family business back on track.

Nicodemus had forwarded an offer from a theater company in Edinburgh for her to perform there. Tempest politely declined that invitation as well.

"One farewell show," Winston pleaded. "If I can't convince you to do more than that, at least set the record straight by doing one night of the show you were going to perform on opening night. Give your fans that closure. I'll look into getting it filmed. Let me make some calls."

She hung up after agreeing to think about doing one final show, and looked out the window of her secret turret toward the Fiddler's Folly hillside. She was home.

Chapter 59

The sunlight cut through the trees onto the Fiddler's Folly tree house deck and landed on Tempest's left arm. Her beloved silver bracelet was back in its rightful place on her wrist, missing only one piece.

Liam had scraped the silver away on the four charms bulky enough to potentially disguise a hidden gemstone and obliterated *The Tempest* book charm with a hammer after attempting to extricate the rubies intact had failed. One of the contacts in Ash's box of business cards was a skilled jeweler who was able to restore the three injured charms quickly and was currently creating a new book charm from photographs.

Between her index finger and thumb, Tempest held the large key made up of the charms. This was the stronger version Ivy had cast from the fitted plastic pieces. If Tempest found whatever it opened, this key should hold. Now all she had to do was find where it was supposed to lead.

"Jacket potato." Grandpa Ash handed her a plate with a crispy stuffed potato brimming with Kashmiri chili-spiced white beans and mushrooms sautéed in ghee. Jacket potatoes were almost as ubiquitous in the UK as fish and chips, a hearty simple meal you could easily customize that would keep you warm and nourished on a blustery day. Ash's recipe called for baking the potatoes until their salted and oiled skins blistered with a satisfying, crispy crunch, with the filling being far more flexible. He'd found trumpet mushrooms at the farmer's market, so mushrooms it was, to go with the spiced cannellini beans.

A crisp breeze was blowing through the hillside that day, swirling Tempest's hair around her face. She pulled it back into a ponytail and sat down at the outdoor dining table next to her grandmother.

"Lunch is served!" Ash called over the side of the tree-branch railing.

The sound of children's laughter floated up from below the deck. Justin and Natalie were playing with Abra, while Dahlia, Vanessa, and Calvin looked on from their lawn chairs. Dahlia and Calvin held mugs of jaggery coffee, but Vanessa had opted for the homemade apple juice the kids were drinking.

"I figured it out!" Justin called back. He and Natalie were the first to climb the tree house stairs and reach the deck. "Ms. Morag." He grinned as he reached Grannie Mor. "I figured out the riddle. I'm Justin Knight. In your riddle, it was one *knight*—a person in a metal suit—not 'one night' like 'one day.' So when one knight, one blacksmith, one baker, and one candle maker crossed the bridge, there were four of them. Enough people for the faeries to trick them. It was a puzzle of how the words were spelled. Is that right?"

Grannie Mor's eyes sparkled. "You're a clever one."

While everyone settled in around the table and Ash brought out the rest of the feast, Tempest looked at the wonderful family and friends that surrounded her. There was something else in what Justin had said. *A puzzle of how the words were spelled* . . . Tempest repeated to herself.

There wasn't room for all twelve of them around the table. Four people fit on each of the two benches on opposite sides of the table, Tempest and Darius took stools at each end, and Morag brought up one of her art desks to make a kids' table. Tempest poured Abra a small bowl of his food next to the kids. She needn't have bribed him. Abra happily basked in the kids' attention and forgot about the food.

"Pass the hot sauce, Mom?" Darius asked. Morag handed the glass mason jar to Ivy, who passed it to Gideon before it reached the end of the table. Gideon looked warily across the table at Sanjay, as if wondering how they had ended up seated across from each other.

"Justin guessed the first riddle," Natalie said. "Can you give us another one?"

"Ay," Morag said before dipping her fork into her steaming potato. "Let's see if I can remember a good one by the time we get to dessert."

Satisfied that everyone had been served, along with a small glass of champagne for the adults and sparkling apple cider for the kids, Ash sat down in the empty spot between his wife and Tempest.

"A toast." Ash raised his glass. "To my clever granddaughter. You solved so many puzzles to bring justice to that poor girl."

"Not quite all of them," said Tempest. *A puzzle of how the words were spelled . . .* She repeated it to herself again, then leapt up from her seat and dashed down the stairs.

"Where's she going?" Darius's voice echoed behind her.

Tempest didn't stop running until she'd reached the Secret Fort. Ivy arrived at her side as Tempest was reaching up to touch the imprecise lettering.

"This lettering." Tempest turned to her oldest friend. "I never guessed it might have been done badly on purpose."

"You mean how the 'T' is a little bit off-kilter?"

"Secret Fort . . ." Tempest tapped on the carved lettering. "It's not *Secret Fort* at all—it's *Secret for T.*"

"Secret for Tempest," Ivy whispered.

"It's here." Tempest stepped inside and spun around in the center of the unfinished tower. *The circular tower shaped like a lighthouse.* "Wherever this key leads, it's here. My inheritance."

"Didn't you already search the grounds?"

"I did, but there are so many crevices where a key could fit." Tempest dashed out of the door.

"Where are you going?"

"Grannie Mor's art studio. The painting with the key my grandmother didn't paint."

Tempest found the painting where her grandmother had left it resting on a tilted easel. The tower lighthouse in the night sky of the watercolor painting shone its beacon of light into the indigo ripples of the sea. She leaned in closer. "The key my mom added doesn't look like the charm bracelet key. It's more like the stained-glass key light in the tower."

"Where does the light shine through the window?"

"Let's go find out."

The sunlight cast its warm light through the stained-glass key window, falling on the opposite wall.

"It's impossible," Ivy said. "Not only don't we know what time of day to see where the light falls, but there can't be a door here."

Tempest raised an eyebrow at her friend. "First of all, it's not like these bricks are an ocean. We can inspect the whole wall. And I agree the stones don't look like a door, but you're the one who's been working with Secret Staircase Construction for years. You know how well things can be hidden."

Ivy shook her head. "It's not that. It's the fact that this part of the brick wall is set into the hillside. There's nowhere for it to *go*."

"What if . . ." Tempest closed her eyes and let her fingers feel the cool stones. They were smooth—at least most of them were. She opened her eyes and looked where her hand had stopped. Nearly invisible to the eye, the shape of a key had been carved into the stone. Tempest took the cast of the charm bracelet key and inserted it into the small space in between two stones. With the key inserted and only the Janus-faced jester and its top hat showing, she held her breath and twisted.

Click.

Nothing happened.

Ivy frowned. "That was anticlimactic."

"But if *I'm* the key . . ." Using the full force of her muscular arms, Tempest pressed on the stones around the key. A four-foot section of stones pushed forward into the hillside.

Ivy gasped. "A cave."

"You coming?" Tempest was already halfway through the small opening.

"Are you sure we should—"

"There's a light up ahead." Tempest clicked off the flashlight on her phone and put it in her back pocket. It wasn't a reflection from her light. Up ahead, a light shone through the darkness. Had her mom strung lights in this place?

"Now I'm really not sure."

"Ivy, get in here." After five feet of crouching, the passageway opened up into a high-ceilinged grotto. Tempest stood up and stretched. The cavern was huge. She breathed in the scents of earth and moss. The air wasn't stale. Fresh air was getting inside somehow.

"How," Ivy asked from her side, "could Emma have built this whole thing without anyone knowing?"

"I don't think she did."

"Your dad would have told you—"

"He doesn't know. That summer when she sprained her ankle and had to stay behind when my dad went to the out-of-town project, she worked on this tower during that time. She knew how to build a secret door, but there's no way she could have carved a whole cave out of the hillside in that amount of time."

"Then what is this place?"

"Close your eyes." Tempest did so as well as she spoke the words. "Listen."

"Water. It's the creek."

"Our hidden creek. When the earth shifted more than a century ago during the earthquake and much of the stream went underground, this place was left."

"That doesn't explain the light."

"I think it does." As Tempest walked forward, the light grew brighter. It was still dim, but the further she walked, the more her eyes adjusted. After stumbling over a tree root, she turned her phone's flashlight back on.

After five minutes, the light of Tempest's flashlight shone on a pile of treasure. No, not treasure. Coins. Pennies. They were below the wishing well. It wasn't a proper well at all, but a structure built to keep the ground stable.

They walked back the way they came, listening to the rhythmic lapping of the underground section of the creek.

"Why all this secrecy to make a hidden key to get here?" Tempest wondered aloud. The light of her flashlight gave her the answer. They'd missed it the first time around, when they were so focused moving forward. But five feet inside the cave was a black steamer trunk.

Tempest knelt in front of the trunk, her heart thudding more loudly than the fake heartbeat they'd created in the Locked Room Library. She grasped the padlock holding it shut.

"The key's too big to fit in this lock." She paused. "But this one isn't." The single charm on her bracelet that hadn't joined in making the large key was itself a small key. She unlatched the bracelet and nudged the key charm into the padlock.

It fit.

The trunk creaked as Tempest opened the lid. Inside were two waterproof boxes. The first one was labeled *Emma's Journals*, the next *Videos for Tempest*. On top was an envelope addressed to Tempest.

If you're reading this letter, it means things didn't go as planned at the Whispering Creek Theater. But you've always been a key who can open any lock, so I know you'll find this.

I've left you my journals, with my magical stories, for you to pull from as much or as little as you want. I've also given you my videos of Elspeth and I practicing our routines.

Even though this letter means something has gone wrong, there's no Raj family curse. Not in the way your grandfather imagined. Whatever has happened to me, please don't try to find out. You have your own life to live, and it's going to be brilliant.

I love you more than anything, dearest Tempest.

Look to the future, not the past. There's no curse, so you can feel free to be whatever kind of magician, or anything else, that you'd like to be.

Chapter 60

Tempest showed her family the grotto, but kept the letter and journals to herself. She hadn't yet decided what to do with the information her mom left her, but she had time—and a family she knew she could count on, whatever the future held.

The following day, Ivy texted Tempest to meet her in the Secret Staircase Construction workshop. "I told him!" She zipped her pink vest until it covered half her face.

Tempest smiled at the familiar gesture that she'd missed so much over the past several years. "I'm not quite to the mind-reading level of our friendship yet."

Ivy unzipped the cuff far enough to free her mouth. "I told Darius that I've been working part-time at the Locked Room Library and that I want to get a master of library science degree." She grinned. "I know that means I need to finish up my last couple of credits to graduate with my BA first. But you were right. He was so happy that I'd figured out what I wanted to do with my life."

Ash cooked his famous Rajaloo potato curry that night to celebrate. He also spelled *Congratulations, Ivy!* out of cumin seeds on the top of a platter of saffron rice.

After stuffing herself silly for a second day in a row, Tempest fell asleep that night smiling. She couldn't remember the last time that had happened.

Tempest woke up before dawn each morning. It was mostly because of her new job. Secret Staircase Construction's one remaining full-time employee was Darius, with Ivy and Gideon working for him part-time, and a cadre of skilled contractors to call upon when needed, including Indigo Bishop. Darius no longer had to worry about making an unattainable payroll for people he felt responsible for, and could figure out what he and Tempest wanted the family business to be. Tempest was excited about the prospect of using her own magic storytelling skills to help him get the business back on its feet.

But she also awoke before her alarm because her mind was racing. Her dreams involved dark ocean waters and a combination of fear and excitement as she caught glimpses of selkies swimming in the sea just beyond her grasp. She hadn't yet had the heart to revisit the past and delve into the boxes her mom had left her. But here in the present, first thing each morning, she checked for news about Preston. It still troubled her that Preston, or whatever his real name was, had killed to protect her. He hadn't been seen since that day he was arrested.

Tempest visited Robbie, who was now awaiting sentencing for his role in covering up the murder of Cassidy Sparrow. Tempest wasn't ready to forgive him, but she had an idea about why he'd risked everything.

"Liam isn't really your brother, is he?"

He didn't answer.

"He's your son."

"How did you work it out?"

"You were seventeen when he was born. Your dad had left years before that, but Liam could still have been your half-brother. But you felt such guilt for doing the same thing your dad had done, not being around, so you were willing to give up your life for Liam."

"He doesn't know, Tempest."

"I won't say anything. Not until you're ready."

Tempest took a quick trip to Las Vegas to begin preparing for a farewell show, during which time Justin watched Abra for her. When she returned home, she stood in the orange light of the stained-glass key window of the Secret Fort. She'd moved a folding table and four folding stools next to Abra's hutch, and now she and Gideon huddled over the blueprints she'd sketched.

"You sure you want to do this?" Gideon asked.

Abra nuzzled Gideon's shoe, but didn't bite.

"The honorable Abracadabra Rabbit has spoken." Tempest scooped Abra into her arms and lifted him back into his hutch. "It's impossible to say no to this face."

"Building a new house, even starting with the beginning of a structure, is difficult. At least twice as much work, time, and expense as you think. Probably more, in this case, to make sure the hillside is reinforced to be structurally sound next to the grotto."

"I've got enough money, thanks to my manager arranging for my final show in Vegas to be filmed."

"There's more than money to consider."

"Exactly. My mom began building this Secret Fort, and it's the spot on the property with the most privacy from my family. Good thing I happen to know a guy who's good at working with stone."

"If he's the guy I'm thinking of, he'd love to help."

"Are you sure you've got time? Aren't you supposed to be applying to architecture school along with working at Secret Staircase Construction?"

"I was going to tell you. I invited my parents over to my home studio while you were gone. They hadn't been before. I always went to them."

"And?"

"They don't understand, but they're finally starting to support my decision to work as a stone carver. They knew I wasn't exactly telling them the truth about becoming scared of heights after falling off a ladder at a previous masonry job. But they could tell I'd been keeping something from them. They hated it, so they're trying to be supportive. I really did have a bad fall last year, but when I was recovering I wasn't frightened. Instead, I knew I had to be true to what I wanted to do with my life. I'm going to be a stone-carving artist. The part-time work I'll be doing for your dad will pay my rent well enough until my pieces start making money. Your grandmother has some contacts in the local art world she offered to introduce me to. But that's for another day." He turned back to the sketches.

Tempest's next step would be to find an architect, but for now, she wanted to come up with sketches for her own home—and her own story.

"This guy who's good at working with stone," Gideon said, "I hear he only works with people who tell him how they fooled him with an impossible magic trick."

"I have a feeling the stone carving artist is so observant that he knows the answer already. He only has to realize it." Tempest rolled up the sketch and tucked it into a poster tube.

"My first thought was that the two people who disappeared were people you knew, who were in on the trick. But that can't be possible. They were there first, before I arrived. I picked the table we sat at, and I was the one who asked you to do a trick. You didn't have a say in either of those things."

"Didn't I?"

"You didn't tell me where to sit. You didn't offer to do a trick."

"Didn't you notice my devilish whisper in your ear?"

Gideon groaned. "The coin you were twirling in your fingers."

"The power," said Tempest, "of suggestion."

"You wanted me to ask you to do a trick. The two diners were working with you."

"I found two art students at a local café, told them I'd buy them dinner if they'd help me with an illusion. If it didn't come up, they'd still get a free meal. As for the seating setup, I did what's called a 'force,' which is most commonly applied in card magic. The member of the audience who picks a card believes they chose the card of their own free will, but there are many ways to influence them, to essentially force them to pick the card the magician wants."

"What about the table?"

"Even though you thought you selected a table of your own free will, I set up the conditions so you'd pick that one."

"You weren't even there."

"You work as a stonemason. There's no way you'd select a wobbly table. Every single table at Veggie Magic wobbles. The tables are all decades old. It's part of the café's charm. They put wedges underneath the legs to even them out. I simply arrived early and pulled them out. I did it because most people who meet a magician ask them to do a trick. You hadn't done so yet, but I knew it was only a matter of time. I didn't know for sure, which is why I didn't mind if I bought the art students lunch without them needing to flip the table and disappear. But I subtly suggested a trick by spinning the coin. If you'd wanted to ask me to do a trick, that would remind you. It was a subtle mental reminder for you, and if you gave in to the suggestion and asked me to do a trick, I'd go forward with my signal to the students. You did, so I waved the handkerchief with a large motion they couldn't miss."

She pulled a red handkerchief out of thin air and waved it in front of his face. When she pulled it away, he'd pulled off a magic trick of his own. He was standing right in front of her. He took her hand in his and lifted her left wrist to his lips. With the softest touch, he kissed the inside of her wrist, the spot where the lightning bolt charm lay. The old-fashioned gesture, the simple touch, shot a lightning bolt of electricity through her.

Gideon held her gaze and caressed her wrist gently before letting go of her hand. "Guess we'd better get to work."

Tempest didn't know what would have happened next if a noise hadn't sounded from outside the doorless entryway.

"You guys got started without us?" Sanjay stepped into the Secret Fort, with Ivy a couple of paces behind him.

"There's a lot to do," said Tempest. "I thought it was time I got started living the rest of my life."

"That," said Sanjay, "doesn't sound like someone who leaves destruction in their wake."

"Maybe I'm growing up." Tempest smiled at her friends.

Sanjay tossed his bowler hat into the air. It landed on the ramparts of Abra's hutch as he took a step forward and spun Tempest around in his arms. "Welcome home, Tempest."

Cardamom Shortbread Cookies

Tempest's favorite cookie. This recipe is a combination of Indian Nankhatai cookies and Scottish shortbread.

DRY INGREDIENTS
   1½ cups all purpose flour, sifted
   ½ cup chickpea flour (*besan*), sifted
   ½ tsp ground cardamom
   1 tsp baking powder
   ¼ tsp salt

WET INGREDIENTS
   ½ cup coconut oil, melted
   ¼ cup milk of choice (both oat milk and almond milk
      work great)
   ½ cup powdered sugar

DIRECTIONS
Preheat oven to 350 degrees F and line a baking tray with parchment paper. Mix the dry ingredients in one bowl and the wet ingredients in another, making sure to sift both flours. Stir the dry ingredients into the wet, bringing it together but not overmixing. Roll the dough into bite-size rounds and press down in the center to flatten them out. Approx. ½ Tbsp each makes around 40 bite-size cookies. Bake for 15 minutes.

Variation: Add a small dollop of jam, nut butter, or chopped nuts in the depressed center of the cookies. See Gigi's

website for a quick and tasty homemade jam: www.gigipan
dian.com/recipes.

Grandpa Ash's Rajaloo Potatoes

Three mix-and-match components that are a mix of East and
West: vinegar-roasted potatoes, cumin caramelized onions,
and a spicy vindaloo dipping sauce. Fix them on their own
or make the full set like Tempest's grandfather does in his
tree house kitchen.

Vinegar is widely used in Scottish cooking, but isn't as traditional in Indian cooking. The acidic balance in South Indian
foods was traditionally achieved with limes, lemons, and
green mangoes before the Portuguese brought vinegar into
the mix in Goa, where Vindaloo originated.

Vinegar-Roasted Potatoes

INGREDIENTS
    1 lb fingerling potatoes, cut into ½-inch pieces
    ½ cup apple cider vinegar
    1 Tbsp kosher salt
    1 Tbsp olive oil

DIRECTIONS
Preheat oven to 425 degrees F and line a baking tray with
parchment paper. Chop the potatoes into ½-inch pieces. On
the stovetop, bring 4 cups water, apple cider vinegar, and salt
to a boil in a saucepan. Add the chopped potatoes and boil for
10 minutes. Strain out water and leave to cool for 5 minutes.

Toss with the olive oil and spread on a baking sheet. Roast in the 425-degree oven for 45 minutes or until crispy.

Partially cooking the potatoes with vinegar before roasting is a great trick to approximate the flavor of fried British chips dipped in vinegar.

Vindaloo sauce

There are many dishes called vindaloo, and the thing that unifies them is spice (surprisingly, not always vinegar!). The sauce below is spicy, but you can make it just as flavorful with less spice by reducing the number of chili peppers. It's a great topping for the vinegar-roasted potatoes above, or any dish that could benefit from a spicy sauce. It also works well as a sandwich spread.

INGREDIENTS

5 dried Kashmiri chilis, deseeded (Don't like spice? Reduce to 2 dried chilis, but don't omit them altogether.)
2 Tbsp fresh garlic
2 Tbsp fresh ginger
¼ cup shallots
¼ cup olive oil
2 Tbsp apple cider vinegar
1 tsp paprika
1 tsp ground cumin
1 tsp jaggery* or brown sugar
¼ tsp cinnamon
¼ tsp salt
¼ tsp ground black pepper

DIRECTIONS

Soak the dried chilis in hot water for 10 minutes, then slide open and deseed. Blend all the ingredients together in a blender until a thick, emulsified paste has formed. Serve as a dipping sauce with the vinegar-roasted potatoes above.

*Jaggery is a palm sugar widely used in India, which can be found online or at Asian food markets in the West. It's not as refined as other sugars and contains molasses.

Cumin Caramelized Onions

INGREDIENTS

   1 Tbsp olive oil
   2 tsp cumin seeds
   1 large onion, either yellow or white, thinly sliced

DIRECTIONS

Heat the oil over medium-low heat in a heavy-bottomed skillet. Add cumin seeds. When they begin to crackle and release their scent, after about a minute, add the thinly sliced onion. Slow cook the onion mixture on medium-low heat for close to an hour, stirring occasionally. The long cooking process will release the sugars from the onion to caramelize the mixture, creating a sweet and savory topping. When your vinegar-roasted potatoes are done, the onions will be as well. Sprinkle on top of the roasted potato mixture for even more flavor.

Note: Ground cumin is not a good substitute here. Use brown mustard seeds if you don't have cumin seeds, or omit altogether—the caramelized onions are still tasty without spices.

Variation: Short on time? Use a higher heat oil and fry on medium high for 10 minutes to crisp the onion. The result won't be as sweet, but will still be tasty.

Want more recipes? Sign up for Gigi's monthly email newsletter to receive a free eBook cookbook: WWW.GIGIPANDIAN.COM/SUBSCRIBE.

Acknowledgments

Tempest would not exist if not for my amazing parents, Susan Parman and Jacob Pandian, who raised me in a multicultural family and took me across the United States, Europe, and India when I was too young to fully appreciate it, but old enough for it to sink in that I was a citizen of the world (and its food!). And James, you've supported my wildest dreams from the start, and life continues to be a marvelous adventure with you.

I began writing Tempest's story several years ago in Edinburgh, Scotland. I had completed a full year of cancer treatments in Northern California, during which time I promised myself I'd seize the day and take my writers' group to a writing retreat in Edinburgh once I was well. I rented a huge flat with views of the castle, and several members of the group joined me. Thank you to Mysti Berry, Rachael Herron, Lisa Hughey, and Emberly Nesbitt for making that trip every bit as inspiring as I envisioned.

Huge thanks to my early readers Nancy Adams, S. A. Cosby, Jeffrey Marks, Emberly Nesbitt, Susan Parman, Brian Selfon, and Diane Vallere. So many others helped with various aspects of the book: brainstorming, fact checking, late-night conversations about classic mysteries, and encouragement as I worked out the last pieces of the puzzle. Thank you to Leslie Bacon, Jeff and Diana Bahr, Adreinne Bell, Juliet Blackwell, Stephen Buehler, Ellen Byron, Lynn Coddington, Shelly Dickson Carr, Aaron Elkins, Tameri Etherton, Martha Flynn, Kellye Garrett, Doug Greene, Gogi Hale, James Lincoln Warren, Sophie Littlefield, Rosa Macleod, Lisa Q. Mathews, Lloyd Meeker, Shannon Monroe, Lorin Oberweger, Winona Reyes, Catrina Roallos, Nancy Sauder, and Steve Steinbock. And a debt of gratitude to the authors who are no longer with us but inspired me through their fiction, especially Elizabeth Peters and John Dickson Carr, whose ingenious novels motivated me to become a mystery writer.

Beyond individuals, so many organizations have been a tremendous help to my writing and life. Sisters in Crime, SinC NorCal, SinC Guppies, Mystery Writers of America, MWA NorCal, Short Mystery Fiction Society, and Crime Writers of Color. Mystery conventions Malice Domestic, Bouchercon, and Left Coast Crime. My small-but-mighty local library. Independent bookstores Murder by the Book (thank you John and McKenna!), Book Passage (you're the best, Cheryl and Katherine), A Great Good Place for Books (you rock, Kathleen), Mystery Loves Company, Mysterious Galaxy, Book Carnival, and all the bookstores helping readers and supporting authors by hand-selling books. I feel so incredibly fortunate for this generous writing community.

Thank you to my tremendous agent, Jill Marsal, who believed in me and my work even when we had no idea where it fit, and my brilliant St. Martin's Minotaur editor, Madeline Houpt, who worked through challenges with me and pushed me to make Tempest's story better. I'm thrilled to be working with you both to tell my stories. And big thanks to the rest of the St. Martin's Minotaur team, especially Sarah Melnyk, Joseph Brosnan, and David Rotstein.

Last, but far from least, a heartfelt thanks to you, my readers. This is my twelfth novel. Hugs to those of you who have been there with me since early in my career, and thank you to new readers who are picking up one of my books for the first time. I'm an avid reader before I'm a writer, and my fellow mystery readers are a big part of what makes this such a fun job. Thank you! I love hearing from readers. You can find several ways to stay in touch and sign up for my email newsletter at www.gigipandian.com.